# DANGEROUS SECRETS

## CAROLINE WARFIELD

SOUL MATE PUBLISHING

New York

DANGEROUS SECRETS

Copyright©2015

CAROLINE WARFIELD

Cover Design by Christy Caughie

This book is a work of fiction. The names, characters, places, and incidents are the products of the author's imagination or are used fictitiously. Any resemblance to actual events, business establishments, locales, or persons, living or dead, is entirely coincidental.

All rights reserved. No part of this publication may be reproduced, stored in a retrieval system, or transmitted in any form or by any means (electronic, mechanical, photocopying, recording, or otherwise) without the prior written permission of both the copyright owner and the publisher. The only exception is brief quotations in printed reviews.

The scanning, uploading, and distribution of this book via the Internet or via any other means without the permission of the publisher is illegal and punishable by law. Please purchase only authorized electronic editions, and do not participate in or encourage electronic piracy of copyrighted materials.

Your support of the author's rights is appreciated.

Published in the United States of America by
Soul Mate Publishing
P.O. Box 24
Macedon, New York, 14502

ISBN: 978-1-68291-013-9

ebook ISBN: 978-1-61935-749-5

www.SoulMatePublishing.com

The publisher does not have any control over and does not assume any responsibility for author or third-party websites or their content.

*To my son who believes I can do anything I want*

*and my brilliant daughter who is happy to help me do it.*

## Acknowledgements

Every writer knows it takes a team to produce a book. I have to acknowledge the hard work of Debby Gilbert and the good folks at Soul Mate Publishing, particularly my editor Tamus Bairen and cover artist Christy Caughie whose hard work brought this story to fruition.

I won't name names lest I forget someone, but I'm dependent every day on the community of writers who encourage, support, and cheer one another on, particularly my email buddies, the Debs, who've seen me through thick and thin. Since the publication of Dangerous Works, that community has grown to include my partners at History Imagined (https://historyimagined.wordpress.com/) and the funny and upbeat women of The Bluestocking Belles (http://bluestockingbelles.com/) who remind me why we do what we do.

Most of all I want to thank the love of my life, Greg, whose patience and unflagging support makes my work possible. I thank God every day for what we have together.

# Chapter 1

Rome, 1820

"Major Bently? Are you in there?"

*Bently?* Jamie Heyworth covered his ears. *Some damned fool wants my Uncle Charles.*

Pounding, urgent and loud, echoed through his room.

He ignored the noise. *Perhaps it will stop.*

It didn't.

"Major Bently!"

There it was again. *Uncle Charles can answer.*

His Uncle Charles lay dead the past eight years. Jamie peeked out from under his ragged pillow and stared at the cracks in the ceiling.

Another loud knock made his cot bounce and vibrate. It sent pain like nails into his already aching head.

"Major Bently, kindly open. You promised."

*Promised?* He never made promises. He rolled to sit on the edge of his cot with a loud groan, a colorful curse, and a gasp so sharp it filled his lungs with pungent Roman air and jiggled his languid brain cells. Memory flooded back.

That morning he had no money, nothing left to sell, and no reason to get up—except more knocking. Louder.

"Stop the damned pounding," he mumbled.

"Major, I heard your vulgarity. I know you are in there."

Jamie's senses began to clear, and he realized some woman pounded on his door. *The vexatious chit from last night*, he thought. The woman had invaded the tavern he frequented like the black crow of death and would not leave.

*The little blackbird had good credit,* he remembered. He eyed the three empty wine bottles on his table. He distinctly remembered only having money for one. He had spent his last coin on that bottle. *She must have funded the other two.* There had been food, too, he remembered, and a very fine cheese. Jamie Heyworth never forgot a good meal.

"Major, please! It is past nine in the morning, and we will be late," the woman's voice called.

*Late for what?* He struggled to recall.

After he plied her with tea and calmed her down, she had fed him some tale about dying brothers, evil nuns, a menacing count, and nieces held prisoner in a tower. *Maybe not a tower*, he thought. He felt sure he remembered the rest correctly.

"Major Bently!"

*Ah! Bently.* Using his mother's maiden name amused him when he gave it to her. Major Lord James Phineas Heyworth, Fourth Baron—and so on—sounded ludicrous attached to his pathetic self even if he didn't have good reason to avoid being found. He preferred not to use it. Bently sounded safer. He hoped it was.

*Did I promise anything?*

"You promised you would meet me by the fountain in the piazza at 8:30 this morning," said the voice behind the door.

Her answer stunned him. He could think of no reason why he would promise some chance-met blackbird anything, much less an early morning rendezvous.

"Are you well?" the voice persisted.

*No, damn it, I feel like the very devil.*

"Yes. I am well. We were to meet at 8:30 in the evening, were we not?" he responded.

*No sane person runs about at 8:30 in the morning.* He began to wonder if the woman really was mad, one of those hysterical females who reads too many novels.

"Don't be ridiculous. The nuns wouldn't let us in the hospital in the evening," she said.

*Nuns again! And more infernal banging.* He doubted the door, though thick as a post, could stand against his ravening crow.

"Major, you promised! You said—"

Jamie threw the door open. The woman stumbled against him. Soft curves pressed against his entire length and jarred his sluggish body awake.

*I'm not dead yet!* The thought improved his mood considerably. He produced his cheekiest grin and made no effort to remove her soft body from his person.

"What did I promise, exactly?" he asked, staring down into a delicately sculpted face, inches from his. He liked the feel of her. *She's hiding her best parts under all that English wool. Doesn't the foolish woman know she is in Rome?*

The chit pushed herself away, slipped under his guard, entered the room, and frowned in distaste. *No schoolroom miss, this one.*

In daylight, she looked more like a wren than a raven. Dressed in sensible brown, she radiated bright, searching eyes and flowing energy. *Too damned much energy for so early in the morning.* Her eyes darted over the bottles, scattered clothing, and the dirty dishes on his broken chair.

"You said that you . . ."

She stopped abruptly and gaped.

He glanced down.

"Luckily, I fell asleep in my shirt," he said, lips twitching. "I'm sure I can locate my trousers and smallclothes, if you'll give me a moment."

For an instant, blue sparks flared in her eyes, which were rimmed by thick honey-gold lashes. Just as fast, she turned her back.

"Quickly, please." She spoke toward the window. He wondered what color she would turn if she knew how well she showed off her derrière when she pulled her frock tightly to one side with white-knuckled fury.

"What exactly did I promise that has brought you running, fleet of foot, to my quarters this morning?" he asked.

He moved with deliberate slowness around the room, picking up clothing discarded the night before and searching his brain for promises discarded just as easily.

"You agreed to speak with the nuns, to interpret for me," the woman said.

*That was it. The wren needs an interpreter, needs one so badly that she let some excitable waiter drag her into a seedy tavern she had no business entering to meet an English "gentleman." More fool she.*

"I should not be surprised you don't remember. You were much the worse for drink last night," she complained.

*She has me there.*

"You're acquainted with the effects of drink?" he asked. *Intriguing.*

"More than I wish. My husband—oh, do hurry up!" She stomped her foot and, much to his regret, let go of her skirts.

*Husband? Pity,* he thought. *Inevitable though.*

"Are you ready?" she demanded.

"You might wait until I'm finished with my trousers. Your husband will—"

"Do nothing!" She sounded furious.

"I beg your pardon?" He buttoned the fall of his trousers.

"My husband will do nothing. He died three years ago."

"Ah, then there is no one to be concerned about your presence in a man's room in a foreign city in which you speak not a word of the native language. What's the hurry?"

"The hurry, Major," she almost spat out his rank, "is that I am only permitted to visit Isabella during very strictly set hours."

"Isabella?"

"My niece!"

*Of course. The niece.*

"Do pay attention. Sister Amelia Maria will be at the

hospital, but I am told the others will allow me a visit, only the briefest visit, in their common room," she went on.

*Ah. No tower. The niece is imprisoned in a—Good Lord!*

"You are taking me to a convent?" he gasped.

"Of course."

"I must have been 'much the worse for drink' indeed, if I agreed to that."

"You did agree. You gave me your word," she insisted.

*My word. When had anyone last requested my word or respected it when given?* The novel idea rolled around in his head. He had given his word.

"You may turn around . . . unless"—he caught a glimpse of wide-eyed curiosity quickly squelched when she turned to face him—"the sight of a man buttoning his waistcoat and jacket offends you."

"Certainly not. I have seen an unbuttoned waistcoat once or twice," she snapped.

"I see. The husband."

Jamie turned to the basin near his bed and shaved with the economy of movement habitual in a man long used to the privations of camp and campaign.

"This would be easier if I knew your name," he said from the side of his mouth. She didn't faint at the sight of a man shaving either.

"I must have—but no, I didn't, did I? I am Eleanora Haley—Mrs. Edmund Haley."

Jamie wiped his face and ran a hand carelessly through his hair to smooth it. He had no brush; its silver handle fed him for almost a week.

"Well, then, Mrs. Edmund Haley—" He choked on the words when he turned around.

"It's what we agreed to," she said, holding out a leather purse.

*She believes she has employed me?*

Jamie stifled a surge of hope. His fingers trembled and brushed hers when he took the bag. He pulled out a silver coin. The imprint of the papal coat of arms gleamed up at him—a Papal scudo, Rome's primary currency.

"It's what we agreed. Don't think you can push for more."

*More?* One scudo alone was worth more than four guineas. He hefted the bag and reconsidered his assessment of the previous night. The woman was definitely mad, no "maybe" about it. At least now he understood why he promised to meet her.

"You paid me this to escort you to a convent?" he asked.

"Certainly not," she said. "For a month of your time. To serve as my interpreter."

*Not so mad then.* He knew he should refuse.

*A gentleman would refuse the money,* he thought.

Luckily, Jamie was no longer a gentleman. His fingers tightened on the soft leather. The money would keep him alive for a month, long enough to do whatever it was the woman hired him to do.

He smiled broadly. "Let's go see these nuns of yours."

## Chapter 2

Nora stole a glance at the major walking beside her through the winding lanes of his Trastevere neighborhood, the seedy district across the Tiber from Rome's better quarters that was home to poor taverns, poorer families, and down-on-their-luck majors.

"They aren't my nuns," she snapped.

"If you say so," he retorted. She saw his lips twitch. The cocky man had the nerve to laugh at her. She stumbled on the uneven cobblestones.

Her employee made a sorry specimen in spite of his broad shoulders and great height. He claimed to be a major, but his shabby coat and unkempt hair didn't look like those of any military man of Nora's acquaintance.

She chanced another sidelong look. *He does appear strong enough. Thank goodness he thought to shave.*

In silence, they passed wine bars, a laundry, and some women whose profession Nora chose not to guess.

"How far?" he asked when they turned toward the bridge to Tiber Island.

"Are you unable to keep up, Major?" She searched her mind for another option—any option—to hiring the man at her side. She had none. *I need the blasted man. I don't like the looks of him, but I need him.*

"Perhaps you should explain more about our mission," he said. "The details aren't clear to me." His deep voice and the unexpected intrusion in her thoughts rattled her. She took a deep breath.

"Do you remember anything of our conversation last night?"

"Of course I do. You hired me to . . ."

*The oaf can't remember!*

"Interpret," he finished lamely.

He had been drunk. The obvious signs of morning-after ravages disgusted her. His skin had the sickly pallor of the habitual drunkard, and his eyes were red rimmed. She couldn't deal with him hung over.

When they reached a small piazza at the foot of the bridge, she pushed him toward a café.

"You'll think more clearly after some tea and biscuits," she insisted.

"Coffee," he corrected, pulling up a chair into the sun and dropping onto it. He didn't pull out a chair for her.

"I beg your pardon?"

"This is Rome, not London. Coffee," he insisted.

*Insolent rogue!* She ignored his ill manners and seated herself.

"Very well, have coffee but also ask for dry bread and water—a great deal of water," she ordered.

"I beg your pardon?" he asked. She wondered if he was mocking her.

"Morning after sickness. You will feel better with something in your stomach," she told him.

"Husband?"

*He would remember that detail.*

"Yes," she said. Edmund had required a great deal of water to ease his headache—and a great deal of time to steady his unpredictable temper.

The major did as she told him with no complaint. That, at least, weighed in his favor. She began to hope he didn't resemble Edmund as much as she first assumed.

Nora swirled her coffee, thick and black, in a plain white mug and watched her employee wolf down a hard roll. Silence bothered him not a whit. Perhaps he had forgotten her.

He snatched up another roll and bit into it.

"You are alone here." His sudden words proved her wrong. He hadn't forgotten.

"Aside from Robert."

"Robert?" he asked.

"My brother."

"I'm confused. If your brother is here, why can't he interpret for you?"

"Robert is ill, in the hospital. I have to act for him," she explained.

"But you came here on your own. Your father permitted such a thing?" he probed.

He reached for another roll. *When did this impertinent man eat last?*

"My father couldn't—no, wouldn't—come when Robert wrote asking for help," she explained. "He sent me as his surrogate."

"So he ordered you to come a thousand miles alone to lecture his son on the error of his ways?" the major asked in between bites.

"Not ordered! Permitted. He has his parish to shepherd. Who could have come with me?" Her father actually tried to stop her, but she left for Rome on her own. The memory made her temper snap. "I'm no schoolroom miss. I can take care of myself," she insisted.

"You've managed without difficulty?" The major looked skeptical.

"Yes!" Nora knew she answered too quickly.

The major raised an eyebrow, and she felt her face warm. *My troubles with the ship and the sailors are none of his business. I managed them.*

"Language is a barrier," she admitted, but he knew that much already. "That's why I hired you. Difficulties have been trivial. Robert's man of business found me rooms and managed to convey me there with signs and gestures. The landlady . . ." She hesitated.

"Landlady?" he prompted.

"Speaks broken English. She tried to make me uneasy. She claimed there were men lurking at the door, but I think she just wanted me to hire a relative as a guide. I refused."

His deep brown eyes widened when she mentioned lurking strangers, but he said only, "Wise. You wouldn't want a guide you don't understand. Didn't your father think you would need protection?"

"He assumes my virtue to be its own shield! His widowed daughter—plain and practical Eleanora—wouldn't need protection." The words tasted as bitter in her mouth as the Italian coffee.

The major, to his credit, ignored that outburst. Instead he asked, "Wasn't he concerned about his granddaughter?"

Nora felt her heart stutter. She took a deep breath before answering. "He doesn't know about her."

The major looked puzzled, waiting for more. Desire to protect Robert's privacy warred with urge to confide in someone. As her interpreter, he would find out soon enough.

"My niece is Italian," she began, "and Catholic. Robert kept his marriage secret."

The shabby major appeared to think that over. "What will your father do with an Italian granddaughter?" he asked at last.

"Deny her. Force conversion. God knows, but it wouldn't be pleasant. Robert must protect her from that."

"Does your brother wish her to live in England?"

"Not in Dorset, not near Father. Perhaps in Italy, but he wishes more for her than the convent school." Nora knew that much with certainty.

"And her Italian relatives?" he asked.

Nora shrugged. "I don't know. My late, heretofore unknown sister-in-law was an orphan but from a large extended family." Robert had once implied there was more, but Nora didn't know any names or places. "What they wish is unknown to me," she said.

"Would they take the child in? That would solve your problems," he suggested.

"Robert seems reluctant about that. He hasn't said why. I think he wants to make sure someone he trusts will see that she is loved, as well as cared for." When Robert first told her about the girl, Nora had warmed at the thought of having a child to care for. Now she vacillated between hope and fear, neither of which accomplished anything useful. *This shabby major doesn't need to know my pathetic hopes.*

The major's thick brown lashes veiled his eyes as well as he veiled his thoughts. "Are your brother's wishes in writing?" he asked.

"I don't know. He pressed a scrap of foolscap into my hand the first day." She rummaged in her reticule. "It has an Italian name on it. He said that if he died I should contact this man." She held out the foolscap for him to see.

"Putting you at the mercy of another Italian," he mumbled, taking the foolscap. The major looked at the name and cursed softly. "And a high class one at that."

"That is not your concern!" She snatched back the note. *This pathetic excuse for a major has no right to criticize Robert!* Curiosity pushed her to ask, "Is he important?"

"Beaumont's legal representative? Prestigious but not political," he said. "Expensive. Your brother must have money. What will you do?"

He would have discovered Robert's wealth eventually, but Nora wished desperately that he actually cared. She knew his real question: What do I have to do to earn my keep?

"I have no idea about the future," she said. "For now, I wish only to get acquainted with Isabella and to assess the situation for myself."

"That's where my services come in?"

"Yes, Major, precisely. I must have accurate information. My own guesses are inadequate."

"We are to visit the child, speak with the sisters, and gather information?"

*He understands my needs accurately,* she thought. *How hard can this be?*

## Chapter 3

Money made most tasks bearable. Jamie thought the hefty purse in his pocket would make the task he had accepted easy. An hour later, he thought differently.

The smell of death, the trappings of wealth, and the hostile glare from the man on the bed all signaled trouble Jamie didn't need. The little bird had led him to a hospital, not a convent.

She introduced the patient as her brother, Robert Beaumont. Any pleasantry from Beaumont's initial greeting to his sister disappeared when he looked at Jamie.

"This is Major Bently, Robert, an English gentleman. I've employed him to assist in interpreting." The little wren's knuckles turned white when she gripped her reticule.

Her brother's face, white as the crisp linens on which he lay, folded into a frown. "Is that wise, Nora? Father—"

"Is in Dorset. I have no choice," she insisted. "I need assistance so I can make the arrangements you wish for Isabella."

Beaumont's dull gray eyes assessed Jamie with implacable distaste for several long moments. Beaumont might have been sick, but Jamie felt his eyes circling him like those of a predator, looking for any sign of weakness.

"Your sister is in Rome without protection. I'll endeavor to give her what assistance I can," Jamie said, holding his ground.

The patient looked away first.

"Protection? Utter nonsense!" Jamie's flustered employer blurted out. "I can take care of myself. I will learn Italian quickly. For now, I need help if I'm to look after Isabella."

Jamie glanced at the door. He considered returning the money but thought better of it. He had already given half to his landlord on his way out. Besides, Beaumont, he guessed from the looks of the private room and level of care, could afford him even if his sister could not. The man lay dying. His disapproval mattered little.

"Perhaps it would be best if I understood the situation fully from your point of view, Mr. Beaumont," he said.

Beaumont shrank into the linens. *Resignation didn't sit well with this one. I wouldn't want to do business with him,* Jamie thought.

"My problem is my daughter," Beaumont rasped. Jamie leaned close. "She is in the care of the sisters who staff this place. They also have a small school—more of an orphanage, I fear. I placed her with them after my wife died when it became clear that I, that is—damn it, obviously I could not go on caring for her."

"Robert cared for her himself until he became too ill." The little bird ruffled her feathers to ward off criticism.

Jamie made an impatient gesture. "Your defense does you credit, but that doesn't help the current situation." He turned back to Beaumont. "Your daughter is well cared for at present, but you are concerned for the future?"

"Yes," Beaumont said. "I don't wish her to be raised in a convent school."

"I don't understand the problem. Can't your sister simply remove the girl at your say-so? Surely the language barrier can be breached that much."

"It isn't that simple." Beaumont closed his eyes, and Jamie leaned still closer. "My wife was Italian. We were married in her church. I converted, Major. I am Catholic. My father doesn't—"

"Approve?"

"Robert, save your strength. Let me finish," Nora Haley soothed.

"Go on." Jamie turned to politely watch the little widow. Her brother appeared to slip beyond speech.

"Father is unaware that Isabella exists, as I told you," she ground out. "He would be outraged by Robert's marriage, if he knew of it, outraged by Isabella."

"He's a vicar?" Jamie asked.

His employer nodded and went on. "For now, she is in the care of the sisters. Her mother's family approves of that arrangement."

"But not of her very English aunt?" he guessed.

Her cheeks flushed, but she didn't shrink. "They don't know about me as yet. Robert wishes—"

"Isabella must be raised Catholic. The Count—" Beaumont's voice, strong with emotion, startled Jamie. The implication startled him even more.

"What count?" Jamie felt his heart pound.

"The Count di Castellimonte, my wife's uncle, and her guardian. He—" Beaumont tried to interject, but his burst of strength ebbed as quickly as it had come. "The Count is of no consequence," he whispered.

*No consequence? The Count di Castellimonte, cousin to the King of Sardinia, the kingdom's eyes and ears in Rome, represented very great consequence—consequence and trouble.* Jamie kept his curses silent.

"Every child deserves a family, Major," Beaumont said before his eyes drifted shut.

Nora Haley touched her brother's head. "Robert," she soothed. "We're going to Isabella."

Beaumont's eyes flickered back open. "Be careful, Nora. Don't trust . . ." His voice trailed into silence.

"Don't trust" sounded like damned good advice to Jamie. *If the chit has any sense, she'd demand her money back, even the half in my landlord's pocket.*

The widow stood. "My brother needs his rest, Major. We're going to Isabella now."

The little wren marched out of her brother's room and into the street without looking to see if Jamie followed. He did, glad to shake the smell of death. He recognized command when he heard it.

"You'll interpret. That is all I require of you. It's simple enough."

Jamie trudged behind his employer.

He believed the tattered remnants of his honor had died when he sold his dress uniform to eat. Now the woman's "simple" requirements threatened to wake that sense of honor from the dead.

*Simple? Only if I forgot that Italians were even less tolerant of independent women than Englishmen. Simple only if Castellimonte couldn't destroy this chit with a word. Simple only if the foolish woman had any hope of caring for a child that speaks no English and practices a religion that would give her grandfather an attack of apoplexy.*

"Major, do you have a question about what I require?" *The damned woman sounds like a governess and looks like she's wound so tightly she might snap.*

Jamie unclenched his jaw and stifled his inconvenient attack of conscience. She hired him to interpret, not to investigate counts. *Interpret. No more.*

She believed his word, and he took her money. He owed her a month. How she chose to use it need not concern him.

"No, Mrs. Haley. No questions. What you require is simple enough."

## Chapter 4

An overwhelming urge to throttle her new employee swept through Nora. Cold seeped through her gown, and her back ached from trying to sit upright on a marble bench in the convent garden while he prattled away with a tiny girl. *The man has no sense. An intelligent person can't even converse with him!*

The major had evaded her questions about his background. When he did speak, he spouted nonsense all the way to Santo Spirito. He feigned subservience and ignored direct orders. He treated ladies with cool politeness and flirted with elderly nuns and small girls.

Nora had watched helplessly while the major bantered in Italian with the irritable sister who guarded the gate. The nun's eyes grew wide. Just when Nora thought they would be turned away, the old woman chuckled to herself and let them in. Whatever he had said sounded like it was inappropriate, but it worked.

"Whatever you do, Major, do not antagonize the superior of the convent," she had admonished when they were shown into a parlor.

"Of course not," he had responded, gazing at the impossibly tall, hatchet-faced nun who swept in to loom over Nora.

The woman spoke in clipped tones and tight-lipped severity. The major spoke back harshly. When the woman stepped out, anger marred her face.

That's when Nora snapped. "What are you doing? We have to work with these women!"

"That woman is not the superior. If Hatchet Face had the power to deny you, she would have. She didn't."

Before Nora could respond, the major had led her to a sunny garden, fragrant with jasmine and humming with bees. Within moments, Robert's daughter appeared. She had immediately batted long black lashes at the shabby major, prattled adoringly in Italian, and ignored Nora completely. Nora's rumpled employee appeared to encourage the girl.

Nora took in a deep breath and let it out slowly to tamp down her growing irritation. The smell of jasmine mingled with something sweet and cloying. She riveted her eyes on the sight in front of her.

*The little imp is a natural flirt, and he has no shame. Blast the man! What have I gotten myself into?*

Nora made out one word. "Papa." That word and the sadness that darkened Isabella's eyes kept Nora from interfering with his nonsense and demanding the child's attention.

Major Bently turned to Nora at last and said, "She asks after her father. He is, she has been told, very, very ill."

Nora nodded. She looked down at the little girl who scrutinized Nora for the first time.

"She says you look like her papa. His hair is also the color of grass," he told her.

"Grass! Green?"

"Not in Italy in August," he explained. "It is light brown and gold. Come, let's try to talk to this little person."

The major sat next to her, reached down, and pulled Isabella up into his lap. The little one went without question, leaned her head against him, and sucked her thumb, as if a man's shoulder was the most natural place for her to rest. Nora resisted the temptation to like him better for it. *Men can be charming when they choose,* she remembered.

"I am your father's sister," Nora said and waited while the major translated. She looked directly into blue eyes that were exactly like Robert's but utterly out of place with black hair and an olive complexion. The incongruity stunned her.

The little girl tipped her chin sideways to look skeptically at the man and spoke. He answered her briefly in Italian and then translated. "She said she didn't know adults had sisters. I assured her that they do."

"Ask her if she is doing well. Ask her if she is happy here." *Robert trusts these sisters. Should I?*

More words Nora didn't understand. She clamped her jaw shut to avoid voicing her impatience.

"Sister Cecilia told her she was naughty this morning for picking the green tomatoes from the vine," he said at last, "but usually she is better behaved."

Nora smiled at that, and the little one smiled back. Nora felt the warmth of it down to her toes while the major spoke to the girl softly in Italian and the little one responded once again.

"I asked her if Sister Cecilia was very tall and prone to frowning like our grim vision in the parlor. She said yes."

Nora crinkled her nose in distaste. "How—that is, where does she sleep?"

"In the dormitory with the bigger girls. She informs me she is no longer a baby, but she does still have her *bambola*. Doll, I think," he said.

The little girl put a hand to the major's face and spoke to him again.

"The *bambola's* name is Marietta," he told Nora. "She came with Isabella from her father's house where she has many dolls. They have their own little bed. She says they learned to be very quiet because her mama was sick."

"She remembers?"

"Apparently."

"Ask her about her mama," Nora demanded.

He looked reluctant but didn't argue. He conversed gently with the little girl before translating.

"She is an angel," he said at last. "Isabella has been told she went to heaven, and this makes her sad. Her papa is going to see her mother, but he doesn't want—no, he 'refuses' to take Isabella." More swift Italian words. "Isabella is not pleased with Papa for refusing."

When Robert died the little one would have the nuns and her distant Italian relatives. Nora would have no one at all. All that would remain in Dorset would be an angry old man and a cold vicarage. Tears flooded Nora's eyes. She thought she detected sympathy in her interpreter's face. *Foolish notion.*

The major turned and whispered something to the little one. Isabella's giggle caught Nora off guard.

"I asked if there was a fairy in the rose garden," he explained. "She tells me fairies are not real and that I'm silly. I told her we should check."

Soon the major and tiny girl peered into the fountain and peeked under rose bushes, conversing companionably. His face folded into a comical mask of disappointment every time they failed to find fairies.

Nora allowed her bleeding heart to rest in the privacy he provided. The little girl appeared to be well fed, clean, and cared for. She had the laughter of childhood and the glow of health. *Perhaps Robert chose wisely when he sent her here. Does she even need an awkward English aunt?*

The little girl let out a gasp of outrage and shook a finger at the major in a charade of adult behavior. Nora had no idea what made them convulse in laughter.

She felt certain loneliness lurked in the precious little face also. *No child should grow up lonely,* she thought. A fierce desire to provide something better gripped Nora and would not let go.

Lost in emotion and captivated by the game the major invented, Nora missed the sound of footsteps in the cloister.

Isabella had better hearing. The little one looked up with joy and threw herself at a tiny nun standing just behind

Nora. The woman scooped Isabella up in an encompassing hug, her billowing black sleeves wrapped around the tiny body like a comforter.

"The sister asks if she is enjoying her aunt," the major's voice whispered in Nora's ear. "Isabella says you are not an aunt. You are her father's sister."

Nora watched the smiling face of the woman holding the child, watched easy warmth and affection radiate between them. Iron bands of jealousy constricted her chest. Nora clamped her teeth and told herself to be sensible.

"She is explaining the meaning of the relationship," the whisper continued.

A few words of Italian and a second sister appeared from the shadows to take Isabella by the hand. The little girl looked disappointed but didn't shrink back. Both nuns turned to Nora expectantly.

"She is being taken back to the classroom. They seek your permission to end the visit."

"No!" Nora exclaimed. "That is, yes. I think it is best for this first time."

Sudden fear seized her as she watched the little one disappear into the locked and protected walls of a foreign convent. Every lurid story she had ever heard about convents, no matter how foolish, flooded her memory. She frowned at the tiny nun who had remained behind and spoke defiantly to Jamie.

"Tomorrow. Tell her I will visit tomorrow." Nora's voice rose. "And every day after that. Tell her now."

## Chapter 5

Jamie brushed a hand across the back of his neck. *The little bird has talons. But attack now? Damned poor choice of tactics.*

He stared down at the woman swathed in yards of black silk. Sharp black eyes looked steadily back.

"I am Reverend Mother Margarita," the woman said.

Silent laughter racked him. The tiny woman who had just lavished warmth and affection on Isabella commanded this army. *Like any good commander, this one is a master of surprise!*

"Reverend Mother, is it? My employer, Mrs. Nora Haley," he said, gesturing toward the wren. The daft woman glared back. *Keep that up, Nora Haley, and you'll ruin your chances before they start.*

Mother Margarita smiled warmly, but Jamie wasn't fooled. Intelligent eyes danced over Nora, taking in her grim expression. *This one misses nothing.*

He wished for a stiff drink. He needed a diversion before his employer could shoot herself in the foot—or before the shrewd little woman in front of him saw right through him.

"We are aware that Mrs. Haley has come from England to care for her brother," the nun said, prodding him to go on.

"He receives excellent care from your sisters at the hospital," Jamie replied, pulling attention away from the wren. He ignored his employer's attempts to draw his attention back.

"But there is no substitute for family, is there?" he went on, attempting a charming grin.

"Did you tell her what I said?" Nora Haley hissed. He didn't look at her.

"Mrs. Haley is grateful for your care for both her brother and the little one," Jamie gushed on in Italian as if those were the words she had spoken.

Mother Margarita's lips quirked. She asked a question. His employer bobbed her head back and forth between Jamie and the nun in confusion.

"Don't jump your guns," he whispered in English. "She wants to know more about you."

"I need to ask her about Isabella," Nora insisted.

"In due time," he said and returned his attention to Mother Margarita with a charming smile.

"Mrs. Haley is a widow," he began in Italian. "She lived until recently with her father in—" He bent toward Nora and asked in English, "Dorset was it?"

The wren nodded, but a fierce frown twisted her features. She obviously didn't wish to discuss family. If she bit her lip any harder, she would draw blood.

"Her father is a vicar." Jamie reverted to Italian.

"Protestant?" Mother Margarita asked.

"Yes. Certainly."

The Reverend Mother looked troubled, but whether it was for the salvation of Mrs. Haley's soul or for the complications it meant regarding the child's care, he couldn't say. In fact, he had run out of things to say.

He watched the two women, both tiny in stature but strong in will, take each other's measure. His employer didn't shrink. She stiffened her spine, put on what appeared to be a righteous confidence like a cloak, and let Mother Margarita observe her. *Good for you, Nora Haley. Stand your ground*, he thought. *Just don't attack.* He had known hardened soldiers with less backbone than the wren.

"You wish to see your niece again tomorrow?" Reverend Mother asked finally. Jamie translated, his jaw tense. *If the wren wrecks this encounter, she might not get back in.*

His employer's fierce expression when she answered yes would have quelled a regiment. There was no need to translate. "And every day," she added.

Mother Margarita launched into a convoluted explanation about prayer schedules, schoolroom demands, and children's naps. Jamie managed to keep up.

"Visits may take place at three for the time being," Mother Margarita decided. Jamie translated. *The wren ought to accept that,* he thought.

"Three? Every day?" the wren demanded to know, red blotches warring with white on her face.

"Certainly," the tiny nun agreed. Mother Margarita didn't say how long the arrangement would last. Robert Beaumont's days had to be few. "For one hour."

"Two!" the wren demanded. Jamie groaned.

"Don't press your luck," he said in English. "That will be acceptable, thank you," he told the nun in Italian.

Nora Haley bit back whatever else she wanted to say. Jamie relaxed his shoulders. *Good tactic. Save the heavy artillery until you need it.* He began to realize that his dainty little employer had sense as well as bottom.

"And who, exactly, are you?" the mother superior demanded.

*Damn! A surprise attack just when I let down my guard.* The woman who confronted him gave no quarter.

"Major James Bently," he said with a slight bow. "Mrs. Haley's interpreter, her employee." He tried, but failed, to look at her directly when he said it. When he glanced back down the diminutive nun's penetrating look, assessing and weighing him, made his knees weak.

The Reverend Mother seemed to choose her next words carefully.

"The Count di Castellimonte wishes to see Isabella. He requests that she be taken to Palazzo di Savoia in the morning. That is, of course, impossible." Mother Margarita spoke directly to Nora in Italian. Jamie had to squash his panic in order to keep up. "It will not do because of the child's schooling. He will see her here. Tomorrow."

"But I thought this count lived in Sardinia!" the wren exclaimed grabbing his arm.

"Piedmont." Jamie corrected her without taking his eyes off Mother Margarita. *Castellimonte here? I won't come near the place.*

"Pardon?" the wren asked.

"His holdings are in the Piedmont, but he has a home here also." Jamie's stomach clenched. *Home? It's a damn palace in the center of Rome.*

Palazzo di Savoia lay close to the papacy, close to diplomatic circles, and close to European intelligence networks. *Too damned close. What a mess!*

"I see."

*She doesn't see. Isabella's family can squash Nora Haley like a bug.* Jamie knew they could also unravel his carefully protected anonymity with the stroke of a finger. He had to wiggle out of his commitment to accompany his employer the next day.

"Mrs. Haley, I don't think we want to encounter Castellimonte just yet," he said. "Perhaps we could skip tomorrow's visit."

"Absolutely not!" His employer raised her stubborn jaw.

A smile played on Mother Margarita's lips. "A problem, Major Bently?"

"What time does the count visit? Will there be a conflict?" He prayed there was.

"Not at all," the little nun said. "He visits at the noon hour." Panic subsided. The man and his retinue would be gone by three.

"What, Major? Please tell me what she said."

"No conflict, Mrs. Haley. We can come at three." *And not a damned minute earlier.*

He suppressed a temptation to shout a warning about Castellimonte. She paid him to interpret. Neither she, nor her niece, nor the girl's family politics were Jamie's problem. He owed her a month. He could stay out of sight that long.

"Isabella must know her family." Nora Haley's melodic voice had steel in it. "Both sides. Tell her." Her lower lip thrust firmly over a chin so stubborn Jamie pitied the man who crossed her. "Tell her," she repeated.

He did. Mother Margarita nodded approval, murmured goodbyes, and slipped silently back into the cloister. The woman, who denied the commands of counts, appeared to favor neither family.

His wren watched the commanding nun disappear into the inner sanctum without flinching.

"The Piedmont?" she whispered several moments later, still staring after the woman.

"The Piedmont is one part, the mountains. The entire thing is designated 'The Kingdom of Sardinia.'"

"Isn't that an island?" She stared at the closed door as if she could will Isabella back.

"Sardinia itself is," Jamie answered, "but the island isn't the power center. Piedmont is the ancestral holding of the House of Savoy. Savoy rules Sardinia from their mountain strongholds."

"And this count?" she spat. Turning to look at him now, attention was hot in her eyes. The brave little bird, both wise and foolish, was taking stock of her enemy, a sleek and ravenous wolf.

"The count is Savoy. Your niece's great-uncle is the king's cousin." He kept his voice flat and followed her to the gate.

"Damned aristocrats," she mumbled.

Black humor twisted Jamie's gut in response to Nora Haley's anti-aristocratic sentiments. *God help me. What would she say if she found out she had hired a bankrupt baron?*

"Isabella's family rules Sardinia and the Piedmont?" she went on without noticing Jamie's reaction.

"Yes." He didn't add that Savoy ruled Genoa also, thanks to the Congress of Vienna, and all the lands in bordering France as a reward for successfully navigating between Napoleon and his enemies. *Devious is the word for Savoy. One little widow poses no challenge to them.*

She paused at the gate. "We'll see her tomorrow."

"Yes, Ma'am," he agreed. *But don't count on the day after.* A shudder ran down Jamie's spine, and he fought the temptation to bolt.

## Chapter 6

*At least the major didn't bolt*, Nora thought. He had been tempted. She was sure of it. She actually feared he would abandon her when she saw panic in his eyes at the end of the first visit to the convent. She had no idea what had spooked him. He came the next day, however, and for each of the four days after.

Nora watched for signs of drink when he met her, rumpled and scowling but on time. She found none. Pallor and a slight tremor when she took his arm seemed to indicate lack of drink rather than a surfeit of it.

They met daily at the little café on the Trastevere side of the bridge. She couldn't visit a single man's room; that first day had taken all her nerve. She certainly didn't want her employee in hers. The sensible solution had been to meet between the two.

*Perhaps the food keeps him coming*, she thought wryly. Nora fed him every day at noon. As usual, the major came on time and tucked into his luncheon with enthusiasm. *The man does like his food.*

"What?" he asked, looking back at her intently.

Her face heated. The shabby major caught her staring at him.

"Nothing," she said. "Finish up quickly so we can see Robert before we go to Isabella."

"I doubt it is 'nothing,'" he retorted. "I can see your mind working."

"You like to eat," she said.

"Any sensible man does," he laughed. "Never know when the next meal will come."

Nora digested that information. The dozen or so questions she had about the major flooded her brain.

"Where did you serve?" she blurted. There seemed no point in asking him when he left service. So many officers had been put on half-pay, so many soldiers jettisoned, after Napoleon finally surrendered.

"Here and there," he answered, neatly deflecting questions once again. He made it clear she didn't pay him enough to interrogate him. She let it pass.

He took a second helping of fish broiled in olive oil and changed the subject. "You're good with children. Do you have experience?"

"You mean do I have children of my own? No." Familiar sadness filled her.

The major ate in silence, but his raised brow encouraged her to go on.

"I did set up a cottage school for girls in my father's parish after Edmund died. It was," she groped for words, "poor in resources." Sadness washed over her briefly. She missed it still.

"Your father didn't support it," he said. She found his shrewdness surprising when it surfaced.

"'Damned foolishness' he called it. He thought it contrary to the natural order to educate women."

"Who educated you?" the major asked.

"My mother and the lending library," she answered. "Behind his back," she added before she snapped her mouth shut. *He has no business asking about my family.*

"Did you say your husband wrote poetry?" he asked.

Nora nodded. "I think I fell in love with literature. Edmund represented everything my father forbad me." She still remembered the elation of that defiance—and the humiliation when she had to crawl back to him.

"Intriguing," he said. "I wonder what else you did to thwart the vicar." Laughter danced in his eyes.

"He forbad my work with the Dorset Anti-Slavery Alliance entirely. I finally had to resign," she told him bitterly. "He managed to defend the greatest evil of our age by twisting Scripture."

Memory of the old man's voice when he threatened to cut her off and let her starve echoed in her head. She stared down into the dregs of her tea. Even now she found her capitulation humiliating. *Some evils demand courage; my courage failed under pressure.*

She couldn't look at the major for a long moment. When she did, she saw that his laughter had ceased. She thought his expression looked pained. Perhaps he disapproved of abolitionists. She reminded herself it was none of his business.

He rose to his feet. "Let's get to it," he said in clipped tone.

She paid the bill, and they set out for the hospital. The major had proven to be dependable and, occasionally, even perceptive. She had the rest of the month to make use of his skills, and she determined to make the best of it. Now he looked surly and irritable.

"Is there a problem, Major?"

## Chapter 7

Jamie's problems began when Mother Margarita started coming a bit earlier than needed. While Nora Haley's curiosity had been easily deflected, the mother superior proved to be relentless.

Isabella, who had quickly decided to use her classroom English to "teach" her aunt Italian, sat next to the wren, laughing and pointing. His employer loved it. Jamie stood in the shade of the cloister walk and watched the wren and her niece trade vocabulary and smiles.

Mother Margarita found Jamie there. "Do you have children, Major?" she asked without preamble.

Jamie choked. He didn't disguise his horror. "I should think not."

"You are good with Isabella," the nun said. "Nieces and nephews?"

"Friends," he said. "They dote on the little monsters. I play with them and leave."

"Friends are a great blessing," Mother Margarita said. He again felt as though she could see right through him.

"That they are," he managed. They had once been the best part of his life. "The Cohort" they called themselves, friends since boyhood.

"Are you close to your friends?" she asked.

"Not any longer." *Not since I fled in shame.*

"What part of England is your home, Major?" she asked.

He hesitated. He tried silence. The Reverend Mother waited him out.

"I grew up in Rossmoor, Mother," he explained at last, "a tiny speck deep in Derbyshire—that is the Midlands—not a place you are likely to recognize." He rushed on before she could pursue that line of questioning, "And you, Mother, where do you call home?"

"My home is here, of course," she smiled, "but I suspect you mean my place of origin. The answer is quite dull—Rome. I have not traveled far afield." Her look of innocence didn't fool Jamie. She pushed on before he could think of another tactic.

"Do your parents still live in Rossmoor?"

Jamie groaned inwardly. *Here it comes*.

"My father died three years ago," he said. Jamie clamped his jaw shut and determined to say nothing more. *The foul old man died with a knife in his chest on a table covered with the cards his assailant accused him of shaving.*

"Do you have family, Reverend Mother?" he asked before she forced him to describe his mother's circumstances. His question elicited a warm discussion of siblings and their many children.

"Do you have brothers and sisters, Major?"

*So much for diversion.* "One sister," he said.

"Not married?"

"I believe Arianna is past the age where women expect to marry." With no dowry thanks to her only brother's stupidity and little reputation thanks to their father's behavior, Arianna had no hope of a decent marriage.

"She lives with my mother," he continued and then cursed himself for a fool. He braced for the next question. The two women who had every right to expect Jamie's protection lived in dire poverty at the mercy of a miserly old aunt thanks to his incompetence.

Isabella's running assault on her favorite nun put a stop to the questions that day, but not the campaign.

Every day Nora Haley went to visit her niece. Every day Jamie facilitated until the two of them went off on their own. Every day Mother Margarita's interrogation continued.

He began to think the tenacious general at Santo Spirito had intelligence gathering skills Wellington would have welcomed. She never let up.

The nun quickly recognized that Jamie would not be forthcoming with details and began evasive tactics. He resolved to be careful. He still owed Nora Haley three weeks, and he wanted to finish it.

Mother Margarita tried literature, politics, and, finally, money.

"Poverty isn't the greatest evil," she probed that afternoon. "Debt is unfortunate but needn't be permanent or cause for shame."

The Mother Superior undoubtedly knew that Englishmen often slunk to Rome to avoid debtor's prison.

"Quite right. Pockets to let is no disgrace," he said.

"One can seek the help of friends." She would remember that.

"Of course," he said. Jamie didn't object to living off his friends, or even asking for a loan. They could all afford to help.

"Friends can be generous," she went on.

*Or horrified if they knew I attempted the vilest of methods to multiply my miserable inheritance. Even that failed. They would despise me.* He felt sick.

"Major?" she repeated.

Jamie stared into an abyss. His mind filled with the fate of one hundred and thirty-two souls chained below deck of a ship bound for the Charleston slave market. It sank with all hands and Jamie's inheritance. *Of course they would despise me if they knew. I despise myself.* At the thought of losing the respect of the friends who mattered most, despair filled him.

"So, Mother," he began on a shaky breath, desperate to change the subject, "how do you think—"

That time the chapel bells rescued him, chiming time for Isabella to leave.

He walked his employer to the gate.

"I'll bid you good night, Major Bently," Nora Haley said.

His only response was a grunt. She raised an eyebrow.

"Aren't you going to offer to escort me to my rooms so that I can say no?" she asked, amusement plain on her face.

It had become a ritual with them. Every afternoon he offered to escort her home. Every afternoon she refused, saying she didn't pay him to escort her; she paid him to interpret. Every afternoon he pretended to give in and then followed her home.

Sunk in his own hell, he had no response.

"Until tomorrow then," she said.

"Of course," he growled sourly. *Tonight the stubborn woman can have her way.*

Jamie had other concerns. The screams of one hundred and thirty-two drowning men echoed in his head. He knew he could never tell his friends. *I certainly won't tell my abolitionist, temperance-happy employer,* he thought. *I need a drink.*

Nora sucked in a panicked breath and wished she had allowed the major to follow her home. Someone else had. She sped up.

The footsteps sounded behind her soon after the major had turned away toward his own rented room. She knew it wasn't the major. Cold needles of fear stabbed at her spine.

When Nora began to run, the steps kept pace. She glanced over her shoulder, but the furtive little man kept to the deepening late afternoon shadows.

She stayed to the center of the road, avoided alleys, and sidestepped dark doorways toward her boarding house. Her rooms lay uphill in a more respectable neighborhood across the river from the major's dilapidated room. Respectability made it empty and quiet.

She felt a fool as she scurried to her rooms. The major's teasing haunted her. *Why didn't I let him walk me home?*

Nora climbed the stairs, locked the door, and hurried to the partially shuttered window in the back from which she could look down on the inner courtyard.

A man passed through the passage to the street, the passage Nora had used to access her stairway, into the courtyard. Tall, thin, and somberly dressed, he bent in furtive conversation with her landlady. Coins passed from his hand to hers before an oily smile slid across his face and he disappeared into the passage.

On the stone pavement below, the landlady counted coins, dropping them one by one into her pocket. *The evil old woman!*

Nora sagged against the wall, utterly alone. *Who can I dare trust in this place? Even the sisters have other loyalties, ties to country, to Church, and to family.* Nora had only Robert, and he faded daily.

The major's shaggy head with its sad brown eyes swam before her. Whatever plagued him after his conversation with Mother Margarita, she wished again that he had followed her home.

The tremor in her hands and the fluttering of her heart embarrassed her. She loathed weakness but knew her pride for the root of her problems. Another woman would have let him walk her home.

"Don't be a chicken heart!" she said to the empty room. *I never succumb to nerves. At least, I never did before.* She had managed alone in Dorset, in her own home, among people she knew.

*At least the major understands me when I talk.* She didn't know when that had begun to matter, but it did now.

"He owes you nothing," she told herself. "You hired him to interpret, not to be your watch dog."

The pounding of her heart would not be quieted. *It wouldn't hurt to have a simple conversation with my employee would it? With the furtive little man gone, it would be safe enough to go to him, wouldn't it?*

Within minutes Nora hurried toward the winding streets of Trastevere, clinging to the west bank of the Tiber. No one followed, but she walked faster when the streets narrowed, the sun sank lower, and the cafés grew seedier.

## Chapter 8

"Major!"

Jamie took a step, gripped his wine bottle, and fought the urge to run. *What is that damned woman doing here at this hour?*

He breathed in, allowing the stink of street offal to mingle with the sour odor from the barroom door and pummel his senses. *At least I can tell I'm alive. Is there time to hide?*

"Major!" the familiar voice demanded, closer now. "I need you."

*Of course she does, the inconvenient chit. I've been ten days sober, and she needs me the one evening I need oblivion.* Jamie pulled the bottle closer, cradling it in the crook of one elbow, and turned to face his employer.

"What are you doing here?" he demanded.

"I—" Her breath heaved in and out. "I—"

Jamie glowered down at her. At least he tried to. Her face stopped him. *The damned woman shivered.* Something brought her running like a scared rabbit, and he didn't like it one bit. He reminded himself that she wasn't his problem. *She isn't,* he repeated to himself, *there's no need to go soft on her.*

Nora Haley's eyes hardened as if she read his mind.

"What is that under your arm?" she asked.

He held up the wine bottle. The cork rested askew, the bottle open, but the contents almost full.

"As you see," he said. *Damned if I'll apologize. We were done for the day, weren't we?*

"Did you need something?"

She looked hesitant. *She wouldn't hesitate if Beaumont died. What else could it be?*

"Yes, I have a paper for you to translate. Can we sit somewhere?" Her eyes darted unerringly toward the window of his room high on the side of the dilapidated house across the street.

"I think not, Mrs. Haley. Follow me." He put a hand on her arm and led her to the café next to the disreputable tavern where she had first accosted him.

Jamie examined his nearly full bottle of wine, feeling his mouth water, while the waiter brought tea. *Get on with it,* he thought.

"Do you want to tell me why you are here?" he asked impatiently. The sooner he got it over with, the sooner he could drink himself to sleep. "A paper, I believe?"

The woman sipped her steaming tea and pursed her lips. He could see rosy streaks rise up her neck. *She's not as confident as she wants to appear. What spooked her?*

"The paper?" he repeated.

The redness deepened when she bent to open her reticule, fetched out a familiar looking piece of foolscap, and handed it to him.

Jamie gave it a perfunctory glance. "'Signore Antonio Salvia, Legal Representative,'" he read. "Do you want me to translate the address?"

She shook her head, unable to meet his eyes.

"You showed me this days ago." He tossed it down in front of her. "Why are you really here?"

She told him.

Jamie Heyworth could curse in six languages and still remember to be grateful the woman across from him only understood one. He avoided English. At least she finally recognized danger when it forced itself on her, recognized it, and ran for him. *Interpreter? She needs a damned keeper. I didn't agree to be her keeper.*

"Describe him," he demanded.

"Describe him?" Her blue eyes clouded in confusion, their sparkle gone in the gloomy café. He hated it. *Her eyes should shine with all the reflected light of her quick mind.*

Jamie tamped down any thoughts about her eyes and felt his anger rise. "Describe—tall, short, thin, fat? English? German?" he barked.

"Italian," she answered. "I heard him speak, and his hair was dark."

He waved an impatient hand to indicate he needed more detail.

"Thin and tall. Very thin, I'm not sure how tall. His face is narrow, and I want to say—" she bit her lip, searching for the word.

"Ferret faced?" he interrupted, "Narrow like a weasel?"

"Yes," Nora sputtered, "Exactly like that."

"Wearing a plain suit?"

"Like a secretary or a clerk. Yes, a suit," she said. "You've seen this man?"

"He works for Isabella's uncle." *Castellimonte's Ferret.*

"The count? But how do you know?" she asked.

His job was to interpret, but his instinct and his inconvenient honor were another matter. He had made it his job to know.

"My employer lets me go early each day. It's a simple matter to reconnoiter the count's compound. The Ferret comes and goes often," he told her.

Nora chewed her lower lip. "The count's man? He watches me," she said, "and you watch him."

Jamie forced a smile he didn't feel. "That is often the way it works among adversaries."

Nora made no reply.

"Shall I escort you home?" *Oblivion will have to wait.*

"Please," she said.

"No argument? The man must have frightened you badly," he said.

Nora Haley bobbed her head.

"You're wise to be cautious. Keep your door locked, and don't wander the streets without an escort." Jamie pointed a finger at her when he said it.

She started to sputter protest and bit back the words. She nodded again.

Jamie acted as if he hadn't noticed. "I don't think you need to fear for your physical safety, but you might take a care for your reputation."

"My reputation?" Outrage put fire in her voice. The blue eyes shot sparks. He liked sparks. "How can that man know or care about my reputation?"

"He has you watched. A child's future is at stake. Have a care, Nora Haley," he said. He rose, extended his right hand to Nora, and picked up the bottle with his left.

"That can stay here," she said tartly. "I need you sober."

"What I do on my own time—" he began.

"—impacts me," she asserted. "You're the one who said I should look to my reputation. An escort carrying an open wine bottle won't enhance the impression I make on the Count di Castellimonte's spies."

She stared until he dropped his eyes. *The damned woman has a point.* He didn't resist when she took the bottle and signaled for the waiter. "Major Bently won't need this," she told him. "Kindly dispose of it."

Jamie's mouth watered. His hand shook with the need to pull it back. He needed just one night, just one blind drunk. *Does she have any idea how badly I need it?*

His night turned inside out and she went on speaking.

"Besides, Major," she said, "If anything happens to Robert, I may need you at any time of day. I need you sober."

If the count's man came after her, he'd be no help in a drunken stupor. He owed her two more weeks. *Apparently I owe it to her sober.*

## Chapter 9

Jamie crouched behind a fragrant verbena bush and wondered how he might avoid Mother Margarita. She continued to waylay him every day.

Every conversation had been nothing but a series of feints and sorties designed to expose his flank. Once when she got him to admit he hadn't been a model student of the classics, she said, "You are better educated than you would have her believe, aren't you, Major?"

*Thank God I never mentioned Cambridge or that two of my three closest friends have titles. I didn't have to. She probably guessed.*

Routed by a five-foot elf in a black habit, he now resorted to cowering behind the bushes. Much more and she would expose him to his aristocrat-hating employer and undermine his efforts to stay hidden.

"Dreading my company, Major?" Mother Margarita peered around the shrubbery and smiled in greeting; she spoke Italian as always.

Jamie rose to his feet. She was not alone. The figure of a tall, white-haired monk, austere in a black Benedictine habit, followed her. Big tired eyes and a gentle expression dominated the monk's lean face.

"Dreading your company, Reverend Mother? How could I? You are always charming." He turned on the smile that had once oiled his way through the finest drawing rooms in London. He spoke the truth; she used charm as a weapon. *I ought to know. I do the same.*

"What nonsense! You are adept at light conversation, but you keep yourself well-hidden. Does Mrs. Haley know as little about you as I do?"

"Less." *I certainly hope so.*

"As I thought. She is foolish to trust a stranger."

"Yes, but she has few choices." He felt compelled to defend Nora Haley. Reverend Mother nodded sadly. They both knew Robert Beaumont's days were numbered.

Jamie looked expectantly at Reverend Mother's companion, hoping to distract her.

She took his hint. "May I introduce Padre Barnabas?" she said with a twinkle in her eye.

Jamie bowed. "I am honored to make your acquaintance, Father. Are you the chaplain here?"

The old man's tired eyes, deep set in a narrow face that tapered to a strong pointed chin, lit up.

"When my duties permit it," he said. "Madre Margarita is my cousin. I like to look after her." The two smiled at one another with good humor as if from some familiar private joke. "My cousin told me about her English friends. She tells me the lady is lucky to have found a protector."

A flush of embarrassment shot through Jamie. "Interpreter," he said. "I am merely an employee. It may be, as Reverend Mother says, that she is foolish to trust a stranger, but she has few choices."

"Perhaps not. She is lucky then to have found someone so trustworthy," Reverend Mother said.

"You can't know that!" The words were out before Jamie could think. *The damned woman had no idea.* He thought of his mother and sister. *No woman should trust Jamie Heyworth.*

Mother Margarita smiled at the monk but spoke to Jamie. "Isabella trusts you. Children are wise about the true nature of people. That alone would have been enough to convince me."

"You can't be—"

"Can't be certain? Perhaps not, but I am usually right." She said it with certainty, and Jamie noticed that the wizened monk found that very amusing.

"Whatever it is that you hide may be to your shame, Major, but it is not to Mrs. Haley's harm, nor would it harm Isabella. You will carry out your obligations to her," Mother Margarita asserted.

"I promised a month. She will get a month."

"And if she needs you longer?" Father Barnabas seemed genuinely interested.

"I can't promise anymore." Jamie closed his mind to any other possibilities.

"Oh, look she has seen me!" Mother Margarita opened her arms. Isabella threw herself into them.

"I teach Aunt Nora Italian, Mother!" the little one exclaimed in her native language.

"Padre Barnabas!" The little girl dropped a deep curtsy to the cleric. Father Barnabas, obviously an old friend, planted a kiss on the top of her head. Mother Margarita tucked the little one under her left arm and held out her right to Nora Haley.

Warm sympathy passed from Mother Margarita to his employer; it needed no translation. She never failed to ask about Robert Beaumont, even though Jamie suspected she had more accurate medical information from her nursing sisters. Her compassion buoyed his employer.

Jamie translated their few words and facilitated an introduction to Mother's elderly cousin.

Nora colored when the old man warmly took her hand and offered her his blessing. She dipped her head when Jamie translated the words.

On a whisper of black silk they were gone, taking the child with them.

Nora followed Isabella with her longing eyes and spoke without looking at Jamie. "Who was that priest, and what was that about?"

"Her cousin, she said, a visitor. That's all." Nora looked skeptical but let it drop. She turned toward the gate.

Jamie didn't blame her skepticism. He couldn't shake the feeling they had been inspected. Why the opinion of an elderly monk mattered, he didn't know. *Spies everywhere,* he thought.

"It won't be much longer, now. What will I do then?"

*How the hell should I know? Any fool can see this woman longs for a child, and the good Lord knows I am eight kinds of fool. Anyone with eyes can see it. Nora Haley, good English wren, would pull out her own feathers to make a nest for Isabella.* Jamie squeezed his eyes shut. It would bring the woman only grief, he knew. *They will never let an English widow have the girl.*

He couldn't fix it for her. He owed her two more weeks. He planned to enjoy it in peace.

Nora climbed the steps two at a time, gasping for air. Her lungs hurt. She had run the entire way from her rented rooms to the major's as soon as Mother Margarita's message reached her.

"Major! Wake up! I need you!" she gasped.

She heard the bed creak. She didn't normally meet him until lunch. The sun still lay low in the sky. She could hear him moving around.

She pounded on his door. She didn't care how early it was. She needed him.

"Major! I need to speak with you!"

This time she didn't fall into his arms when he yanked the door open.

"Good morning, Mrs. Haley. Welcome to my palace." Her shabby major bowed his most ironic obeisance, but not, she noticed, before he scanned the hallway behind her.

"You shouldn't be here. Reputation, remember?" he whispered.

She ignored him. "Reverend Mother sent word." She pushed past him into the little room.

"Your brother?" he asked. His face darkened. "Has something happened to Isabella?"

"Fine, both. No, no. Not that." She gulped for air. "It is Castellimonte. He wishes to see me."

"Now?" The major began to shrug on his jacket, his face furrowed in thought.

"At two this afternoon." Nora breathed, wide eyed with fear.

He stopped. "What time is it?"

"Just past nine."

"Merciful heavens, woman. You have five hours!"

She dipped her head in shame. She wouldn't spell out her urge to share fear.

He must have been able to read it on her face as his tone changed. "On the other hand, you have time to prepare," he said.

"Prepare? How?" she demanded.

He began to shave. She suspected he had no idea.

"You'll want to look your best," he said at last.

Nora sputtered indignantly. "I certainly don't need to put on airs for some worthless aristocrat. Do you think I have a splendid afternoon gown hidden away? I don't waste my days sipping tea in fancy drawing rooms. What's good enough for Isabella and Mother Margarita is good enough for the Count di Castellimonte."

"You will want to rehearse your answers," he went on as if she hadn't spoken.

Nora glowered at the man's back. He ran a towel over his face and turned back to her.

"Fine," he said, "you stay here, then. Let the count's spies make what they want of it."

Anger drained out of her. "Do you think they followed me here?"

"Perhaps. I didn't see them, but that doesn't mean they aren't out there."

She sank into his rickety chair. "I don't know what to do," she said.

His chin jerked up as if at a sudden thought. "Do you feel at risk at your own premises?"

"How could I? That ruffian you had me hire sticks like glue. I left him in the piazza."

Jamie glared down at her.

"That 'ruffian' knows his work. Wat Jones is a good English soldier come on bad times," he told her. *I was damned lucky to find him.*

"He refuses to come in," she mumbled.

The thought of Wat Jones, former sergeant and current miscreant taking tea at Nora's table distracted Jamie briefly. *Of course the man wouldn't come in. The fool woman should realize putting a guard at her door had put a stop to lurking strangers.*

"Are you frightened?" he repeated.

Nora puffed up indignantly. "Of course I'm not frightened! I just . . ." She couldn't cover her bluff.

He had to get her out of here. *Five hours gives her too damned much time to anticipate disaster. How can I keep her busy?*

"As I said, stay here if you wish. Let the Ferret judge you as a light skirt." He ran right over her gasp of outrage. "Or go back to your rooms as you choose. Wat is there."

"I told you he is in the piazza. He followed me here," she said.

He combed his hair swiftly and walked to the door just as swiftly. "Good," he said. "I have some appointments to keep."

"Appointments?" she squeaked.

"I have a life, Mrs. Haley," he said.

*Let her think I have business to conduct. I need to run as far from this count as I can. But where?* Nothing came to him.

The wren's eyes flitted around Jamie's pathetic little

room with desperation, seeking an argument to hold him, and his defenses began to crumble. *Damn it to Hell.*

"I could accompany you," she said.

He caught her eye, warning her.

"No, I don't suppose I could," she agreed. "I can't very well stay here. My reputation, Major," she said, as if it was her own idea. "I'll visit Robert and meet you by the fountain in the hospital piazza at 1:30."

*Excellent choice. She would be both occupied and not alone.* He nodded agreement.

Jamie glared over at his image in the mirror, astonished to find that he actually planned to meet the count. He choked on the thought. He was in no condition for it. He barely had time to visit the barber around the corner, and could do nothing with his only coat. He pictured his dress uniform, long gone to pay for meals and more wine than he cared to admit. *I can't do it.*

"I'm sure the count has interpreters of his own," he began.

Nora, standing at the door with hands in a white-knuckled clasp, couldn't hide the fear in her eyes.

"How could I ever trust a word they said?" she asked.

*She can't.* "I'll meet you at 1:30," he said while he gently unwound her hands, cold as ice, and took them both in his. Warmth began to flow between them. "Never fear. I'll be there."

*He would. Damn. At least "Major Bently" would.* With luck, James Heyworth, Baron Ross would stay far away. Perhaps his old coat would put him beneath notice. If the count stooped to notice him, no secrets would be safe.

She swallowed hard and nodded. "I know. You haven't failed me once. I'm sorry to rush in here, but I had nowhere else to go." She let go of his hands, taking warmth with her.

He placed a hand to the small of her back to guide her to the door. The fragile bones of her back lay in his hand. *How could he leave this little bird to face the wrath of Savoy alone?*

"You worry for Isabella's sake. Don't. We'll face this count together. Besides, you have one powerful protection."

"You are—" she began.

"Not me." *Lord, no, not me. Use sense Nora.* "Mother Margarita. She wants what is best for Isabella as much as you do." How far the Reverend Mother and Nora might differ about just what constituted "best" he left unsaid.

Still, he couldn't take her into enemy territory without good reconnaissance. He watched her on her way, seized with a fierce desire to justify her trust.

An hour later, the clatter of crockery contended with a cacophony of multilingual conversation in Jamie's ears. The snug café near the Piazza Venezia sounded like its cousins in any other capital when the younger sons and shabby clerks of the diplomatic corps paused for luncheon.

The café sat near the embassy of Hanover where England, having no formal relations with the Vatican state, planted its diplomats informally among the representatives of the king's cousins.

With his hair trimmed and his jacket freshly brushed, Jamie looked only slightly less respectable than the regular clientele. He nursed coffee and prosciutto and strained to eavesdrop on several conversations at once. Nothing of value reached his ears.

From his vantage point he could watch the clock tower tick away the minutes until he had to meet his employer. Cursing the wasted time, he had almost risen to leave when he heard it.

"What news from Turin?" The asker spoke German. His companion, a fresh-faced puppy with startling red hair dropped his voice to answer. Jamie heard "Savoy" and "rebels" but little else. He edged his chair closer. *Upheaval in the Sardinian capital*?

"Quiet for now," the puppy said, obviously trying to impress the blunt faced man who had asked. "But we know the . . ." His voice faded. Then Jamie heard, "Nephews and cousins would like to see the king fall." Jamie filled with gratitude for the indiscretion of junior officials.

The puppy rose to leave and almost tripped over the chair Jamie conveniently placed in the way.

"Sorry, sir." Jamie made a gesture meant to indicate the terrible crowding in the café.

"Not a problem," the puppy replied. His eyes narrowed. "English?" he asked. "I don't believe I know you."

"Bently," Jamie said, putting out his hand. He felt sweat bead on his forehead. The last thing he needed was the attention of some eager clerk the Foreign Office planted in the Hanoverian embassy to keep an eye on expatriate Englishmen, yet he sat across from just such a man thanks to Nora Haley.

"Campbell, Archie Campbell," the puppy said shaking his hand. "I'm, ah, visiting Von Reden at their embassy." The fool almost winked at the pretense. "If I can be of any assistance, don't hesitate to ask," he preened.

*You could forget you never saw me.* The puppy probably would anyway. "Thank you. Good of you," he bit out, forcing a smile, certain now that the puppy's position made his information about Savoy mostly accurate.

Archie Campbell swaggered out, looking certain that his position of importance had impressed one more pathetic English traveler. Jamie let him turn the corner before hurrying away.

Upheaval in the Sardinian capital sounded serious, perhaps as serious as the rebellion in Naples. It should keep Castellimonte preoccupied, he thought. Factions in the House of Savoy were another matter. Jamie had no idea whether that would help or hurt his employer's situation.

## Chapter 10

Nora, sitting uncomfortably in the great hall of the Palazzo di Savoia, devoured Isabella with her eyes and struggled to understand why the girl had been forced to attend the audience. *Don't any of these people care about a little girl's misery?*

Her heart ached. *These wretched people go out of their way to make others miserable.* Nora perched herself on a tiny gilt bench and craned her neck upward. Above her, the Count di Castellimonte held court from a massive chair and inspected all with stone-faced hauteur.

Behind her right shoulder, the major interpreted everything that was said, speaking softly into her right ear. "Theater, Mrs. Haley," he whispered. "Don't let it spook you." The warmth of his nearness comforted her more than his words.

"You have come, Mrs. Haley, because Mother Margarita has told us of your interest in my great-niece," the count intoned. He ignored the small body fixed so miserably on a stool to his right. Isabella fidgeted and wiggled; she nearly fell.

Nora opened her mouth to reply, but the old man overrode her.

"This child is Savoy. Her interests are ours," he declared.

Nora studied the haughty face but found no sign of warmth.

"You have come to Rome to visit your brother," the count continued. "You are new here. You cannot be expected to understand."

*Understand what?* Nora opened her mouth to speak again, but the count stopped her with the raise of an imperious hand. He leaned back to confer with Ferret Face who stood behind him to the left.

She tried to hold her gaze on the dour old count and his minion, but her eyes strayed over and over to Isabella who teetered, twisted her hair, and stared down at them. Nora longed to hug the child. Isabella's gaze, however, focused on Major Bently. She shot daggers at him as if to demand that he rescue her.

"The little one is not happy with us," he whispered in Nora's ear. Nora glanced back. The major watched the count steadily and refused to meet the little girl's eyes. "She doesn't like him much."

"Can you make out what they are saying?" Nora asked.

"Not well, but Ferret Face seems to be filling him in on our activities."

Behind Nora's back, Isabella finally slipped from her seat, with a loud thump. At her cry, Nora rose from her seat.

The count clapped his hands with a crack so loud Isabella jumped and stopped wailing.

"Enough!" he barked in Italian. "The child will go back to Santo Spirito."

Nora sputtered, but the count overrode her in impeccable English. "The child will go back."

A young maid picked up Isabella to carry her out. The little one opened her mouth, looked at her great-uncle, and closed it again, sullen but resigned.

Nora sank back onto the little bench.

"Sit, Mrs. Haley. Chin up. Stand your ground," the major said softly. "There's my girl."

"He speaks English," Nora whispered while the maid escorted Isabella out.

"Of course he does, the old wolf."

The count's voice boomed down. Nora managed not to jump at the sound. "You may visit her there at three. That is permitted."

*My visits do not require your permission.* Mother Margarita didn't need the count's permission. On the other hand, she thought, the nun had not been able to prevent him from bringing Isabella to this audience.

"Of course," Nora said firmly, "I always do." She held his gaze. She would not show weakness before him.

When the door closed, the count waited a full minute for total silence.

"Now we will deal with this matter," he said. "You have affection for this child. That is natural. You are a woman." He didn't make it sound like a compliment.

"She is my family, my lord," Nora said as calmly as she could.

"She is of the House of Savoy and of Castellimonte," he continued in English. His look challenged her to deny it.

"Every child has two families," she retorted. Nora refused to shrink away. Pride held her voice steady and her spine straight.

The count assessed her more keenly, and Nora felt the major's hand come to her shoulder. She hadn't needed him to translate after all, but his presence kept her steady.

"She is Savoy. She will remain at Santo Spirito until she is sixteen. I will arrange a good marriage for her."

"She is only a child!" Nora exclaimed. The major's hand, warm on her shoulder, held her in her seat.

The count glared at the interruption. "As you say, she is merely a child, and a girl at that. It is for her elders to decide what is best."

"She needs more than convent school. Her father wishes more for her," Nora insisted.

"Robert Beaumont is a fool. We permitted his marriage to my sister's daughter because his business prospered and she lacked a dowry. She, too, was a willful woman like her mother before her. Beaumont, though a good man, stupidly contracted a disease at so young an age!" the count declared.

*As if poor Robert could help it!*

"He wants Isabella to have a family, Excellency." She spoke quietly, but no one would mistake the steel in her voice.

The count stared down his aquiline nose. "You have courage. That speaks well for the child's blood. However, you have neither wealth nor breeding. You have no husband. Robert Beaumont's father is a heretic preacher. It is unthinkable. She will remain at Santo Spirito." He made a gesture as if to dismiss her.

Nora would not be dismissed. She shook off the major's hand and rose to her feet.

"My great uncle is Viscount Stansbury. My parents were both English gentry. Robert and I may not have the pedigree you wish, Count, but Isabella, as you say, is of our blood also, and we will not be excluded from her life."

The count glared at her. At last he gave a nod so slight it was almost imperceptible. "We shall see, Mrs. Haley, how strong you are. We shall see."

"You're a foolish woman," Jamie told her after the count swept out with his courtiers.

*Foolish but magnificent. Did I see her as a wren? This woman who sails, head high, across the audience chamber is an eagle.*

"Are you really Stansbury's niece?" he asked, skipping to keep up. He shuddered at the thought that Stansbury, a disgusting old roué, might be related to Nora. Jamie had seen him more than once in some of London's most disreputable gaming hells, places Jamie himself wouldn't admit to visiting.

"Yes, to my shame." She bit her lip.

The count might not know what a worthless and debauched lecher the old viscount was, but Nora clearly did. Jamie didn't like to think about how she knew. *No wonder she despises aristocrats.*

"Should I be impressed?" Jamie goaded.

They passed a liveried footman and moved through double doors into the grand foyer with its vaulted ceiling and regal pavement of parquet tiles.

"The count is the fool if he weighs Stansbury in my favor," she said tartly, when they were safely past.

"He has no right!" Nora seethed under her breath. Her slipper-clad steps on the tiles were soft, even in her anger.

"Perhaps no right, but he has a great deal of power," Jamie told her.

"This is not Piedmont. This is Rome. What is Sardinia?" she asked rhetorically.

"A powerful state," he answered, "the most influential on the Italian peninsula, and an ally of England."

Jamie felt his breath catch from the exertion of keeping up. He climbed down the steps behind her, almost tripping when she suddenly turned.

"He said she was 'Savoy.' You mentioned it before," she said. "They are a ruling family? Does he mean she is royalty?"

*She really doesn't know? She never let on during the confrontation.*

"The House of Savoy is the Sardinian ruling family. They are related to the House of Stuart, though I don't remember the genealogy. Isabella is probably descended from Charles I." *Damn it. Nora, these people have way more power than your disreputable English viscount uncle.*

"Stuart? Like Prince Charlie? The Jacobites?" She wrinkled her nose.

"Exactly like the Jacobites. The current king, Victor Emanuel, is, in fact," he explained, "next in line to the Jacobite claims, such as they are. Neither the king nor his brother before him has given any indication they would actually make any such claims. They probably view the throne of England as inferior to that of Sardinia. That doesn't stop lunatics back home from making claims on their behalf. England watches them closely."

She grimaced and, just as suddenly as she had turned to face him, swung around to walk down the stairs and into the light. They crossed an immaculate courtyard and left through iron gates that loomed over the watchful eyes of two disdainful guards in the colors of Savoy.

They were far down the road, instinctively headed to the convent and to Isabella, before she spoke again.

"No one owns another human being," she suddenly spat out. "Titles and pedigrees don't give them the right!"

Jamie felt his mouth quirk in the shadow of a smile and just as quickly sobered. *Some titles may be worthless—mine, for example—but power wins in the end every time.*

"How can I protect her?" The cry torn from her heart lacerated his.

"Do you fear for her at the convent? Surely the nuns can protect her."

"Yes! No. That is, no one will harm her physically. Mother Margarita wouldn't permit it. She deserves better, though."

*Better than the wealth and power of Savoy?* Jamie wondered. *Better than the stern care of the Sisters of Santo Spirito? Is the woman daft?*

"I'm sorry," she continued, dismissing him. "You have no way to help. I wasn't thinking."

"You need a solicitor." Jamie blurted out the words before he stopped to think.

"Yes! Of course! This is a country of laws." She turned to him with hope alive in her eyes.

"To an extent. This isn't England." Jamie knew too well the limits of law in the face of absolute power, but he didn't want to deflate her.

"It is the Papal State, not Sardinia," she said.

"Yes, but it is still an absolute monarchy. Pius VII's rule is the only law. You might do better here than in Sardinia, however."

"Where will I find an English Solicitor?" She didn't say "might."

Jamie scratched at his ear. He had agreed to be her translator, not her knight errant.

"Franz von Reden is minister of the Kingdom of Hanover in Rome," he began thoughtfully.

Nora looked confused. She shook her head as if to bat his words away, but he held up a hand and went on. "He frequently has house guests—representatives of Hanover's cousin King George in London, unofficial British envoys here. Some of the 'guests' are permanent."

"Of course!" Nora's eyes lit up. "Excellent suggestion. We can go tomorrow."

*Not bloody likely. I'm not going near that place, even for Nora Haley.* He suspected word would shoot straight back to London, and he knew that if his friends got a whiff of his whereabouts they would descend like rescuing angels—and leave in disgust when they knew the entire truth.

"Not 'we.' You! You don't need a translator to speak with the King's representatives." *Or even his minor clerks.*

She looked for a moment as if she were going to order him to come. He held his ground and watched her eyes, bright with irritation, while she sought a counter argument. She had none.

"Very well. I will go in the morning."

That was the Nora he had come to know, all backbone. *The fools at the Hanoverian embassy will treat her well enough. Has anyone,* he wondered, *ever cared for Nora the way she cares for Isabella?*

## Chapter 11

Nora watched a young, obviously English, clerk take her information. He introduced himself as Archie Campbell. After the impressive German-speaking guards she passed through to get to a dark little office, the clerk disappointed her.

"You were right to come to us," he said, puffing out his chest. "We can't have these Italians bullying a good English lady."

*The man looks like a powder pigeon,* she thought.

He raised his quill, one pinky finger raised delicately above the rest, and looked at her inquiringly. "The father of the child? English also?" he asked.

"Yes. Robert Beaumont. He is," Nora took a breath, "ill."

"And Mr. Beaumont wishes you to care for the child?"

"Yes, that is it precisely." *Get on with it! Have you no sense of urgency?*

"No question he would want his English family to care for the child," the man clucked. "If the other relatives are Italian, well . . ." The powder pigeon left the rest unsaid.

"And the name of this relative who troubles you?" he asked.

"The Count di Castellimonte."

Nora watched the blood drain from the young man's face until it was white as the paper in front of him. She doubted that boded well for her case.

A sudden longing for Major Bently's help washed over her. *Where had the blasted man gone?* Nothing she said the previous evening convinced him to accompany her to the Hanoverian offices. He claimed to be busy, but she suspected he had an aversion to the place. *Typical man—when I need him most, I can't depend on him.*

The powder pigeon regained some of his composure. "The man you need, Mrs. Haley, is Arthur Wentworth," Campbell sputtered. "Been here the better part of twenty years. Fled Napoleon with the rest, of course, but stayed in touch with the papal court for all that. I can make you an appointment some time later this month."

Panic set in. "You don't understand. My brother is dying. I must see him immediately. Please ask!"

The clerk started to protest, but Nora overrode him. "You will inquire now, or your superiors in London will hear how you failed to protect an English lady in dire need." As a threat, it lacked teeth. *What would the major have said?*

In the end, he sniffed his disapproval but went to do as she bid. In short order, he returned to show Nora into a strange little room with gilt cherubs on the vaulted ceiling, bookshelves around the walls, and a massive dark wood desk crouched in the center of the floor like some bear in a cave too small for it.

Arthur Wentworth, a bluff Englishman of the gentry class dressed in tweeds even in the heat of Rome, looked up from behind the desk. He did not stand; she noted the breach of manners. She saw no approval in his eyes.

"I have but a moment, young woman, but perhaps you can give me a quick description of your problem. We will decide what must be done," he growled.

Nora ignored the man's obvious irritation at the interruption and described her brother's condition as quickly as she could.

"Beaumont? Of course we know Beaumont." She thought his attention sharpened at that. She outlined the arrangements for his daughter's care, Robert's desire that Isabella not grow up in the convent school, and the anticipated opposition of her mother's family.

"And the count who is so concerned about the girl, do you have any idea who he is?" Wentworth asked.

"I believe he is a cousin of the King of Sardinia," she said.

"Cousin and Secretary of State. These are not people used to having their wishes challenged."

"I should think Napoleon would have corrected that notion," Nora snapped, thoroughly sick of hearing about the power of the Italian aristocracy.

The old man chuckled. "One might think so, but since the Congress of Vienna, they are back and more powerful than ever. Victor Emmanuel has made it his business to remind his people about the divine right of kings, and he sends Castellimonte here in case the Pope forgets."

"Still, there are laws," she said.

"Yes. Even Italy has the rule of law, whether the House of Savoy understands that concept or not." He sighed wearily. "What is it you wish, Mrs. Haley? Let's get down to it. Do you believe you can raise this little girl yourself?" Wentworth looked doubtful.

"Yes!" she gasped, struggling to breathe normally. The depths of her need to have Isabella shocked her. "They don't want her—not really. They plan to leave her in the care of the sisters. She deserves a family."

"Your brother's wishes? What are they?" he asked.

"He does not wish her to grow up at the convent. He has said so."

"Is there a will? No court, Mrs. Haley, in this or any other country, would present the child to an impoverished widow over a wealthy and powerful family. Without a will, there is little I can do."

In the moment, Nora saw herself as Wentworth must have seen her, a drab widow with no prospects. She doubted he could conjure a less likely a candidate to provide family for a small child. Her heart sank. *How could she convince this man to help?*

"I don't know about a will," she said. She pulled the creased and tattered piece of foolscap from her reticule.

"Robert gave me this. He said to contact this person if anything happened to him."

Wentworth's expression shot from bland to interested astonishment.

"Antonio Salvia is a legal expert. We might call him a solicitor. He is one of the best," he said. "Your brother may indeed have a will, but what it stipulates and how unbreakable it is remains to be seen." Wentworth made some quick notes. "We'll investigate. Perhaps I can at least clarify your position. That's all I can promise."

"Thank you, Mr. Wentworth." She took the paper he offered and quickly wrote down where she could be found. "If I am not there, you could contact me through the Convento Santo Spirito. Mother Margarita will know where to find me." His bushy eyebrows rose again at that, but he didn't comment. He dismissed her with a careless wave of his hand.

In the end, Wentworth's information about Robert's will reached Nora two hours after news of Robert's death.

Nothing comforted Nora, not the cool comfort of the hospital's marble courtyard, nor the tender care of two nursing sisters who pressed "inglese" tea on her.

She sat, back rigid, numb with grief, and awash in sorrow while the women buzzed like bees in Italian, burdening her with unwanted compassion.

The major, who had brought her to the hospital and certainly ordered the tea, stood guard in the shadow of a Corinthian column. Nora saw compassion, for once unquestionable, clearly on his face. A fierce desire to be held and comforted engulfed her. *Absurd wish! Who would comfort me? This man?*

"Oh, Mio Caro!" A swish of black muslin engulfed Nora and two arms came round her. Mother Margarita didn't wait to ask; she simply hugged her. Nora understood only her name, felt only concern, but it was enough. She wept as if her heart would break.

When the tears finally ended, a gentle hand touched her chin and pulled her face upward. She looked into Mother Margarita's caring black eyes. Soft words washed over her.

"She says you are a strong woman." The major's deep rich voice, suddenly near, rumbled through Nora.

She sniffed wetly and glanced up in disbelief, shaking her head as if to deny it, and took the handkerchief Mother Margarita offered.

"She says even strong women cry when faced with loss."

Nora nodded numbly. Mother Margarita, satisfied with what she saw, stood up.

"Today you may cry and rest," her major translated. "Tomorrow is time enough to face what must be faced. She asked her sisters to bring you a light supper here."

Nora started to protest. "I couldn't eat!"

"She's right," Major Bently insisted. "She says you will need your strength."

"The funeral. I have to make arrangements," she protested.

"Your brother made arrangements when it became clear he would not get well. Mother Margarita gave the information to me two days ago."

"To you?" she asked, outraged.

"You had enough on your mind." He waved some folded papers. "You don't need to worry about planning the funeral."

"Isabella?"

The little nun spoke directly to Major Bently.

"The Reverend Mother agrees that Isabella is the most important thing. She asks if you are able to tell the little one what has happened."

Nora nodded fiercely.

"Good. She says that you may see her this evening after you have eaten something. Mother herself wishes to talk with you about Isabella tomorrow. She is very firm about that," he told her.

The nun handed her some folded papers before she could speak.

"This message came from the embassy," the major translated.

Nora took it nervously, glancing at Mother Margarita. The missive was sealed, but she had a feeling the nun knew what it held. She broke the seal and read. Wentworth, blunt and to the point, did not waste ink on trivialities. Her heart gave a leap of hope.

Your brother, it appears, was a careful man. Salvia crafted an excellent will. He shall leave his entire estate to his only daughter, Isabella. He stipulates that you are to oversee her care. There are other stipulations—conditions you may not wish to accept.

Nora mentally amended "shall leave" to "left." Wentworth included few details, but there appeared to be a house and enough for Isabella's care. She looked back and forth between the Reverend Mother and Major Bently as though either might enlighten her, but, of course, neither knew the conditions.

She handed the message to the major who scanned it quickly.

"Good, on the whole." He said when he had reread it carefully. "Good I think."

"We'll know when we hear the conditions," she said. The major's eyebrows rose at Nora's use of "we," but he said nothing.

She pointed to the note. "He also says that advocates from Castellimonte have already contacted Robert's legal representatives to indicate their interest in the estate—and Isabella."

Major Bently looked at Mother Margarita. "Shall I translate?" Nora nodded and then listened while he translated the message. Mother Margarita's frown deepened. She spoke to him quietly.

"Is there a problem?" Nora demanded.

"She says, 'We shall see.' Just that. 'We shall see.'"

## Chapter 12

Jamie downed strong coffee as if it were the brandy he fervently wished for. Nora had gone to meet Wentworth and Salvia alone under protest hours ago. He would not, could not, go near the consulate.

*She should have returned by now.*

"More Signore?" the waiter asked for the tenth time.

Jamie looked beyond him to a little man pouring glasses of rich red wine. His mouth watered. Brandy would be better. *No wine, no brandy. One wouldn't be enough, and more would be too much. Nora will need me soon. She needs me sober.* He took another currant bun instead.

*Where is the damned woman?*

He refused to regret sending her alone. She paid him to interpret, and he did. He had translated for the nursing sisters, the hospital officials, and the priest who informed, not asked, Nora about the funeral arrangements. He even translated the Catholic funeral Mass Robert had requested, astonished he remembered enough Latin to do so.

He didn't owe Nora Haley an explanation for his behavior or his reasons for avoiding English diplomatic staff.

In four more days, the month he had promised her would be over. He took another swallow of coffee and let the bitter dregs burn his throat. *So where the hell is she?*

"Major!" His little brown wren came in a rush, out of breath and frantic.

Jamie leaped to his feet. "What is it? Did it go badly?"

She struggled for breath. "No. I, well, yes, but not

entirely." She leaned one hand on the table, breathing deeply. "We're late. We promised Mother Margarita—"

"Calm yourself. Don't talk. I know what we promised, and you are over an hour late. I was—" he almost said 'worried' but thought better of it "—going to send a messenger to the convent to warn her, but here you are."

He motioned, and a cup of tea appeared before her. While the waiter refilled Jamie's cup, he watched Nora take a sip. She gave a deep murmur of pleasure, hung her head back, and closed her eyes. The graceful line of her throat made his blood run hot, to his amusement. He wouldn't have guessed the little English wren could do that to him.

The lines around her eyes froze his heart. *What had those bloody legal hawks said to her? I should have gone with her. Did Castellimonte's envoys try to browbeat her?*

Cowardice shamed him. He didn't have the courage to bring himself to the attention of the embassy where some functionaries probably didn't give a fig about his identity. No, the torture he feared would come if his friends found him, and find him they would once the embassy had his scent, find him and reject him once and for all.

"Thank you, Major," she said. "I needed that more than I realized."

Absorbing the sadness of her smile, he realized his greater fear. *Nora might learn the truth.* He didn't know when Nora's opinion began to matter or, for that matter, when she had become "Nora" to him, but she had. He swallowed coffee, scorched his throat, and coughed.

"Are you well?" Nora handed him a napkin.

"Only careless," he wheezed. At least he managed to distract her. "What did they say to you? What did they do?"

"I'll tell you on the way to the convent. You have to translate for the Reverend Mother." She hurried him from the café and out into the piazza. "I don't know where to start."

"The conditions."

"Yes—good. One I might have guessed. Isabella must be raised Catholic."

"You knew her father's wish."

She nodded. "I should have anticipated the other. She must reside in Italy. Visits to England are permitted, but her primary residence must remain here."

"Where the count can keep an eye on her," he mused.

"Probably, although I think Robert made the stipulation. He may have made a promise to her mother. In any case, the count's representatives raised the issue of my willingness to stay here so far from home," she told him.

"Is that all?"

"Those were the only two conditions of the will itself. The count's people demanded others," she said.

"So what are their other issues?"

"I don't know Italian. The representatives spoke English most of the meeting. When they got to my language skills, they were positively scathing," she went on.

"That's easily rectified. Learn." Jamie wondered if she wanted to and how she really felt about Italy. He knew she would do whatever it took to keep Isabella. "What else?"

"The count does not want Isabella raised by an unmarried woman, even a widow. He disputes the claims that a childless woman could provide better mothering than the convent school will provide," she sighed.

Outrage flooded Jamie; he balled his fists in anger. "Stupid man. Anyone who saw you with her would know better."

She looked up at him, and her gratitude made his knees weak.

"It's loyal of you to say so, but he hasn't seen much of me, has he? And he is not alone. The three of them—even Wentworth—seemed to agree on that point," she explained glumly.

"But the will?" he prodded.

"Yes, the will. My brother's wishes weigh heavily. Wentworth doesn't think the count can break the will, but—"

"But what?"

"He can make it difficult," she said.

*Understatement.* He opened the convent gate, holding it so she could pass under his arm. She looked up at him.

"There's more. There are demands."

## Chapter 13

Nora clenched her jaw as if to fend off words she did not wish to hear.

"A man like the Count di Castellimonte has obligations," Mother Margarita murmured from behind her rough wooden desk in the Spartan convent office.

"Surely you see that any honorable man would care for the well-being of a family member." The Reverend Mother tented her hands thoughtfully and waited while the major translated.

"Men again!" Nora sputtered with indignation. "Isabella has more than one family!"

Mother Margarita smiled at that. Nora sank back in her chair. Most of the nun's advice seemed sound, and Nora forced herself to admit it gracefully.

"You will settle in Rome." The major's translation of Mother Margarita's words did not come out a question.

"Of course I will!" She already planned to live in Robert's house and send Isabella to the convent as a day student. *All that awaits me in Dorset is a cold vicarage and life as Father's drudge.* In Rome, she had Isabella.

Nora's eyes went unbidden to the major who stood beside her, listening intently to the Reverend Mother. His unruly hair brushed his neck when he leaned over to listen. His strong hands gripped the back of a chair. Nora shook her head to clear it. The major's hands were not her concern.

"She believes you will learn Italian quickly," he said. "Isabella makes a good teacher."

"Of course I will," she said. The words sounded petulant to her ears. Major Bently raised a warning eyebrow.

"I'm sorry, Mother. It isn't you. When I met Mr. Wentworth, he, they—" Memory of the man's arrogant disdain gave her a frisson of resentment.

"Men again?" Mother Margarita smiled.

Nora felt her face heat. "Learning the language is only common sense," she said. "The Major—"

"Will not always be near," he finished for her.

She suddenly realized he only owed her only two more days. *Is the sadness under those thick lashes real or am I imagining it?*

"The count has demanded that you visit Turin."

"Sardinia's capital. Yes, I know. Tell her I do not wish to go there, even on a visit," Nora insisted.

"She knows that. She agrees. There is danger. She urges caution, however, before you defy the count. He can force the issue."

"I know. I know. He can tie up the will in court indefinitely. With no funds, I can't care for her. It might become difficult to even stay in Rome," Nora said wearily.

Without Robert's money she couldn't even afford a translator much longer. *What will I do without him?*

"I will take her to Turin if I have to," Nora said. At the look on Mother Margarita's face, an ugly thought struck her. "Would it be so dangerous to travel to Sardinia?"

"It most certainly would be." The major raked his eyes over her until Nora squirmed in her chair. "And you, Mrs. Haley, are just foolish enough to rush in."

"I wouldn't put Isabella at risk," she said.

She felt his eyes bore into hers. *Impertinent man.*

"Mother says he will stand by his insistence that Isabella visit Sardinia," he went on. "She also says Isabella must not go. Once there, she could be forced to stay."

"Stay? Why?"

The major glanced over at the nun and shook his head. For a moment Nora thought he would laugh. *Had the man no sense of propriety?*

"This woman has an astute grasp of politics," he said, humor lurking in his voice. He sobered. "Sardinia teeters toward instability. Isabella could be used as some sort of pawn. When the count said he would make a good marriage for her, he meant one that is beneficial to the family."

Mother Margarita rose from behind her desk and walked around to speak to the major directly in Italian. He shook his head in denial and did not translate. Mother Margarita began to gesticulate and speak forcefully as if attempting to persuade, and he answered her in Italian.

"What is it? What is she saying?" Nora demanded.

Major Bently ran a shaking hand through his hair and squeezed his eyes shut.

"Translate for me! What is she saying?" she repeated, frantic to know.

He let out a long breath and looked at her. "She says that if you concede the point, the will can be processed, and you can take apply for guardianship."

"Then we will go to Turin."

The flow of Italian continued. There was more being said. There had to be.

"Major!"

"The situation is unsafe!" He made no pretense of subservience. "You cannot go."

"I will be under the protection of the Count di Castellimonte. Surely he means Isabella no harm." She believed it.

"You would be under the protection of a wolf!" he exploded.

"There is nothing for it. If Isabella must go, I must go to protect her."

"You would march into hell for Isabella, and that may be exactly what you will be doing!" he shouted back.

Major Bently leaned his head back, caught himself, and puffed air out of his cheeks. "Mother Margarita says there is another way," he admitted, "a way to convince Castellimonte to let go."

"What is it? I'll do anything," she told them.

"Foolish woman. You would, too," he growled. "She says you need a husband."

"Husband?" The word hit Nora like a brick, driving the breath from her lungs.

The major continued speaking, "A husband would not only add countenance to your claim of making a home for Isabella, but a husband could also forbid travel to Turin. It's unfair, but she is right."

Nora snorted and sat down abruptly. "Nonsense. Who does she think I can find to marry me?" She looked up into his face, and what she saw there brought a lump to her throat.

"Me," he said sadly. "She thinks you need to marry me."

"Doesn't she understand?" Nora asked.

"That we are strangers? That you are my employer? I think she does." He looked pained.

*He doesn't wish to marry me—of course he doesn't*. She would do anything to get Isabella, even marry a stranger, but she couldn't burden Major Bently with her problem. *Isabella is not his family, and I mean nothing to him.*

Nora felt Mother Margarita take her arm and pull her to her feet. The nun gently but firmly walked with her to the door and urged her out into the garden.

Isabella looked up from her seat on an ornate bench and smiled at her; Nora could not resist. She opened her arms.

The door closed behind them. The major and Mother Superior were inside. Alone.

Jamie blinked at the sunlight and the tableau in front of him. *The dull little bird I met disappears when she holds*

*Isabella, and a creature of grace and light emerges.* The sight of the two of them drew him like a bee to honey.

Cold fingers of shame crept down his neck and gripped his heart. He slouched back into the shadows of the cloister, trying to order his roiling thoughts. He failed.

"Did you manage to convince Mother Margarita that I am perfectly capable of managing for myself?" Nora asked.

*The idiotic woman has no idea what she would be taking on alone whether she went to Turin or not.*

"No. She is a stubborn woman." *And a shrewd one.* The nun had played him like a fish, tapping every weakness: poverty, honor, even his attraction to Nora. *No, not honor. Honor demands that I tell them the truth.*

"But, Major, surely you convinced her."

With a sigh and exaggerated effort, he went down on one knee in front of her. He let raw need—to protect, to have a few more weeks of Nora Haley's life—push honor, honesty, and sense to the ground. He reached for the book in her hands.

Nora pulled back, wary. He took the book from her and put it on the ground and wiggled his eyebrows at Isabella who giggled in her aunt's lap.

"Mrs. Haley, I am aware what a poor specimen of a man I am. However, for Isabella's sake"—he said the last three words with exaggerated care—"would you accept my hand in marriage?" He thought that if she had any sense she would run all the way back to Dorset.

"You can't wish to marry me." She looked like she had been slapped.

"Can I not?" *I need to do this for her,* he thought, refusing to examine his own desires.

"We hardly know each other," she said.

"I quite agree that in the normal course of things you wouldn't even notice me."

"It isn't that." If she knew the truth, she denied it. "We don't know, that is, I'm not—" She fluttered to a stop, eyes wide.

"Listen to me, Nora. Listen carefully," said Jamie. He noticed she didn't object to the use of her name. "You would be in danger in more ways than you can imagine in that world. You could be retained."

Her eyes grew wide.

"You could—you *would*—be forced into some sort of subservient role in the count's household. If Isabella became a pawn, you could not save her."

Nora paled even further at the mention of the girl. Isabella was the lever he needed. He took it.

"Isabella is what matters," he went on calmly. "Your brother feared her fate enough to draw you here from England. Marriage could keep you in Rome where Isabella is safer."

He held his breath. The need to do one good thing clawed in him; he had no doubt that protecting Nora Haley would be very good indeed. Despair almost choked him when she didn't respond.

"Agree to marry me," he went on, caressing Isabella's head where it tipped onto his shoulder, "and we can see to her welfare, whatever that may be." He had come to love the little imp. Whatever else happened, he would make sure her aunt could protect her.

Nora continued to frown. She raised her hands in a helpless gesture.

"I may not be much," he went on, "but my protection is far better than none." He held his breath to wait for her reply.

"Yes, but *marriage*!" The words burst from her in rush. "We hardly know one another, Major." She did not, he noticed, make use of his given name. "The intimacy and, and the *totality* of marriage is difficult enough with someone you know well." She looked ready to cry.

"Oh, Nora, I thought you understood. It wouldn't be that sort of marriage. It may not need to be marriage at all." *Of course it wouldn't.*

"What sort of marriage would it be?"

"To begin with it would be merely a betrothal. That may be enough."

Hope flared in her eyes.

He went on quickly. "Even if we're forced to carry it out, it wouldn't be a marriage at all, except on paper. Our relationship would be the same—employer and interpreter—only perhaps we would add 'bodyguard.'"

Her brown eyes, large and alert, studied his.

"Name only," she said.

*Not even that. False identities and marriage vows don't mix well.* Jamie tried to suppress the thought and could not.

He held her eyes and waited for her to go on. *This is bound to end badly,* he thought. *She will discover my real name, discover she has consorted with a "blasted aristocrat" and realize she is betrothed to or married to a man who participated in the slave trade, however unknowingly. Then there will be hell to pay. I'll lose her now, or most certainly lose her later.* He chose later. He could protect her in the meantime.

"Name only," he repeated, "and easily annulled when you're safe and your guardianship of Isabella is secure."

"You could go on with your life as it was before I disrupted it?"

"Yes," he said. He almost cried. *I had no life before you came.* He would let her believe it.

"If that is the case, then, yes, Major, I will marry you."

He had won. For an awkward moment, he stayed on his knees, clutching her hands. He had the absurd notion that he should kiss her and found that he wanted to very badly. Instead, he squeezed her fingers gently and rose to his feet.

"There is one small change I think we should make." She blinked up at him. *She probably wonders if I will transform into tyrant already.* "You are going to have to bring yourself to call me by my name—Jamie. My name is Jamie."

A spark of light sputtered to life in her eyes ahead of her smile. She looked at Isabella. "What do you think? Shall we call him Jamie?"

Isabella giggled. He chucked her under her chin. "That would be *Uncle* Jamie to you, chick." He repeated it in Italian. He liked the sound in any language.

"What do we do now?" His practical English wren had returned.

"Now we concoct a betrothal—and quickly," he said.

## Chapter 14

"You cannot simply manufacture a betrothal!" The prim little Italian legal consultant, Antonio Salvia, bristled, offended at the very thought.

They sat side by side across Salvia's exquisite inlaid desk in a sunny chamber filled with discrete artifacts, any one of them valuable enough to keep Jamie in wine for years.

"But you see, Signor Salvia, marriage benefits everyone. The little one will have parents, and the count's requirements will be met," Nora said. Only a little twist of movement showed Jamie her agitation.

"The count will not be pleased, Signora," Salvia insisted.

*Let Nora peck her way through this barnyard.* Salvia limped along in English. She didn't need translation unless they asked her to sign papers. Jamie would examine papers carefully.

"How could the count be displeased?" Nora demanded. "You and Mr. Wentworth both assured me that marriage would answer."

"Marriage, *sì*, but this?" Distaste twisted Salvia's face. The skin on the back of Jamie's neck crawled when the man flicked a glance at him. "Marriage must not be entered into lightly." Salvia waited for understanding. Nora gave him no response.

"Have you spoken to Mr. Wentworth about this man?" he went on.

Nora sputtered, taken aback. "What do you mean?"

"What do you know of him?" Salvia asked.

Unholy amusement bubbled up. *Good question, Nora,*

*what do you have to say to that?* Jamie leaned toward her, listening intently.

"This man served my country. He is a man of honor and courage," she said. "If your concern, Signore, is with his appearance, you should know that some elements of my country—to be frank the highest of our so-called nobility—have treated our soldiers very badly."

Hundreds, turned off after Waterloo without the means to survive, roamed English roads. *Nora cared. I should have predicted that. No wonder she hadn't objected to hiring Wat Jones.*

"Desperate men make poor husbands, Signora Haley. In the normal course of things, your father would look into the match. If you would let yourself be guided by wiser heads, perhaps we can sort this out."

Jamie cut in, "My fiancée does not require your guidance, Signore. Your job is to carry out her brother's will."

Salvia cast Jamie a contemptuous glance but kept his attention on Nora.

"Signora," he wheedled, "I have a daughter myself. I do not want to see you lost and confused, allow me suggest—" Nora, straight-backed, pulled herself even higher, ready to do battle. Still, she had no answer. Jamie did.

"My fiancée has already told you what she wants," he bit out. "She intends to act on her brother's wishes, and she expects you to help her."

Salvia turned the full force of his scrutiny on Jamie. His eyes missed nothing, not the frayed cuffs, the overlong hair, or the eyes Jamie suspected still showed the effect of drink. Jamie met his gaze directly. *The windbag may be correct in his assessment of me, but he will not bully Nora.*

Salvia lifted a quivering chin and spoke to Nora without taking his eyes off Jamie. "You insist, Mrs. Haley?" he asked.

"Yes, sir, I do," Nora answered.

"Very well, Signora. Perhaps it will make a difference with parties who have interest." *Castellimonte. We will have to do better with Castellimonte.*

"Uphold the law, Signore," Jamie snapped. The thought of Isabella as a dynastic pawn sickened him. "Leave Mrs. Haley's niece and her family to us."

Salvia ignored him. He addressed Nora. "You will want a protestant minister to conduct your wedding." It wasn't a question.

She caught her lower lip between her teeth. "I hadn't thought about it," she temporized. *Of course not. She didn't plan an actual marriage.*

"You will want that the marriage is legal in England as well as here," Salvia droned on.

"Mother Margarita assured me something could be arranged, that the marriage would be perfectly legal." Nora's voice sounded rushed. *Of course she wouldn't want an English ceremony. Too legal. Too hard to dissolve.*

"I will talk with Signor Wentworth about your laws and customs. Perhaps he will suggest something."

*Wentworth. Diplomacy. Law. Questions.* Suddenly the kind of ceremony mattered very much to Jamie. "My fiancée is satisfied with Mother Margarita's suggestions," he asserted. "When she is ready, a Roman ceremony will suffice." *And keep your nose out of it.*

Nora shot him a grateful look. Salvia's eyes shot daggers.

"As you wish Signora," he said. He launched into practical matters including release of some funds from Beaumont's estate.

"Decisions about the child's residence will, of course, take time. As to guardianship . . ." He shrugged. *Of course. Time and Castellimonte's approval.*

Nora, overwhelmed by the size of the allowance Salvia proposed, nodded dumbly. He droned on.

"I will report your betrothal to the Count di Castellimonte," he said finally and shot another hateful look at Jamie. "I will speak with Mr. Wentworth about this Major Bently."

*Damn.*

Several hours later, Jamie tossed what few items he owned into a cloth sack with shaking hands. Salvia must have sent a footman to the Hanover's embassy at a dead run. Wentworth's summons lay crumpled on Jamie's equally rumpled bed.

*I will run south,* he thought. Revolution might just serve. Some army might hire him. Naples in flames might push visions of Nora in trouble from his mind. *Unlikely.*

He tossed a broken comb into the sack. *Austrians in Naples will draw Whitehall's agents.* Whitehall meant Jamie's friend, the Marquess Glenaire. His spy network there would outshine his network in Rome. *Not south.*

He flung open drawers. Empty. Two steps backward and he hit the wall of his tiny room. He slipped slowly to the floor, laughing. *Packing? I have nothing to pack and no place to go.* To the north lay Sardinia and the long arm of Savoy. Greece? *No funds for passage. No Greece.* The thought of sailing brought Jamie's nightmares up from the depths. He covered his ears to close out the screams of dying men.

"Major! Jamie!" Nora's voice. *She will despise me when she founds out. The respect of my friends and, God help me, Nora will die as surely as the poor souls on the* Avante.

"Jamie, are you there?"

She only came to his room when absolutely frantic. He decided she could despise him later; she needed him now.

He flung open the door, heart in his throat, and gripped her shoulders. "What happened? Isabella?"

"Castellimonte." She shrugged away and swung into the room, collapsing into his rickety chair.

Quick inventory found no injury, not the visible kind anyway. She waved paper.

"He got my message requesting a meeting. He replied with a summons. He wants to see me tomorrow."

"You got a summons also?" he blurted out without thinking.

"He summoned you?" she asked.

"No, Wentworth. Not important." He waved a hand as if to push away the thought.

She blinked up at him. "We must see Castellimonte."

*Can't. If Wentworth doesn't dig up the truth, Castellimonte's minions will.* "What exactly did the message say?" he asked in order to buy some time.

"Nothing. 'Mrs. Haley's presence is requested.' What did you expect?"

"No mention of me?" Relief flooded him, followed quickly by guilt. He suppressed both.

"No, but if we're going to announce our betrothal, we need to prepare, don't we?"

"They invited you alone. I can hardly join you," he began.

"I can't announce a betrothal alone," she pointed out.

The sack on his bed drew her eyes.

"What is that?" she demanded, accusation stark in her eyes. "You gave your word you would stand by me." *Foolish woman.*

"Trash." *Everything I own, but rubbish all the same.*

It seemed to satisfy. Something in her face when she looked back at him changed. She examined him carefully. "Perhaps I could go alone this time," she suggested. "We don't want to aggravate him. I could go and mention the betrothal. To feel him out. Then later you can accompany me to reassure."

"You don't like how I look?" he demanded irrationally.

"The count," she began. Confusion gave her face

vulnerability that wrenched his heart. A sudden vision of Nora standing alone in her black bombazine before the ravening wolves of Palazzo di Savoia brought Jamie's racing mind to a halt. *The betrothal,* he remembered. *His promises.*

"No," he said. "That will not do." He owed her at least one attempt to fool Castellimonte into giving her Isabella. One attempt. Then he could run. "We have to go together, and we have to do better."

"Better?" she asked.

"Salvia didn't believe the betrothal for one moment. For one thing, you're still in black," he explained.

"I'm in mourning!" she exclaimed.

"You wore black before your brother even died. Perpetual widowhood does not become you," he told her. *Never mind that Italy has widows in black aplenty.*

"Edmund may not have been much of a husband, but he deserved respect," she said.

"Three years of mourning?" he demanded.

Her shoulders slumped. "My father didn't believe the expense of new clothes was warranted," she mumbled.

*Not perpetual mourning then.* That thought shouldn't please him, but it did.

"Besides," she added tartly, "Robert certainly deserves it."

"Robert deserves attention to his wishes regarding Isabella," he said.

*Damn. Tears.* He hated his lack of handkerchief. She pulled a scrap of lace from her reticule and dabbed her eyes. Her shoulders sagged in surrender.

"A newly betrothed woman might be excused for putting off full black. It might lend credence," he suggested.

"It isn't possible to arrange a wardrobe by tomorrow," she sniffed.

"You have the funds. Money unlocks doors," he said. That was certainly true. Signor Salvia had obtained a generous advance of funds from Isabella's estate. Finding an obliging modiste would be little trouble.

"What of you?" she countered.

He looked down at his stained and shabby jacket, the same one he had worn every day since she met him, and frowned.

"I'll see a barber," he said. The words sounded lame, even to him.

"You'll buy a suit," she insisted.

"I have no money." Embarrassment made the words harsh. He had said they would still be employer and employee, but he couldn't stomach the thought of a salary.

"I didn't expect you to buy it yourself," she said. "As you pointed out, I have the funds. I can't very well let you escort me in that horrid jacket, can I?"

*You have taken her coin for a month. Why should you stint at a suit?* His pride, when swallowed, almost choked him. He would have to let her buy his clothes.

"Fine, Mrs. Haley," he grumbled. "If you wish your hired man tricked out in livery, I suggest we outfit him properly."

Nora opened her mouth to protest, but some demon drove him on.

"Shall we say three suits? And shirts, six shirts."

If they were to present a strong front as a betrothed couple, he couldn't go looking like a beggar. He needed more shirts. She would require an entire wardrobe. He suspected she would fight him on that point more than the suits.

Her jaw snapped shut.

"Think of it as armor," he said. "If you go into battle, you must go armed." *Especially if I am likely to abandon you after the first skirmish.*

Determination lit her eyes. "I defy you to find a modiste before tomorrow afternoon," she said.

## Chapter 15

Nora fought discomfort in an anteroom of the Palazzo di Savoia and tried to look serene. *Armor indeed.* She pulled at her newly fitted dress. The soft muslin in deep lavender for half mourning, with its tiny embroidered rose buds and modest neckline, became her. That made it worse. Robert deserved better.

Her confidence melted under Jamie's glare. He stood, erect and tense, his body framed by ornately carved shutters and an exquisite gilded window frame. He scrutinized her under worried eyebrows.

"Do sit down!" she snapped. He ignored her. She stared back. *Honestly, the man's tension does not help,* she thought. *Either he feels concern for Isabella that equals my own, which I beg to doubt, or some private demons drive him. Not that he will share it, the irritating man.*

She went back to fidgeting. "You shouldn't have ordered so much," she complained.

He had conjured a fitting out of thin air and then forced orders for an entire wardrobe on her. When he requested a formal gown, she tried to put her foot down, but he had insisted, "If you must consort with counts, you must look the part."

"I shouldn't have bought so many gowns," she repeated irritably.

"You will need them," he murmured.

"You certainly needed new clothes," she retorted. *Stupid man! You ought to be grateful. Some beggar in a Trastevere back alley, warmer tonight in your filthy old coat, certainly is.* Before she could form a tart comment on ingratitude, a door opened on silent hinges.

Nora sprang to her feet. Just as swiftly, Jamie took her arm and whispered, "Easy now. Don't look too anxious. Try to look madly in love, dearest."

*Dearest? The dratted man is right, of course.*

She attempted to give him a coy look when they entered Castellimonte's reception room. His cheeky wink sent flaming tendrils up her cheeks.

"Perfect," he murmured.

"The Count di Castellimonte," a voice said. The Ferret.

A younger man followed Castellimonte. "And the Baron Victor Filiberto," the Ferret intoned. It was clear by the resemblance to the count that this was his son. He flaunted expense and foppish excess. Nora, suddenly grateful for the new gown, felt dull by comparison.

The count gestured for Nora to sit. Unlike their previous visit, he placed her on the same level. *That bodes well, doesn't it?*

Jamie didn't wait to be asked. His hand, warm on the small of her back, directed her to a chair. He sat next to her and moved his own seat so close their knees met. His hand never left her back. The feel of his body warmed her until she felt tension leave her shoulders.

"My son," the count began, "takes an interest in family affairs." The younger man smirked. His eyes raked over Nora until her skin crawled. Jamie took her hand in his free one and gave it a squeeze.

"I see you have put aside mourning, Mrs. Haley," the count said.

Her heart sank. She tried to form a response, but Castellimonte, stone-faced, did not pause. "What is it you wished to see me about?" he asked.

*Stupid question.* A calming breath stifled the temptation to sputter. "My brother's will, Count, and guardianship of Isabella."

He raised a regal eyebrow and regarded her dress but nodded for her to continue.

"My niece must remain in Rome. I accept that. She must be raised Catholic. Mother Margarita and the sisters at Santo Spirito will help me see to that. The terms of Robert's will have been met."

A cold stare met her statement. The letter of the will would not suffice.

"Your legal representatives explained that you have additional concerns. I must learn Italian. I have begun to do so." Isabella made a great tutor. The thought gave her courage.

"The greatest hurdle, at least the one reported to me, is my unmarried state."

Victor Filberto, Castellimonte's son, leaned back, his smirk deepening.

"That much is obvious," the count said with a dismissive gesture.

Jamie's hand, warm against the small of her back, urged her on. She leaned into it for strength.

"I have come, that is Major Bently and I have come, to inform you of our betrothal." She took a steadying breath. "I have tempered my mourning attire in deference to that happy event."

"Foolishness," the count snapped. "Families contract betrothals carefully. One does not leap into such an arrangement lightly. What has your father to say to this?"

"I am a widow, Count, and my father lives far from here. I do not require his guidance in this matter."

"Unwise and inadequate," the old wolf pronounced.

"My fiancée—" Jamie leaned slightly forward and broke in. He pronounced each word with force and repeated them, "My fiancée makes her decisions for herself. She does not require your guidance."

The old man shifted his glare toward Jamie. "You do not have permission to speak."

Jamie continued as if Castellimonte had not spoken. "The matter is simple. Robert Beaumont left a will that clearly stated his wishes. You hinder the courts from carrying it out. Honor demands that you remove those hindrances."

"You lecture me about honor?" The old man's face turned purple. His son sat up sharply.

*Foolish man! Don't anger the count.* Jamie ignored her discreet tug on his hand. Panic set in. The assessing look on Victor Filiberto's face did little to calm it.

"The honor of Savoy is legendary," Jamie went on smoothly. "That's why you will follow the dictates of Beaumont's will." He said it as if it he believed it. She tugged again. He squeezed her hand without breaking eye contact with the count. He astounded her. *Where did my shabby major learn to defy counts?*

Castellimonte's imperious stare never wavered. The young baron's eyes glittered with an eager, vile look, one Nora had not seen since Edmund had dragged her to a bull baiting.

"We do understand," Jamie went on, "that you will want to take time to become acquainted with Mrs. Haley."

Her shoulders almost relaxed under his soothing tone. She avoided looking at Victor.

"You will no doubt want to see for yourself how well your great-niece thrives in Mrs. Haley's care."

"No doubt," Castellimonte repeated dryly. The silence that followed was blessedly brief. The count's expression remained stoic. She thought she saw a flicker of amusement, but when he spoke, his voice didn't betray any.

"Very well, Mrs. Haley. We shall see about this betrothal. In the meantime, you may attempt the role of guardian. For now."

A mixture of English and Italian followed, a blur to Nora's ears. The count, it seemed, found the thought of Isabella's guardian in rented rooms an abomination. The keys to Robert's house would be handed over. Nora left the details to Jamie. Two words reverberated in her mind.

For now.

## Chapter 16

Any hope Jamie had of running when they left the count lay in ruins.

Nora demanded to see Isabella as soon as the ordeal ended; he couldn't refuse. When she snuggled up with Isabella on a garden bench to continue their Italian "lessons," he knew with a sick heart he couldn't leave. *Two little birds at the mercy of a wolf...*

"Is that not so, Uncle Jamie?" Nora asked.

He squashed the surge of delight that ran through him at the sound of his name on her lips and crushed Wentworth's summons. He stuffed it back in his pocket.

"Sorry, Nora, I wasn't attending."

She gave a disapproving sniff. "Isabella wishes to know if it is true that her Papa wanted her to stay with me."

He crouched down in front of the little girl. "Your Papa loved you very much. He wants you to have a family, your very own aunt, now that he can't take care of you himself."

"What of my uncle, the count?" the little girl asked, eyes wary. The quiver in her voice tore Jamie's heart. The count had given temporary cooperation at best. At worst, he would use Isabella as bait in Castellimonte nets. Nora had no defense against the man. He knew she couldn't secure her claim if he left.

"He wishes what is best for you also," Jamie said. *That might even be true, in whatever way the man sees "best."* "He agrees your aunt should care for you."

The little one's intense concentration exploded in an unexpected outpouring. He rocked back on his heels when she threw her tiny hands around his neck and laid her head on his shoulder, unable to speak.

He wrapped her in his arms and, God help him, his heart. He rose to sit next to her aunt. He could not leave. *For now*.

"Aunt Nora will never fail you, Isabella," he said. "She will always be there for you." *Unlike me*.

He passed the little girl into Nora's lap. Nora reached for her instinctively. In doing so, her hand closed over his. She swiftly pulled it away, her warm brown eyes full of consternation.

*You aren't so indifferent to my touch, are you Nora? What would it take to make you want me? And how long would it last?* He rose to his feet.

"Can you manage alone?" he asked. "I am expected by Wentworth."

Nora sat bolt upright. "I forgot! You must go. Of course, you must go. We need his help. Isabella and I will do fine."

"Leaving so soon, Major Bently?" Mother Margarita came briskly through the convent door into the walled garden. "Can you spare a moment?"

"Alas, no, Reverend Mother." He escaped through the gate before the interfering woman could stop him and complicate his life further.

*A month ago*, he thought, *I had privacy, peace, and some last shreds of pride.* He hurried away from the little nun.

When he reached the street, he remembered his errand. If the nun roiled his peace, Wentworth could destroy both privacy and pride. *A month ago my belly was empty and my purse emptier.* He could manage hunger if he had his pride. *A month ago I didn't know Nora Haley and her imp of a niece. What is pride worth compared to them?*

"You're Mrs. Haley's, ah, friend?" The officious little clerk, Archie Campbell, let his voice trail off and his smirk show.

"My fiancée is no business of yours," Jamie snapped, grateful the puppy didn't recognize him from the cafe. He had enough of fools; he leaned into the man's face. "Tell Wentworth I'm here and do it quickly, if you want to keep that pretty face of yours."

Wentworth wasn't much better. When the clerk ushered Jamie into his office, he looked up with undisguised distaste.

"One gathers you wish to help Mrs. Haley secure custody of the niece," he intoned. "How noble." He peeled back his upper lip when he spoke and twisted "noble" into something base.

"That woman appears willing to go to any length to obtain what she wants," Wentworth went on with a dismissive sniff. Jamie felt like a fool for directing Nora to the pompous windbag in the first place.

"What my fiancée wishes and what the child's father wished are one and the same," Jamie retorted.

"Yes. Beaumont. Pity that. We could have used him."

*Used him how?* Jamie shuddered to think. The old man made no pretense of being anything other than what he was: the Foreign Office's agent in a country where England never let lack of formal relations get in the way of a healthy spy network. Cold fingers began to climb up Jamie's spine.

"The woman possesses courage, though, or blind foolishness, defying Castellimonte," Wentworth went on. On that at least, Jamie agreed. "Foolish or not," the man shrugged, "The situation may unfold to our advantage."

The cold fingers climbed higher. Wentworth's eyes bore into Jamie, probing and assessing.

"Your name is Major James Bently?" Wentworth picked up a quill.

"As you well know." *The bastard wants to take notes?* Cold fingers climbed another step.

"Peninsular War?"

*Good guess.* Most of England's lost veterans could claim the same. Jamie nodded.

"Waterloo?"

Again a nod.

"Unit?"

Jamie thought furiously. He rode with the Blues but his so-called reputation for bravery, or rat-stupid recklessness as he called it now, made him known among most officers in the Peninsula. "The 14$^{th}$ Foot," he replied. It was the least distinguished, smallest unit he could conjure up.

"14$^{th}$ Foot? I don't believe I know it," Wentworth paused quill in mid-air.

"No reason why you should. Look, Wentworth, what does this have to do with Mrs. Haley?" Jamie demanded.

"If you wish Mrs. Haley to secure guardianship of her niece, I can help you. To do that, I require information," Wentworth said.

*Information. The coin of choice for diplomats.* Wentworth didn't bother to say that he could hinder Nora just as well.

"You know what you need to know about me. If my fiancée is satisfied, you should be," Jamie snapped.

"My dear Major Bently, you are not at all what I expected. I believe there is a great deal more to know about you." Wentworth skewered him with probing eyes.

Jamie stared back. The cold fingers reached the base of his neck and threatened to choke him. Wentworth looked away first.

"Be that as it may, I require information. You could be of assistance." Wentworth put the quill down.

Jamie raised both eyebrows. "Information, Mr. Wentworth?"

"The Count di Castellimonte is of interest to his majesty's government," the man intoned.

*Interest? As goldfish are of interest to the cat.*

"What does that have to do with Mrs. Haley?" Jamie asked.

"Come now, Major, don't pretend to be naive. The woman has embarked, foolishly or bravely, to adopt the count's great-niece and to deal with the man and his court. This opens up certain opportunities." Wentworth gestured broadly.

Jamie refused to speculate; he waited in stony silence. He didn't have to wait long.

"You wish Mrs. Haley to keep her niece," Wentworth went on. "I can help. You can help me. Beneficial all around, not?"

"Help you how?" Jamie asked.

"Nothing strenuous. When you or Mrs. Haley meet with the count or his people, information may come to your attention," Wentworth suggested, "tidbits, you know, small things. All I need is for you to keep us informed."

"You want me to spy," Jamie spat.

"I wouldn't be so harsh, Major. I—"

"I would. I won't be your bloody spy. Bribe his servants," Jamie snarled.

Wentworth's lips twitched, and laughter gleamed in his eyes. *They have already bribed the servants. He wants more.*

"One can never have too much information, Major. I remind you Mrs. Haley wishes to keep her niece. If you wish my assistance, you will work for me. There would be compensation."

The ice shards in Jamie's spine exploded in the heat of his rage.

"I won't be your bloody spy," he repeated through clenched teeth. "I won't take your bloody 'compensation!'"

Wentworth sat back in his chair, tented his fingers, and smiled like a well-fed spider. "Spy? Not if you say so. But you will help us."

Jamie did not respond.

"Think about it," Wentworth said. "Visit Mrs. Haley and her niece. Come back when you have made your decision."

Jamie rose so quickly he knocked over the chair. He leaned the knuckles of both hands on Wentworth's desk.

"I won't do it," he spat.

Wentworth's smile never faltered. "Take your time. That will allow me to correspond with Whitehall about your service."

Jamie knew that for the threat Wentworth intended. He stumbled from the office. *Do I have any choice? None unless I find a way to disappear.*

## Chapter 17

Nora seethed with irritation in front of an imposing villa in a prosperous neighborhood that the man who identified himself simply as Capello claimed was Robert's. It was many blocks and a universe away from her little apartment. How or when Robert had acquired it eluded Nora. Apparently this palace even had a name—Casa Beaumont.

Jamie had failed to respond to Nora's hastily written note when the man moved up the time to hand over the keys to the house.

Neither Nora's rudimentary Italian nor Capello's broken English were sufficient for the task. Besides, the man watched her like a hound on the scent. She needed Jamie. *Where has the irritating man gone?* The sun beat down mercilessly where they stood on the street.

Nora finally gestured impatiently for the man to open Robert's house. The heavy oak door opened on silent hinges, and she stepped into a new world. No English house had walls the color of apricots and lemons. No English house opened to an interior garden fragrant with oleander. *No English house ever called to my heart. This one does.*

She rocked on her toes, anxious to explore, tempted to dart in every direction at once. She took a shuddering breath and tried to bring herself under control.

"Shall we wait Major Bently?" Capello's voice, tight and high-pitched, stumbled over English words. Jamie had disappeared from Santo Spirito the day before and never came back. She silently agreed that they should wait.

Her eyes darted around the dim entrance, a broad tile-lined foyer. Shutters closed over windows facing the street. Heavy drapery covered all but one of the French doors opening on the interior courtyard directly across from the entrance. She traced patterns in the tile floor—red, brown, and orange patterns swirling outward from the center.

"Signora?" The man's question didn't require language. "Where is this fiancé of yours?" his eyes seemed to ask.

She looked at the door as if to call him forth, but it remained firmly shut. *Do I need him? The house belongs to Isabella. It will be our home, not his.*

Corridors opened to the left and to the right. Nora strode toward the one on the right, and the little man scuttled after her, notebook in hand, sputtering in Italian. She made out the Italian word for fiancé, one word she had cause to learn.

Robert's house looked dim, smelled of dust, and echoed her every step. She adored it. The corridor led past two anterooms to a large chamber filled with furniture under Holland covers.

She wondered if Italian houses had drawing rooms. Drapery covered one wall of the room. Nora peaked behind the drapes and found floor-to-ceiling windows that opened to the sunny courtyard filled with overgrown beds and marble statuary. She pictured the shabby gray room at the vicarage her father called a drawing room, clapped hands over her mouth, and giggled.

"Hello?" a voice called. *Jamie!*

Nora's companion scurried down the corridor and began a spate of Italian. Jamie answered him in the same language. Nora couldn't make out the words, but she understood the tone. Her faux fiancé had arrived thoroughly out of sorts.

"What is it?" she asked him when he strode into the drawing room.

"This person tells me the count insists he deal only with

me," Jamie complained. His red-rimmed eyes made her heart sink. *Has he been drinking?*

"But he's Robert's employee!" she exclaimed.

Jamie shot her a scathing look. Lines around his eyes and the crease between his brows added to her unease. *Drinking or simply lacking sleep?*

"Let's get this over with," Jamie growled. "Who knows what game the count is playing?"

The hound darted a speculative look between the two of them. Jamie spoke a few sharp words, and the man led them toward the opposite corridor. When the man glanced over his shoulder, Jamie took Nora's hand, kissed it, and placed it formally on his arm.

"Look delighted," he whispered. "We're betrothed, remember?"

Nora plastered a smile on her face. "You might do the same. What's the problem?"

"The man's accent. Piedmontese," Jamie said under his breath. *Piedmontese. Like the count.* "This," he translated, more loudly, "is the family wing."

Four modest sleeping chambers lay on either side of the corridor. In one, a finely embroidered coverlet and a tiny bed full of *bambole* proclaimed it to be Isabella's room. The little dolls in their tiny silk dresses smiled back at Nora.

"On the first floor?" she asked. In an English manor, the nursery would be tucked high and away.

"Why not?" Jamie asked.

*Why indeed.* Beaumont's villa had no second story to block sun to the courtyard. Robert and his wife must have wanted Isabella close. Nora opened a door and found a closet full of small girl's clothes and bows that clearly had no place in convent school. A second door led to a room for a nursery maid.

Jamie leaned into the doorframe while she fingered toys and treasures. She wondered whether he was being patient or feeling too poorly to care. A small music box began a familiar melody when she opened it, but ran down. She looked up at Jamie and caught sight of the little man eyeing them both.

"What is in the other rooms?" Nora asked. When Jamie took her hand, she felt sparks in her fingers.

"He says they are unused," Jamie told her. She opened a door and found the room as empty as the man said.

"For additional children," Jamie breathed from behind her left ear.

Heat shot up Nora's arm to her face.

"Or so the man said. For Robert and his wife," Jamie added belatedly. *The irritating man probably meant to make me blush. All for show.*

At the end of the corridor, an ornate door stood facing her. The corridor took a sharp right turn at that point.

Robert's man reached past her with an oily smile to open the door.

"The master suite," Jamie translated.

The door swung open to reveal a spacious room. With her hand warm in Jamie's, all she saw was the massive bed that dominated the room. Nora later remembered a vague sense of tasteful decoration and carefully arranged furniture.

Robert's man continued speaking, but Jamie didn't translate.

"What did he say?" Nora prodded.

Jamie looked down at her. "He said, 'This will be your room when you are married.'" She felt the blood drain from her face, and then, in a rush of heat, pour back in.

"Excellent blush, my dear," Jamie whispered. "That is exactly what we want him to report to our nosy count."

He dropped her hand and strode to an interior door. It opened on a massive, empty dressing room. "My shirts will get lost in here," he said.

She pushed past him. The door on the other side of the dressing room opened to a pleasant little sitting room.

"Perhaps it is behind that door yonder," Jamie said. "The lady of the house's chamber? Isn't that what you wanted to see?"

*How had he guessed? Surely there would be separate chambers.* When they married, if they married, there would have to be separate chambers.

Another door opened off the sitting room. They looked into the room together. A delicately crafted bed and flowered hangings proclaimed it to be what Nora hoped. The richness and beauty of the chamber lay far beyond anything she would have known to hope for in Dorset.

She looked up at Jamie. Concern, caution, and a lack of sleep all registered in the slant of his mouth, the slump of his shoulders, and the lines around his eyes. *No drink.* She felt sure of that. Relief filled her. *When did he last sleep?*

"We can manage this," she said.

"We won't have to," he retorted.

"But if we marry—"

"When we marry," he said, loud enough for their hound to hear, "this will be perfect."

*Does Jamie expect to contract a real marriage? Of course not.* What mattered was that the count believe it.

Robert's man, or the count's man she now understood, conducted the rest of the tour quickly and with little detail. Perhaps he had seen what he needed to see.

When they arrived back at the entrance hall, he produced the keys but did not hand them over. A spate of Italian and answering words followed. The two men disagreed about something.

"He wishes to hire servants for you," Jamie said.

"Of course," Nora said, relieved. "I can afford it, and the house is large."

"You can afford a staff," he agreed. "You will need a staff for this place. I told him you would do it yourself."

She puzzled out his point; it didn't take long. *If this man spies for Castellimonte, so will any servants he hires.*

"I certainly can," she replied, looking at the man. "I wouldn't think of putting him out or inconveniencing the Count di Castellimonte for something as mundane as hiring servants."

Jamie's lips twitched. She made out the count's name when he translated and saw the little man's agitation.

The hound clutched the keys to his chest; Jamie held out his hand in an unmistakable gesture of command. Capello glared, but he handed over the keys. When Jamie passed them to Nora, the man paled. He said nothing and made no move to leave; he remained rooted in place as if he expected more.

Nora had no warning. The feel of Jamie's arms startled her; the touch of his mouth on hers crushed her. Knees buckled. Sensation muddled her brain so badly she almost missed the words he whispered against her lips. "Give him something to report. We may as well make it good."

Her world exploded. Nora's mouth softened under Jamie's, and he nudged hers open. His gentle invasion set her reeling. After what felt like a lifetime, he slid his hands to her elbows and put her away from him with a wink. *Cheeky man.*

The count's little watchdog scuttled off under Jamie's fierce glare. Nora slumped against Jamie. He put a steadying arm around her and watched the man go.

"That report should be interesting," he said, dropping his arm and putting distance between them. Nora was shaken and thoroughly disgusted that what had rocked her to her core meant nothing to him apart from show.


Four hours later Jamie could still taste that kiss. He had meant a simple salute to her lips, but, once tasted, he couldn't hold back. He couldn't regret the passion, even if it meant nothing to Nora beyond fooling the count's little spy.

Jamie approached the embassy for a second day after a night of tossing about for some way to both salvage his pride and keep Nora safe. He found none.

Wentworth's clerk's knowing smirk did nothing to soothe his foul humor.

"Tell Wentworth I'm back. If you say that I need an appointment one more time, you'll pick up your teeth off the floor," he roared.

"Tut tut, Major, we need finesse. Violence will not do." Wentworth himself spoke from the doorway, a picture of English tweed and pomposity.

Jamie swallowed the need to tell him where to put his finesse, stormed past him into the office, and sank into a chair across from Wentworth's desk.

The older man moved with considerably more dignity, spoiled only by the amused look on his face. He raised an eyebrow. "Major?"

"There are conditions," Jamie said.

Wentworth did not appear surprised. "Indeed."

"First, keep Mrs. Haley out of this. You will stay far away from her."

A broad smile spread across Wentworth's devious face. "Easily promised," he said. "I will assign a clerk to the guardianship process. You may have to warn her away, however. I'm under the impression you sent her to me." He looked ready to laugh. "Any more?"

"I won't take money," Jamie insisted.

"Possible. But you may want to reconsider," Wentworth objected.

"There's more. Do not mention me to the Foreign Office," Jamie went on.

Wentworth swallowed a chuckle. "Who shall I give as a source? A down-at-his heels English major? What will they make of that?"

"They can make whatever they damned well please. There are enough shabby majors in Europe to choose from." They both knew that to be true.

Wentworth sobered. "No mention of Major Bently in dispatches regarding Castellimonte?"

"No mention of any kind." Jamie held his eyes steady on Wentworth's. "What is the usual phrase, 'our contact in Castellimonte's circle'?"

"The euphemism for servants," Wentworth murmured. Jamie understood the man's knowing expression. *The bloodhounds in London won't accept that for long. Hell, Glenaire won't accept it for a moment.* His friend would sniff out deception. It would buy time, though, and that's what Jamie needed. Time to see to Nora. Once she had legal claim, he would leave.

"Accurate then," Jamie shot back.

"My dear fellow, no servant can report what is said over port once the ladies are dismissed. You are about to be catapulted into that circle," Wentworth pointed out.

Jamie snorted. "I beg to differ. I'm hardly about to become the House of Savoy's new confidant."

"On the contrary," Wentworth said. "I have it on good authority you will receive a dinner invitation this very afternoon."

*Servants. Damn. Deeper and deeper.*

"There may not be anything of value to report," Jamie suggested.

"Oh there will be. Report everything and let me sort it out," Wentworth ordered.

"No mention in your dispatches," Jamie repeated through gritted teeth.

Wentworth sighed. "As you wish."

Jamie rose to leave.

"Major," Wentworth called. "Take the money." Before Jamie could open his mouth to refuse the cursed money, Wentworth went on, "Or do you intend to live off your wife's money entirely?"

Jamie's jaw snapped shut; he stood frozen in place.

"Shall I set up a discreet bank account? She needn't know, of course."

He thought furiously. With money, he could buy his own shirts. He could find small gifts for Nora and Isabella. *Hell, I could acquire some damned handkerchiefs for the next time she needs them.* With his honor long gone and his pride in tatters on the floor of Wentworth's office, it made no difference.

He took the money.

## Chapter 18

The wealthy and the titled merely irritated Nora most days. Waiting for the count's dinner to commence, her skin crawled and her shoulders tightened to bands of steel under the furtive stares of well-polished luminaries. *Have I grown another head?*

Victor Filiberto bowed over her hand while his eyes roamed over the rest of her.

"You look lovely tonight," he said in English. *Perhaps he means it. Perhaps he thinks I wasted Isabella's inheritance on this gown.* His leering eyes gave away little.

She believed she did look rather well in the shockingly expensive, deep blue silk Jamie had insisted she buy. She squeezed her eyes shut. She thought the finery inappropriate, and she didn't like the baron slobbering over her hand.

Jamie's palm came to rest on the small of her back. Any feelings of safety the gesture might have brought warred with other less familiar emotions. The sudden sharp memory of his kiss sent sensation dancing along already frayed nerves, spreading liquid warmth through her middle to pool in places that brought a blush to her face.

"My betrothed does look particularly lovely tonight," Jamie said through narrow lips. The word "betrothed" sounded unbearably intimate when he said it, as if it were true.

"You make a happy couple," Victor responded. No warmth reached his eyes. "When is the wedding?"

"We have no date," Nora rushed in breathlessly. "There has been little time."

"You will, of course, keep us informed," he replied and, with a nod at Jamie, moved off to greet other guests gathered in the anteroom. Jamie followed him with his eyes and then resumed scanning the room.

Nora expelled a breath. "I don't like him," she whispered.

"Good," Jamie replied, reaching to shake the hand of a man who introduced himself with a minor title. Jamie translated introductions, small talk, and then, "When is your wedding?"

She answered as she had to Victor. When the man moved on, she asked in undertone, "Why do they keep asking that?"

"A politeness when addressing a betrothed couple," he replied. "Wouldn't you ask the same?"

Nora nodded, smiling at a woman who now spoke to Jamie in Italian. More small talk. The woman moved on.

"Or," Jamie said smoothly without looking at her, "they wish to ascertain if your betrothal is real."

Nora choked.

"Smile, *mio caro*," he said.

What little comfort she had mustered failed her. She managed a weak smile. Head high, she struggled to respond to niceties. *Why did I let Jamie convince me to perpetrate this sham betrothal?* She prayed for another way to cement her claims to Isabella. No ideas came.

When the old wolf himself stood in front of her, she leaned into the support of Jamie's arm.

"Good that you could join us, Mrs. Haley," the Count di Castellimonte said in English. She curtsied deeply and rose to an assessing look on the old man's face. "We wondered whether mourning would keep you away."

*I knew it. This, all of this—the dress, the dinner—is inappropriate.* Her heart sank. The small pat of reassurance she felt on her back kept her knees from doing the same. *The count invited me. Why should he disapprove?*

"Some might say otherwise, but your good news changes

things, of course," he went on. If Castellimonte declared her dress appropriate, it was.

"The modesty of your dress does you credit," he continued. "It is appropriate for a betrothed woman to attend a simple family dinner, even one mourning a loss."

*Simple family dinner? There must be fifty people here dressed in outfits that would feed a family in the village back home for a month.*

Nora tried to control her breathing.

"We are pleased to have you and your betrothed join us," the count said with every appearance of sincerity. If he decided her presence was appropriate, then it was.

She replied with her wobbly smile. Jamie gave her back a discreet push.

"We're honored to be here, Count," he replied when Nora remained mute.

"Normally one would expect a wedding to wait after so sad an event," Castellimonte said, "but with the child to consider, perhaps you wish to settle matters quickly."

Jamie did not respond.

The count looked directly at Nora. "When will you marry, I wonder. Soon?"

She could not breathe. *Stop behaving like a fool. This sham will not last.*

"My fiancée has many things to decide, Count," Jamie answered for her. "There has been so little time."

"Yes, I can see that," the man said. "When and where are big questions. If you need assistance, you need only ask. It will not do to move the child into the home of a single woman."

Nora's heart lurched. Jamie's reply sounded far away, muffled by the pounding in her ears.

"Thank you," Jamie ground out. "But no. Mother Margarita assures us such arrangements are a simple matter."

"Perhaps. If she cannot arrange matters, I will."

Nora thought later that perhaps his voice sounded pleasant, but his words did not. Before she could consider it, she fainted.

"Give her room!" Jamie demanded, lifting Nora in his arms. His own heart raced.

The count's staff reacted with perfect efficiency. *The blasted household runs like a well-oiled machine, one with a hundred searching eyes.*

He felt those eyes on his back. He didn't give a damn, but Nora would. His little wren weighed even less than he had guessed. He could feel the delicate bones of her shoulder against his chest and loosed his hold lest he break something.

He strode as quickly as he dared toward the small salon a servant indicated, sheltering his precious burden. The room was lit when he came through the door. Servants moved tables and opened space around a silken settee. He placed her on her back and pulled the coverlet that appeared at her feet up over her shoulders. Two footmen bowed out.

Footsteps sounded behind him. The door swished shut against the crush of people who surged forward to see, and all sound died away. He leaned over Nora. Her soft breath, barely audible, brushed his ear. He sagged against the settee in relief.

"Nora, sweeting, can you hear me?"

Her eyelids twitched but did not open.

Jamie slid Nora's gloves off and held one hand, dainty in his huge one, gently rubbing her hand with his thumb. "Nora, come back to me," he whispered.

Her eyes flickered open. A smile twitched at the edge of her mouth. "Sweeting?" she slurred. "Foolish man." Her eyes fluttered shut, but faint hints of color returned to her cheeks.

Jamie caressed her hand. "Rest for a moment, Love," he said. If endearments distracted her, he would use them.

The door swished behind him again, and another voice broke the silence. "Water. Then English tea," commanded an imperious voice.

Jamie glanced over his shoulder. They were alone in the room except for the Count di Castellimonte. The old wolf shut the door on a departing servant.

"A physician has been summoned," he said.

Nora gasped and pushed herself upright. "Count—" she began, turning paler.

"Easy, Nora, easy," Jamie said. She didn't resist when he put an arm around her shoulders and maneuvered her back down. "Give yourself a moment." She lay quietly, but her eyes stayed open in alarm. Her breath looked too rapid for Jamie's taste.

Castellimonte pulled a small chair up close to the settee.

"Where is your so-called physician?" Jamie snapped.

"Coming," the old man said. He grasped Jamie's shoulder for a moment. From any other man Jamie would have found it reassuring. *What is the old wolf playing at?*

Nora blinked up at the count. "I'm sorry. This isn't like me," she said.

"No, it is not," Castellimonte replied. "That causes concern. You usually have courage."

Color rushed into Nora's face. *Damn it.* Jamie clutched her hand.

"She lost her brother. She's far from home. She worries for her niece. She shouldn't have to put up with bullying," Jamie spat over at Castellimonte.

"Quite right." It wasn't an apology, but Jamie doubted Castellimonte would ever come closer to one.

A man in a gray silk suit entered the salon. He pushed Jamie aside. The count rose and urged Jamie back down. "She will need your skill," he said.

Jamie blinked for a minute. *Skill? What good can I do?* The physician took Nora's hand and asked a question.

In Italian. She needed a translator of course, Jamie's skill. He leaned close.

Jamie explained the man's question and described the event. "Does it happen often?"

"No." Jamie didn't wait to ask Nora.

"Has it happened before?" the physician asked.

Jamie ran his hand through his hair. He asked her. "No. Never," he told the man.

"Has the signora recently become pregnant?"

"No!" Jamie snapped.

"What is it?" Nora asked. He told her. Her eyes darted among the three men. "How can he think that?"

"Is there no possibility?" the physician asked.

"No, none," Jamie responded. He glared at the count. *If that old wolf attempts to have this man examine her, he will regret it.* Castellimonte returned his gaze serenely. *Is that why he sent for a physician, to check if she is pregnant?*

"Tell him," Nora said. Jamie raised a questioning brow. "Tell him I'm a widow. No children. Ever. I can't."

Jamie translated her words. He didn't need to translate the bitterness.

The physician seemed to accept that. He checked her pulse, peered into her eyes, felt her forehead, and sat back on his heels. He stood with a shrug.

"A faint. The crush perhaps. She is well. She will recover momentarily." He addressed the count directly and ignored Jamie. He left as quietly as he had come.

Jamie sat on the edge of the settee, took her hand, and related the physician's conclusions.

"Of course," she said tartly, "but I never faint. It must have been the heat."

Jamie grinned down at her. "Mrs. Eleanora Haley is not so easily put down."

"Help me up," she demanded. He did.

A liveried footman appeared with an ornate silver tray carrying water, tea, and cakes. He set them on a table within reach. The count dismissed the man.

The count himself poured her water. She gaped at him; he smiled back. "Do you think me incapable of something so simple as pouring a glass?" he asked. Nora colored further; it seemed to please the old man.

"Come, Major," the count said. "Let us give Mrs. Haley a moment to recover."

The count led him to chairs on the other side of the room.

"You care for her," the old man said.

Jamie would have denied it, but he couldn't. "We are betrothed," he said.

"This marriage will take place." It wasn't a question. Castellimonte's eyes held Jamie's. Jamie looked away first.

"In due time," he said.

"She cannot have children. Does this not bother you?"

"We will have Isabella," Jamie said. That time he did not look away. The truth of it grieved Jamie sharply. Nora would have Isabella. He would stop at nothing until he made sure she did. Jamie would have them both while he could.

"You will come to Turin," the count pronounced.

"No. We will not," Jamie told him flatly. "As her husband, I will forbid it."

The count looked at him for a long while and then gave a sharp nod. "Come to see me tomorrow without Mrs. Haley. I have business to discuss," he said.

## Chapter 19

The garden at Santo Spirito glistened green and gold in the sun as always, but Isabella's face didn't light up at the sight of Nora. She threw herself into her aunt's arms and sobbed inconsolably. Nora looked up at the young nun who had escorted her to the garden for their daily visit and raised her brows in question.

The sister gestured helplessly and spoke in rapid Italian. Nora shook her head. She understood none of what the young woman said and only one word in Isabella's incoherent tirade.

"Bambola?" she asked. "Doll?"

The sister pursed her lips, groping for the word. "Um, lost," she managed.

"Sister Cecilia says it is nothing," Isabella sobbed in English, her little body rigid with outrage. "She called it *una piccola cosa*—a small thing." Her face crumpled, and she threw herself back on Nora's shoulder. "My Marietta!" she wailed.

Nora took the little face in her hands and wiped away the tears with her thumbs. "Tell me what happened. Tell me all of it."

"I am allowed a doll. Mother Margarita said it," the child sniffed. "She sleeps in my bed every night."

"What happened today?" Nora urged.

Isabella's face twisted up again. "Today I woke up, and Marietta was gone."

"Did you look for her?" Nora asked.

"I looked everywhere!" The child sounded indignant. "Under the bed, in the place I keep my clothes." She lowered her voice to a whisper. "Under Ursula's bed, too. She wanted my Marietta from the first day."

"Does Ursula have a doll of her own?" Nora asked.

"Yes, but it is cloth, and its face is painted on," Isabella told her. Marietta apparently had "real eyes and hair."

"Marietta is different from other girls' dolls?"

"Some have none," the little one said. "They say they are too old, but I think they want a doll all the same. I looked under all the beds," Isabella confided. "No Marietta. Sister Cecilia would not let me look in the trunks where the other girls keep their clothes. She told me I was selfish." Nora considered that was the longest speech in English Isabella had ever managed.

Isabella convulsed in sobs again. Nora looked up to see a look of sweet compassion on the face of the young nun.

"Not find," the sister said sadly with a shrug. She patted Isabella on the back and left them alone.

*Did one of the other girls take the doll?* Nora could see where a finely dressed, very expensive doll would tempt a child who had none.

She hugged Isabella to her breast. "I want to go home," the child wailed. "I don't want to stay here."

"You won't have to stay much longer." Nora hoped that was true.

"Uncle Jamie said we could be together," Isabella accused. "Where is Uncle Jamie?" The child jerked upright as if she just noticed his absence.

"He has gone to visit your great uncle, the count," Nora told her. Jamie had insisted he had no idea why the count commanded him to come. Ignorance did little to calm Nora's fears.

Her anxiety over Castellimonte's possible actions or motivations accomplished nothing. His words from the night before, however, echoed in her mind. "It will not do to move the child into the home of a single woman," he had said.

Nora put her face on the little girl's hair and breathed in the sweet clean scent.

"I want Uncle Jamie," Isabella wailed. "I want to go home."

"Soon, darling," Nora soothed.

"Uncle Jamie will—" Isabella began.

"Uncle Jamie will do what?" a familiar deep voice demanded. At the sound of his voice, Isabella leapt from Nora's lap and threw herself at Jamie. A flow of dramatic Italian words and gestures enacted the great tragedy of Marietta. The stomp of a tiny foot seemed to indicate a demand.

"Of course you will come home. Didn't Aunt Nora tell you?" Jamie asked.

At his urging, Nora told her about the visit to Casa Beaumont.

The child bounced, the look on her face swiftly changing from despair to delight as only a child can. "When can I go there?"

Nora felt sick. *When indeed.* Jamie seemed to read her mind. He shrugged. He offered no help.

"There is much to do," Nora began. "The house has been empty for so long. We have to clean."

"Servants do that," Isabella sniffed. A thought seemed to strike her. "Mother Margarita told me it is good for a lady to know how to clean and to cook as well. Can you clean, Aunt Nora?"

"I clean very well," Nora said. *Isabella,* she thought, *would be surprised to find out just how hard I can work.* There were no servants in her English grandfather's house.

"Please do then. Quickly," Isabella insisted.

Nora leaned over and kissed the little girl. "We will," she said, "and you will come to live with me there. Soon."

Isabella's radiant smile tore at her.

Determination filled Nora. *If the count wants marriage, he will get it. Whatever it takes, Isabella will come home.*

"We have to go through with it." Nora attacked as soon as the convent gate swung behind them.

"Go through with what?" Jamie asked even though he knew with sickening certainty what she meant.

"A wedding, of course." She drew breath to go on, but he held up a hand to forestall her.

"Before you explain what sort of worm is at work in your brain, feed me. I haven't eaten today." *I think more clearly when well fed. Besides, a walk at least will buy me time to think.*

Nora huffed indignantly but set out toward the little café near the bridge to Tiber Island that suited them both, the one they had come to think of as "their" café. Isabella's missing doll drama turned his little wren into a fierce mother hawk.

He had hoped for time to drag out the farce that was their betrothal until they wore down Castellimonte. Jamie snorted at his own idiocy. They may as well try to wear down a mountain. *Castellimonte—Mountain Castle. Mountain indeed.* His mind ran its circular track again and again looking for a way out. He found none.

They reached a table in the sun. He watched Nora cup her hand over pink roses stuffed unceremoniously in a milk jug. Their color, delicate but bright, perfectly reflected her smooth English complexion, bringing him a smile and a rush of sadness, as if he already missed her. *I will soon enough,* he thought.

A smiling waiter brought coffee to Jamie. "Tea for lady comes," he said. Nora ordered sandwiches.

"Now you must see—" Nora started in as soon as the man left.

"Tell me about Isabella," he interrupted.

"You know very well. Someone hid her doll. I suspect Sister Cecilia!"

*Or one of the girls. Or the laundry maid*, Jamie thought. In a group home, belongings are fragile things. *A child's emotions are even more fragile.*

"You don't know that," he said.

"It doesn't matter, not by itself. They mean well enough. We have to get her out of there."

"And we will. Patience, Nora."

"Patience? How can you say that? The count thwarts Robert's will, and we dress up and bow."

Hot coffee choked him. "'Dress up and bow?'"

"Like the chorus in a play. Only he keeps the script, and we wander foolishly through the scene."

"Have you been to many plays? In London?" *Intriguing.* It hadn't occurred to him that a vicar's daughter would have had opportunity for the theater.

"Some. When Edmund was alive, he liked to go, but that is neither here nor there," she said.

Nora's eyes lit up suddenly. "I forgot. You just saw Castellimonte. What did he say? Did he complain about my foolish faint?"

"He asked how you went on," Jamie said. "The man gave every appearance of genuine concern." His little wren huffed at the thought. "I agree that his sincerity would be difficult to gauge."

Sandwiches and tea arrived. Jamie began to wolf his down.

"That's it then? He dragged you over there to ask express concern? I beg leave to doubt it."

"No, not that. He offered me work," Jamie replied. He took another bite. Ham and soft cheese melted over his tongue. Jamie liked food. Food was simple. The machinations of counts and governments were not.

"He is plotting something," Nora said.

*Why did I ever think of her as simple?* What she lacked in deviousness in herself she identified quickly enough in others.

"I don't trust him," she said.

"I don't either."

"What did he offer?"

Jamie brushed crumbs from his hands. "He wants me to tutor the young men who make up his household."

Nora's jaw went slack. Jamie shrugged. He had not been able to puzzle it out either.

"He wishes me to pound the King's English into their thick Piedmontese heads," he said.

"Language, of course! Your fluency could be a valuable asset," she said.

"Except that the young sprigs of Savoy could have the benefit of a university. Except that he could hire any one of a dozen Englishmen—that poet Keats who lives over by the Spanish steps for one. Why me? Why now?"

"Keep your friends close," Nora quoted.

"Keep your enemies closer," he finished. "Which are we?" *Wentworth would have no doubt*. "He claims we made a positive impression."

"Must have been the clothes," Nora cracked. She colored lightly, pinker than the roses. They both knew how hard she tried to avoid buying that wardrobe.

"I suspect he respects someone who speaks up to him, who is not cowed," Jamie said.

"He must love you then," she replied.

"Doubtful. Respect perhaps. One can respect an opponent. Respect them but watch them closely." He swallowed his coffee before he told her the rest. "He offered a respectable salary."

"But that's wonderful." Nora bounced up in her chair. "We don't need money, of course, but you—" She stuttered to a stop. "Sorry. I didn't mean to imply—"

"Don't apologize. I know what you mean. It would feel good to have cash of my own, I admit," he said.

"Will you take it?" she asked.

"I don't see how I can refuse. We can't afford to insult the man," he said.

The work would give him access to the Palazzo. *I could trundle over to Wentworth with tidbits of information*, he thought. If the count began to pump him for information about the English, he could do that, too. *It would serve the two of them right. Maybe they would forget about Major Bently.*

"It's honest enough work. You should take it," Nora said.

*Honest enough? What would she think if she knew I took money from both Castellimonte and Wentworth. What a coil!*

"If I do, perhaps we can delay 'going through with it' as you call it."

Nora sobered. "We can't leave her there. If the count insists I be married first, we have to do it." She leaned forward and put her hand over his. "I know it worries you, but it may be needed."

"How can you say that? Marriage would be serious trouble," he said.

The little wren shook her head insistently. "It needn't be real if you don't want it. Once Isabella and the guardianship are safe, you can leave. You will have your life back."

She misunderstood him miserably. *I have no other life.* He began to think he wanted no other life, but marriage to him would bring her nothing but grief. That much he knew for certain.

Nora pleaded with watery blue eyes that destroyed Jamie's defenses. He covered her hand where it lay on his.

"It will not come to that. We mustn't let it. We'll find a way to convince him to give Isabella over to your care," he promised her.

"I want her now, Jamie. Not a year from now," Nora retorted.

"I'll take the work, Nora," he said. "I'll do my best, but I make no promises."

Lunch sat like a rock in his stomach. *When has my best helped anyone?*

## Chapter 20

A blushing maid let Jamie into Nora's house with a curtsey. He knew the house had become Nora's because sunlight filled the foyer, and the dim, the drapes, and the dust were gone. Tile sparkled in the courtyard beyond. His little wren had been busy nesting.

While the maid scurried to find *signora*, Jamie went to the tall windows which opened to the interior courtyard. Overgrown beds, plants in need of pruning, and dirty statuary met his eyes.

Jamie's mind drew a picture of Isabella and Nora on their own bench next to the statues of naked cupids while water danced in the now-dry fountain. Try as he might, he couldn't see himself in that picture.

"Jamie! What a relief! I'm so glad you are here. Did I interrupt your work?"

He turned to see her in a shaft of sunlight with linen wrapped around her old bombazine dress, a white bandana covering her hair except where honey-colored locks had escaped, and a gray smudge running across her nose and down her cheek. Her adorable disarray took his breath away.

"Jamie," she repeated, concerned by his silence, "did my message disturb your work? Was it trouble?"

"No, no," he said, clearing the lump in his throat. "We were finished for the day." His presence, as it turned out, would be needed half days three times a week. He had wished for less free time, less time to brood about Nora, and less time to brood about his own fears. Her message had been a relief.

Her broad smile made his blood sizzle. How a woman

wrapped in shapeless layers of fabric could make his entire body react astonished him.

Nora didn't notice. She swept up and took both his hands. "It goes well?"

"As much as I can tell after two days, yes," he replied.

"How many students?" she asked.

"Usually four or five, if you can call gawky young men with various duties about the Palazzo students."

"Victor?" she asked, wary.

"Am I to tutor our preening baron? No. I haven't seen him," he told her. "I suspect his English is already better than he lets on."

That answer seemed to please her.

"Did you see the count?" she asked.

"Not once. Nor have I sought him out to plead your case. Patience, Nora."

She sighed and dropped his hands. Her tongue darted out to wet her lower lip. He stared at her mouth hungrily. Memory of the one time he kissed those lips pushed all other thoughts out of his mind.

"You have the oddest expression," she said. "What is it?"

"You," he said, "your, uh, dress. Is linen this year's fashion?"

She gave her skirt a twitch. "This is the dress of a good English housewife doing honest work, thank you very much."

"I met one maid. How many did you hire?"

"Four so far. Two maids of all work, and two temporary, although one of them may work out as a nursery maid when Isabella comes." Her eyes slid from his when she said it, and she looked shifty. Jamie felt the hair on his neck rise.

"Did you hire them yourself?"

She didn't look at him. "One or two," she said.

"Nora? You let Capello hire the rest, didn't you?"

She nodded. "Finding them myself would take time we don't have. I know you think they will all spy, but, Jamie, we have nothing to hide. Why not let them?"

She looked at him for approval, eyes bright and clear. *Nothing to hide? A bogus betrothal for one, a relationship that exists only for show, a major with a past to hide.* He tilted his head and spoke through tight lips. "Nora—" he began.

She rushed on. "These girls are simple peasants. They speak no English."

"That you know about."

"Seriously, they don't. They work hard. I like them."

"Why the relief at my arrival then? You need help giving these maids who don't speak English orders?"

Nora laughed. "Hardly. The work is obvious and easily demonstrated. We're scrubbing room by room. I promised Isabella, remember?"

"Why me then?"

The wary look came back. "There's one more," she said, "Or there may be. Capello is sending a housekeeper."

*Housekeeper. The manager of the household. The dragon of the staff. At least, Nora shows sense about that.*

"See, I'm not completely lacking in care," she rushed on as if she could read his thoughts. "I promised only to speak with the woman, not to hire her. You warned me about spies."

"Yes, but you seem to have let the door down anyway," he pointed out.

She looked sheepish. "We have little to hide," she said.

*Nora has nothing to hide. My name, my title, and my deepest sins. Those are mine to hide.*

She peeped at him under lowered lashes. "You can see why I need you."

"You need me?" The thought pleased him. "To begin with, I suggest that you freshen up."

"What?" she sputtered. "I do not need to put on airs for a servant, at least!"

"There are no bigger snobs than upper servants," Jamie said. "The housekeeper always knows everything."

He hoped Nora didn't think about how he knew. He spent more than his share of visits as the pockets-to-let friend of the upper classes. Housekeepers had been particularly skilled at keeping him in his place.

"If you want the woman to respect you," he went on, "you have to look the part of lady of the house."

"Very well, I'll change my clothes." She turned with a swish and started down the family corridor. Jamie followed her.

"You brought extra?"

"I brought it all," she said, looking sheepish again. "It seemed wasteful to keep rooms while this house sat empty."

Blood rushed to his head. "You moved in? Alone?" *Of course she lives alone.* Jamie cursed himself. *How could it be otherwise?* "Where is Wat?" he demanded.

Nora turned toward the lady's chamber and smiled over her shoulder. "Keeping watch, of course," she said.

Jamie stopped dead where the corridor turned to the right. "Where shall I meet you?" he called.

"In the foyer," she replied. "Or you can wait in the sitting room," she said, gesturing to the little salon he remembered between the lady's bedroom and the master's.

He groaned. He refused to go further toward the master of the house's private quarters. "I'll be in the foyer," he called back as she disappeared into her bedroom.

An odd sound held him in place—a giggle. It appeared to come from the room next to him. He opened the door. Two maids bobbed curtsies, rags in hand. They were polishing the four-poster bed in the master suite, the husband's room, the one he had no intention of using. Both women blushed scarlet when he stared at the bed. He mumbled some words of praise for their work and sprinted back to the foyer.

Nora paused at the entrance to the foyer, lifted her chin, put on what she hoped was a lady-of-the-manor expression and swept in. If Jamie thought she needed to play a part, play it she would.

She found him on his knees, and her theatric airs evaporated.

"What are you doing?" she laughed.

"This lock has been loosened. Did you force it?" He didn't sound amused.

"No. I noticed it was loose when I arrived," she said. "I had to jiggle the key to open it."

"Was it like this when Capello showed you the house?" he asked sternly.

Nora searched her memory. So much had happened that day she could be certain of very little. With his head bowed and his back to her, Nora couldn't think clearly. The set of his shoulders and the ripple of muscle in his back distracted her too greatly.

Jamie turned and looked up at her. "Nora?" he asked. "Was it?"

"He opened it without trouble," she said at last. She felt her cheeks heat and hoped he hadn't caught her gawking like a schoolgirl.

Jamie rose in one fluid motion and brushed his hands. "I'll hire a locksmith. Someone damaged that lock. What did you find disturbed this morning?"

"Nothing! That is, I don't think so, but I don't really know the house, do I? The valuables are still locked at Robert's bank. I didn't see anything missing," she said.

"Think, Nora. Was anything rearranged?"

"What other reason could there be to break in except to steal?" Something in Jamie's intense gaze frightened her.

"Wait," she said. "There was one odd thing, but too small to be of any significance." She shook her head.

"Nothing is insignificant, Nora. Tell me," he said, brown eyes boring into her.

"A doll. I went to Isabella's room to find a replacement for the missing Marietta," she said.

"And?"

"Nothing looked disturbed," she told him, "except, when we were here before I thought there were five little dolls in the doll bed. This morning there were four."

She knew Jamie's spew of foreign words were surely curses. Nora felt blessed she didn't understand them. "What? How can a missing doll be significant?"

"An intruder came in here and made it to Isabella's room. Isabella!" he exclaimed.

Nora put her hand on the wall to steady herself, suddenly lightheaded. "Why?" she whispered.

"I don't know what it means, Love, but I don't like it, especially with you living here."

She grasped his offered hand and clung to it just as she clung to his calling her "Love."

"More foolish if I bring Isabella?"

He nodded.

"You'll have the locked fixed," she said, "surely that will help."

"We'll get every window and door checked, fixed with sturdy locks, and secured," he told her. "That will only slow down a determined intruder. You shouldn't be here alone."

*Come to me. Live here with me.* The words stuck in her throat.

Whatever she might have said died with a firm knock on their door. Nora reached for the handle, but Jamie reached out and pulled her hand back.

"Lady of the house, remember?" He made shooing gestures toward the little anteroom Nora guessed to be the household office. She lifted her chin and swept across the tiles. The chuckle that followed her almost ruined the effect.

She sat on a delicate gilt chair behind the small writing desk inlaid with patterns and color. She didn't have long to wait.

Signora Capello turned out to be tall, stern, and as intimidating as Jamie suggested. Nora thought she rather resembled Sister Cecilia; she looked as disapproving.

"Is the signora related to my brother's man of business?"

The woman shrugged. "A cousin, a distant cousin," Jamie translated.

The woman shot him a filthy look.

"Do you speak English?" Nora asked. Jamie looked expectant. His eyes met Nora's; he seemed to approve. They both looked at Signora Capello.

"Some. Little," the woman said at last. She turned to Jamie and spoke in her native language.

"She was given the impression this was to be an Italian speaking house," he said. His eyes held a warning.

"The household will speak Italian," Nora said. Her agreement to raise Isabella in Rome, to learn the language, to send her to Santo Spirito day school all implied that they would.

Jamie raised an eyebrow. She didn't back down. Having said it, they would live with it.

"However," Nora went on, "I need someone who can understand me while I learn Italian." She looked directly at Signora Capello. The woman nodded. She understood Nora's English.

They dealt with her extensive experience, exemplary references, and immediate availability in a rapid series of questions in Italian.

"What is your role at the Palazzo di Savoia?" Jamie asked in English abruptly. If the woman had been taken off guard, she hid it well. She sat straighter and spoke to him directly.

"I have no role at the Palazzo," she replied in perfect but heavily accented English.

"Who do you know there?" he asked without breaking eye contact.

"My nephew serves the count," she said. When he looked expectant, she added, "Eduardo Mora."

Jamie grimaced. "One of my 'students,'" he told Nora.

"You have no role at the Palazzo. Piedmont perhaps?

What Castellimonte family household employed you last?" he asked.

For a long moment Nora thought the woman would not answer. In the end, she said, "I had the honor of serving the count's mother until she passed away last month."

"Noble of you," Jamie said.

She reverted to Italian.

"She tells me most families would be honored to hire the housekeeper of the Contessa. She's probably right." Their would-be housekeeper gave Nora a knowing look.

"Thank you for your time, Signora," Nora began. She should send the woman on her way.

"We will be in touch tomorrow," Jamie interrupted.

He escorted the woman out.

"We can't possibly hire her," Nora said when he returned.

"She's qualified. She'll manage the staff for you."

"But she's the count's person!"

"The next one likely will be, too, and less brazen about it. Hire her," he told her.

Suddenly the weight of it descended on her, and she collapsed back into her little chair so hard it rocked. "Jamie," she said, "I'm afraid."

"Fear is good, Nora. Fear will keep you vigilant."

"Not for myself. I don't want to lose Isabella, but I don't want to put her in danger. I can't be alone here." She caught his eyes, urging him to understand. "You said it didn't have to be a real marriage."

"We can fix the locks," he repeated.

"But Isabella. We need to move her here. We need to keep her safe," she said.

"You need a butler," he told her.

"Butler?"

"Wat Jones may not look like one, but you need him inside your household to keep an eye on things. You need a servant loyal only to you."

"Butler?" she asked, trying to picture it.

"Butler, footman, gardener, whatever pleases you," he replied.

"We can do that, but it isn't enough," she said. She knew it would help, but not as much as a husband. She wished Jamie could see that, but he refused to respond. *Stubborn man!*

"Jamie, please. Eventually I can do it alone but not now." She hated the sound of her own voice pleading.

Still no response. "Would it be so terrible?" she whispered.

Her major looked back sadly, his brown eyes full of regret, his dear face raised in the smallest of smiles. "Not terrible. No. But not good for you either."

*Marriage is the answer*. Nora was certain. *If we marry, Isabella can come home. If we marry, Jamie can see to any intruders. If we marry, the count will be satisfied.* Jamie said it didn't have to be a real marriage.

*It doesn't have to be, but it could be.* God help her, she had begun to hope it might be. She wondered if he thought she feared a physical relationship. *How can I convince him that isn't true?*

# Chapter 21

"An intruder? What do you intend to do about it?"

The Count di Castellimonte staged spectacle and pageant and played the role of haughty autocrat perfectly. Jamie wondered if he could also dissemble with the skill of a stage performer, but he doubted it. His outrage didn't seem feigned.

"Fix the locks. Hire a guard," Jamie replied to the count's question.

The count made a dismissive gesture. "Easily overcome."

"I know," Jamie replied. "The intrusion has to stop." He glared at the count.

"You think I play at these things?" the count demanded. "If I wanted something inside, my people wouldn't be so careless with the lock. If I wanted to frighten, I would leave a clearer message. No. This is the work of amateurs."

Jamie felt a smile dance around his lips. The count hadn't attacked Nora. He sat back and relaxed. The two of them were alone in the count's private office. Castellimonte had been irritated when Jamie demanded an audience, and more so when Jamie insisted that the Ferret leave the room. His report of intruders had driven those concerns away.

"If not you, then who?" Jamie asked.

The count ran a hand through his silver hair in an uncharacteristic gesture. The man wasn't lying. "I don't know. I can't be sure."

"But you suspect."

The count shrugged. "These are troubled times."

"In Rome? Or in Piedmont?" Jamie asked.

"Both. Naples. Milan. None of them want Napoleon, but the people beg for the return of his law code. Others want power at any price," Castellimonte said.

"What does Savoy want?" Jamie asked.

"Stability and safety for our people," Castellimonte replied without hesitation.

"What of safety for Isabella Beaumont? What do your political problems have to do with her?" Jamie asked.

The old man looked closely at Jamie. He appeared to come to a decision.

"There are factions in my country," he began. "The dissatisfied and the greedy think they share goals, the fools. They look for weakness. They look for levers. A child makes a compelling hostage."

"Why Isabella?" Jamie asked.

"A child related to the royal family makes an even better hostage. I had hoped it was not so, but someone broke in yesterday. Now I fear."

"She isn't close enough to the throne to matter," Jamie said, but he thought he knew the answer. He wanted the old man to say it.

"There are persons that care about her who are close enough. She could be used to force cooperation," the count said.

"Such as her great-uncle?" Jamie asked.

The old man's face showed little.

Jamie went on, "You will set up a guard on the house." It wasn't a question.

"Of course," the count replied.

"Make it discreet," Jamie requested. "No need to frighten Nora or Isabella."

"Isabella is safer at Santo Spirito. She should stay there," the count said.

"Mrs. Haley will not stand for that," Jamie told him.

"Your fiancée's courage is foolish. It will bring her to grief."

*True, but unchangeable*. Jamie chose not to reply.

The old man took a deep shuddering breath. "Marry the woman. Do it quickly. They will be safer with you close by."

"My marriage or lack of it is not your concern," Jamie retorted.

"You care for this woman. I have seen it. Marry her," the old man pressed.

Jamie sighed with head bowed; he shook his head to fend off the order.

"Of my students, Giovanni learns the fastest. He has a gift for languages," Jamie said, diverting the conversation.

"We send him to London next year," the count replied with a wry smile. "He has motivation."

"Eduardo, on the other hand, doesn't try. He is more interested in making jokes at the expense of the teacher."

"Eduardo Mora? I don't remember recommending him. He wishes to be my son's friend," the count said thoughtfully. "The others?"

Jamie reported the progress of his students with half a mind in a few short sentences. Eduardo bore watching. So did Victor Filiberto, whether his father thought so or not.

"Leave Isabella Beaumont at Santo Spirito," the count said, when he rose to leave. "Leave her there or marry her aunt."

It was quietly said, but an ultimatum all the same.


Nora paced the foyer in a swish of muslin. Jamie had promised to come and check on the work of the locksmith. *He promised! Where is he?*

That morning she had hired a cook. When the maids removed Holland covers from furniture in a sunny room across the courtyard and scrubbed it clean, it turned out to be a breakfast parlor. She ordered it set up for dinner. She didn't want to eat alone.

"He has no obligation," she chided herself out loud. She shouldn't expect him to hover. *When Isabella comes it will be different.* When Isabella came, she wouldn't be alone.

A knock interrupted that train of thought. Her new footman moved to the door, but she got there before him.

"Jamie!"

"Damn it, Nora, you shouldn't answer the door. I thought you hired Wat as a butler."

"Is that what I am?" Wat Jones asked with a cheeky grin.

Nora didn't care. She pulled Jamie by the hand.

"Look, look. Look at the lock," she beamed.

"Sturdy enough. The windows?" he asked Wat over his shoulder.

"He is still working," Nora answered. "The other entrances are finished."

"Damn!" Jamie ran his hand through his already mussed hair. She found the gesture endearing. "Sorry Nora," he said. "I just realized I haven't even checked to determine all the entrances in this palace."

"No need. Did that," Wat told him. Nora beamed at them both.

"But didn't the locksmith do a good job on the door?" she asked.

"He's done a better job than Castellimonte's guard," he said. "The damned fool waved to me when I came down the street. He is supposed to be invisible."

Nora gasped. "The count hired a guard? What do you call him, the wolf? Do you want him watching the sheep?"

Jamie's chuckle rumbled up from his chest in the way that she loved. His deep voice said, "Sheep indeed. Things have changed."

Wat nodded. "I'll be watching that locksmith," he said before wandering off.

"Can we find a place to sit?" Jamie asked.

"I almost forgot. Eat first. You are always easier to talk to when you eat," she said.

"I can't argue with that. Shall we go out?"

"No. We have a cook. We have a breakfast room. Dinner is waiting."

"Will there be pudding? I like something sweet with my dinner," he said with a wink.

*Wretched man. Locksmiths, guards, intruders, and he wants his pudding.*

"Not sweet, I think," she replied. "Tart. Especially if you prolong telling me what you meant about things changing."

He didn't rush. She watched him eat steadily through the soup and fish, humming and sighing his pleasure. He still ate like a man who didn't know when his next meal would arrive.

"Keep the cook," he said when the pasta arrived. "She is a genius."

"Do you think you can slow down long enough to tell me what went on?"

Jamie wiped his mouth, looked lovingly at the pasta and told her.

"The count is concerned. I think he means it," he concluded. He tucked into the pasta.

"Can we trust him?" she asked.

"In general, no, but where Isabella's safety is concerned, I believe yes. Whoever took her doll didn't work for Castellimonte."

Nora ate her dinner in silence for a few moments. "If he sets guards, will he let her move here?" she asked at last.

"He thinks she is safer at the convent," Jamie replied.

"Safer, but not happy," she said morosely.

"The count doesn't value that higher than her physical security," Jamie told her.

"That's it then? He will raise objections. I saw Campbell today."

"Wentworth's clerk?" His eyes looked wary.

"Wentworth assigned him to draw up the guardianship

case. He told me marriage is the last barrier." Tears welled in her eyes. "Did Castellimonte offer no way out?"

Jamie tapped a spoon on his empty plate. He didn't look at her. "What is it? What else is there?"

No answer.

"Mother Margarita also says we should not delay marriage!" Nora burst out.

Jamie looked like a trapped animal, eyes bleak. "Is it what you truly want also?" he asked.

Nora knew she should deny it. She should tell him to go. She should not pressure him, but she could not back down. Marriage would solve her problems. Marriage to Jamie had become her dearest hope.

"Yes," she said. She had been determined not to burden him; she wondered if she could make sure marriage to her didn't do that.

"Nora, do you hear yourself? You want Isabella here so badly you're willing to marry an employee?" Jamie forced his voice not to shake. She offered his hope of heaven; if he accepted, he dragged them both to hell.

"You aren't my employee!" she exclaimed. "I haven't paid you since we agreed to the betrothal."

"We agreed the relationship would not change. You feed me. You even bought my clothes. That is not a marriage." Jamie spat out the words.

The little wren's eyes watered up. *Damn! Not tears. I don't need tears.*

"You can't shackle yourself to someone you hardly know," he pressed on. *Someone*, he thought, *who is everything you despise*.

"I know you well enough. I know you keep your word. I know you to be honorable."

*Honorable? I lied to her from the beginning.* Bile rose in his throat.

"I know that you care about people," she went on.

He shook his head to deny it. He cared about Nora and Isabella, yes. But he contributed to the death of one hundred and thirty-two souls. *How is that caring? Do you want to marry a slave trader, Nora?*

She ignored him. "I know you treat me with respect. That is more than Edmund did." Her lips quivered.

He leaned over and took her hand; the touch turned his heart to mush. "Edmund must have been a fool," he said. "Any man of sense would respect you."

Nora drew breath and squeezed his hand. "What is more to the point, you care for Isabella."

"Care? I adore the little imp." That he wouldn't deny.

"You can protect her. You can give her what she needs. She's lost her father. She needs the security of home."

*And what will happen if she loses another father figure?* He could marry Nora and bring Isabella home, but sooner or later it would all crash down on their heads.

"You want this marriage, Nora? Think," he said.

"Yes. Marriage solves our problems," she said as if it were that simple.

"It creates others," he warned, thinking fast. Her adorable frown while she tried to puzzle out his meaning drove him on. "I'm not sure I can manage marriage in name only. Not if I'm living here." *Be afraid, Nora. Run.*

If he hoped the threat of physical marriage would discourage her, her response flattened him. Her eyes glowed in anticipation.

"If that is what you wish, then I wish it, too," she whispered, a blush creeping up her cheeks.

A rush of triumph washed through him; alarm brushed it aside. Jamie groaned. "We won't be able to annul it in that case," he warned in a last ditch effort to turn her decision.

"I'll live in Rome, in this house, with Isabella the rest of my life. If you want your freedom, Jamie, we'll make sure you preserve it." She gave him an impish look. "We have separate suites. Mine has a lock."

Jamie threw his head back and dropped her hand.

"You want this badly," he said through tight lips. "So does Castellimonte."

He lost himself in thought for several minutes. When he looked back across the table, the fearful anticipation on Nora's face decided the matter.

"It appears to be inevitable," Jamie said at last. He put his serviette on the table, folded his hands, and leaned toward her.

"How quickly can Mother Margarita manufacture this wedding?" he asked. "And where is the damned pudding?"

Her mouth spread wide in a smile she couldn't seem to suppress. His heart stuttered. *God help me.*

"You won't regret it," she said. "I'll do my best to make sure you never regret it."

*I already do.*

The footman placed a sweet Italian cake, fragrant with lemon, in front of him.

"Paradise on a plate!" he exclaimed. Her cook would keep him supplied with cakes and biscuits. *That much I won't regret.*

## Chapter 22

Nora sat on her hands to keep them from shaking.

"But it must happen immediately, Mother," she stressed. "In England, we can marry by special license. Is that possible in the Papal States?"

Mother Margarita smiled across the well-worn table that served as her desk and said carefully in broken English, "Not worry. It will be done properly. Padre Barnabas will ensure it."

The older woman leaned a bit forward. "Does the major wish it?" she asked in Italian.

"Sì," Nora said, suppressing doubt. *He makes a pretense of it anyway.* She refused to let guilt at forcing his hand get in the way. "Sì, yes," she repeated.

Two days later, she stood alone, dressed in a manner she wouldn't have contemplated just one month before, and fretted. Her soon-to-be husband failed to appear.

Her dress, a frothy gown of new blue muslin, woven with an open check and decorated with white-on-white embroidered cuffs flattered her. The bonnet she impulsively bought, thinking it might please him, the one that sported lace and blue ribbons, felt heavy on her head. Delight in her appearance eroded moment by moment. She wondered if she had been a fool.

Isabella skipped across the worn stone paving and put her arms around Nora's knees. "Uncle Jamie, he is late."

Nora smiled down at her. "Yes, he is." *A full half hour late. Where is the blasted man?*

The priest complained to Mother Margarita in rapid Italian, accompanied by dramatic hand gestures that made the lace cuffs of his white robe flap around him and the green stole he wore over the top rise and fall.

Mother, who had arranged the hasty ceremony, spoke sternly to the priest and cast a sympathetic eye on Nora. She was to be the sole witness. Nora didn't permit herself to think about how Mother, or her mysterious cousin Barnabas, had arranged it so quickly, how the priest may have been convinced to conduct it, or who had the power to order it.

"He will come," the older woman said.

Nora forced a smile. "Of course," she replied.

She wished she could sink into the ancient paving stones of the floor. Instead, she leaned over and straightened Isabella's hair bow for the fourth time.

"I am pretty," Isabella announced.

"You are ravishing," a voice responded from the doorway.

Nora's breath stuck in her throat. Jamie stood framed in yellow sunlight. *The wretch!* To Nora's eyes he looked impossibly handsome in a new suit of blue lightweight fabric and a new hat set at a rakish angle.

Beams of colored light streamed across the ancient pavement of the side chapel where she waited. Jamie smiled at her and walked confidently through the rainbows of light without taking his eyes from her, his smile growing as he came.

"You changed your hair," he said.

She had. She had thought it nonsense, really, but if Nora was getting married, even a masquerade of a marriage, she would do it looking her best.

"So did you," she said. He had shaved and cut his hair. She suspected he took time with his appearance for her sake, and that had made him late. *It is impossible to stay angry with this man,* she thought.

"I like it. I like the dress, too," he went on.

"Me, too, Uncle Jamie," Isabella insisted.

"Especially you, Angel," he said, chucking Isabella on the chin but keeping his eyes on Nora.

They grinned at one another like fools. Nora sent a silent prayer of thanks that she had given in to impulse and bought the dress. *The admiration in Jamie's eyes matters,* she realized. *It matters very much.*

The priest hurried forward and gestured them to the front of the marble altar and began to pray. Jamie took her hand but didn't translate. Instead, he looked somber, listening to every word. The priest spoke to Jamie in Italian and looked at him expectantly.

"*Sì, con la grazia di Dio, lo voglio,*" Jamie said.

The priest turned to her with the same question. He waited, expecting her reply. She darted a panicked glance at Jamie.

"Repeat what I said," he whispered. "It means 'Yes, I do by the grace of God.'"

She did, hoping she hadn't said anything foolish. She must not have because the priest continued.

Jamie slipped a slim gold band on her left hand. *Where did he get this?* Her mind wouldn't process the thought. *I have nothing for him. Does that matter?*

The ceremony ended as abruptly as it had begun. Jamie turned and looked down at her. Her breath became erratic, and panic came over her at the sight of the well-dressed gentleman with newly groomed brown curls falling down on his forehead dressed like a prosperous solicitor or merchant.

*I married a complete stranger,* she thought. *What happened to my shabby major?*

His warm brown eyes searched hers briefly. Before she knew what he was about, he leaned and placed a chaste kiss on her cheek.

"There are papers to sign and then you can collapse," he said, his familiar mocking voice, a soft whisper. She relaxed on a sigh. *This is Jamie. We will do fine.*

She didn't collapse, thank God. The little wren looked ready to bolt when the priest asked for her vows. She had more backbone than that, though.

"Easy, little one, give Aunt Nora some air," Jamie said.

Isabella danced up and down, clamoring for hugs and kisses, while the priest demanded impatiently that they sign the register.

He led Nora under the arched doorway to the sacristy. When she bent over the register, Jamie watched Mother Margarita take Isabella's hand and speak to her sternly. *The little imp looks ready to explode*, he thought.

"There!" Nora said. "Done."

"Can we have cake now," Isabella asked. Jamie watched her glance at the reverend mother and add a belated, "Please."

Nora bent down and took Isabella from the nun.

Jamie watched the little one dance up and down in excitement. He chuckled, turned to the ledger, and signed his name in a rapid scrawl. He rose to smile at Nora and Isabella.

"Do you plan to tell her?" Mother Margarita asked.

"Tell her what?" he asked without taking his eyes from Nora who tickled Isabella and talked nonsense to the child.

"This," Mother Margarita said. She pointed to the ledger.

He smiled down at Nora's neat signature, "Eleanora Mary Haley," and then bit back a curse. His signature underneath, scrawled, but clear, read, "James Phineas Heyworth."

*Damn and double damn.* His mind had been on Isabella's nonsense. His mind had been on Nora. He forgot.

"Are you going to tell her?" Mother Margarita repeated.

"Yes, of course," he said. *Eventually*.

"When?"

"Are we ready to go?" Nora asked, smiling at him.

Her question saved him from answering the nosy nun. He shut the ledger, stepped in front of it, and took both her hands in a firm grip.

"It's done. This is what we agreed to, isn't it?" he said.

Nora nodded. "Yes. It just feels so odd."

"We'll grow accustomed," he said. He held both her hands a few moments more and then released one.

Nora reached out to Mother Margarita. "Thank you so much for assisting us," she said, "and for arranging to have Isabella's things sent to Casa Beaumont."

The little nun shot Jamie a stern look while she murmured polite congratulations to Nora. He tried to avoid eye contact.

"Come, little wife. Let's get out of this cave and into the sunshine to find cake and show Isabella how happy we are."

## Chapter 23

Nora dreamed of her wedding night when she was a naïve girl, as all women do. Her dreams did not include a five-year-old child and a husband who chose not to bed her. If she felt disappointment, she had known worse before. Her first husband spent their wedding night drinking with his cronies. He vomited on her bedroom floor and fell asleep.

While watching Jamie pretend to drink tea with Isabella's family of dolls, Nora shivered under the burden of memory. Jamie, she realized, had been sober for weeks. She couldn't even recall the moment when she had stopped watching for signs of drunkenness. He drank a little wine over dinner but never to excess. He gave every appearance of enjoying her company. Jamie was not Edmund.

"No more biscuits for you, Uncle Jamie. You will grow stout," Isabella pronounced.

"Never!" Jamie exclaimed. "Ask Julianna."

Julianna, Isabella's newest and most favorite doll, ruled their play. As soon as they returned to Casa Beaumont from church, Jamie had disappeared into his quarters and returned with a package wrapped in silver, overflowing with pink and purple ribbons and lace. Not for Nora, for Isabella, "to celebrate this most momentous day." With wrappings ripped to shreds, Julianna smiled up at Isabella, her bisque face rosy and delicate. The little girl fell instantly in love.

Their "tea" had lasted from teatime, through dinner, and into the evening. Nora's enthusiasm for imaginary treats waned hours before. She sat with her needlework and watched the other two. Jamie, on the other hand, never wavered.

*When I met him I worried about having him around a child. It turns out he is one,* she thought wryly.

Jamie pouted. "Please, Julianna, one more!"

"Julianna says you may have one more to celebrate 'this most momentous day,'" Isabella mimicked.

She wrapped her tongue around the new English word carefully. Nora expected many things to be "momentous" in the next week or so.

Jamie soberly accepted the imaginary biscuit, took a nibble, and closed his eyes as if in ecstasy. That sight made Nora's heart race.

He ruined the effect by opening his eyes and winking at her. "Ah, lemony," he sighed.

Nora smiled back but gave him a pointed look with her brows raised. She tipped her head toward the child.

"Alas, I believe it is Julianna's bedtime," he said.

Isabella's mouth drooped in dramatic disappointment.

"Remember? Aunt Nora said only a few moments more. Time's up!"

A swift hug, some tickles, and a laugh later, Julianna was tucked safely in her little bed and Isabella deposited in the hands of her new nursery maid.

"We'll come back to help with prayers," Nora told her when she kissed the top of the little one's head. "Be good for Alicia."

"Alicia," Jamie murmured when they had closed the door. "Isn't she a bit too young?" He carried a candle and directed Nora toward their sitting room.

"Young perhaps, but qualified," Nora answered. "She is the oldest of thirteen children."

Jamie looked horrified. "Thirteen?"

"Imagine that," Nora laughed. "The girl has seen her share of babies and was wildly eager to get away from home. She will do."

"I'll bet she was!" he exclaimed.

They reached the little sitting room between their suites. He opened the door to allow Nora in but stopped on the threshold.

"I'll leave you to your needle business, whatever it is. Not embroidery."

Nora's heart sank. He planned to leave her alone on their wedding night. "Tatting," she croaked out. She hoped the smile she gave him wavered less than it felt.

She poked at her needlework while the clock ticked, dragging out time. She tore out more stitches than she made. Twenty minutes must be sufficient time for a maid to get one little girl into her nightclothes. Nora bustled down the hall.

Shrieking alerted her. She opened the door to find Jamie tossing Isabella up and onto her bed.

"Ah, Aunt Nora is here. Now we must behave," he said. Isabella moved toward the edge with mocking stealth. Jamie caught her and pulled her back.

"Aunt Nora will read to you and tuck you in." He dropped his voice to a whisper. "And you must be very quiet so Julianna can sleep. She will have a very busy day tomorrow."

"Busy?" Isabella asked. "Doing what?"

"Playing with you, of course!"

Jamie winked at Nora and left. *How can I ever compete for Isabella's affection with the whirlwind that is Uncle Jamie?*

Isabella smiled, and Nora's heart melted. Isabella, she saw with sudden clarity, brought enough love to encompass all of them.

"Read to me, please," the little one said.

Nora slipped onto the bed and opened the book. She pulled Isabella close and kissed the top of her head.

The house lay silent when she finally took her candle and made her way down the dark corridor to her lonely sitting room. Needlework didn't appeal. She would put it away. There were books on a shelf in her room. She would read herself to sleep.

She opened the door to find the room far from empty. Jamie leaned on the mantel, staring at the fire. He raised his head when she opened the door and put out a hand.

"Jamie!"

His smile, soft and welcoming, warmed her to her toes. She saw sadness in his eyes as well but refused to think about it. *Not tonight*, she told herself.

"Come, sit. You must be weary," he said.

He took her hand, tiny in his. Her slight tremor didn't prevent her from gripping him back firmly. *That's my courageous girl. What a day you've had.* He led her to her chair.

Puzzlement clouded her features. "I thought you had work to do." She blinked up at him.

"I have lessons to prepare. I can do that in the sitting room." He stood looking down at her, still holding her hand. Her adorable face tempted him, and the loneliness he saw there battered his heart. He couldn't leave her alone on her wedding night, even on a false one. *Surely,* he thought, *I can spend an hour with her without letting lust overwhelm what little sense I have left.*

"Let's sit together," he said out loud. "Me with my work, you with your needlework." He wagged his eyebrows until she chuckled. "Like old married people." His hand felt empty when he let go, took a step back, and leaned his elbow on the mantel.

The little wren smiled, but her smile wavered when her hand fluttered over to pick up her work.

"I didn't expect you. When you left earlier, you told me you were leaving me," she said. "To my work, that is. Leaving me to my work." She looked taut, like a spring coiled too tight.

"Did I? I went to fetch something," he said.

She looked up at that, raising her eyes in question.

He reached into his coat. He thanked God and Wentworth he had at least a few coins of his own. Silver paper covered the box he pulled out, but only one tasteful bow surrounded it. It fit in his palm.

"As you see, it is something small," he said, "A trifle to remember our 'momentous day.'" She turned it over in her fingers.

"Wait, wife," he said. "First a toast to our wedding, then gifts."

"Gifts, Jamie? A toast?"

"It may not have been much of a wedding, but we deserve some celebration, don't you think? For enduring it, if nothing else."

He poured two glasses of rich red wine and handed her one. She looked at it suspiciously.

"Not sherry, I agree, but much better. You're a big girl. Try it."

To his joy, she did. She took one sip and then another. "Good!" she said, eyes wide.

"Don't look so shocked. People have savored it for centuries without civilization going into decline."

"Don't be absurd," she said and took a bigger swallow to prove that he misjudged her. His newly acquired handkerchief rescued her gown when she choked. *One more reason to be grateful for the blasted money,* he thought.

Nora's face turned red, not entirely, he thought, from choking when he rubbed her back. He pulled his hand away.

"Sip slowly, please," he said. She nodded, and he stepped away.

"To our marriage, such as it is," he pronounced, raising his glass.

She saluted him in turn and took a dainty sip. "Such as it is," she repeated. She put down her glass, raised the little box in her lap, and waved it at him.

"'Such as it is' does not require gifts, Jamie," she said. "I have nothing to give you."

"The polite response is thank you," he said. She had already given him more than he dared hope for: home, food, and the affection of a child, if only for a short while.

"Open it," he went on. "You'll see. It is little enough." Little enough, and yet his heart beat in his throat when he watched her unwrap it.

"Too large for a ring," she said.

He frowned. *Had she hoped for one, a gem-covered ring that would signify actual commitment? Not possible, Nora.*

She opened the red velvet box and gasped at the contents. A delicate gold chain flowed over her fingers. The cameo depicted a young woman with slender neck and soft curls. It had put him in mind of the woman his little wren might be under all her English stiffness, the woman she became more and more every day she spent with Isabella and, he liked to believe, with him.

Wentworth's blood money hadn't stretched as far as the emeralds Jamie thought would suit her. Jamie suspected his highborn friends would have seen the cameo as a trifle. Nora looked at it as if he had presented her with the crown jewels.

"I've never owned anything this lovely," she gulped. She couldn't take her eyes from it.

"Never?"

She shook her head. "My father believes a woman's virtue is sufficient adornment."

"Your father, as we know, is a fool. Did you write to him about your marriage?"

"Hardly." Her laugh was bitter. "I sent word of Robert's death and didn't manage to tell him about Isabella. Did you write to your family?"

"No," he replied.

She held her lips tight.

*Disapproval, Nora?* he wondered.

"Your friends must want to know," she went on, relentless.

Jamie's stomach sank. *What could I say if I wrote?* "*Your friend Jamie Heyworth, lately baron and slave merchant, has married a virtuous English widow under false pretenses. He plans to leave as soon as may be. Do not look for him.*"

"No," he said again. "Did your husband never present you with jewelry?"

"Never. Edmund lived for his poetry. The things of the world had no meaning to him," she said. She looked up then. "Of course he never had two coins to rub together either."

"At least not two for his wife, I think," he said. She looked so ashamed that he deeply regretted saying it.

"The men in your life couldn't see a treasure right in front of them," he said. He vowed never to mention her husband or father again. *She deserved better from them. She deserves better than me, too.*

"Help me with it," she requested.

His hands brushed her neck when he bent to fasten the chain. Her scent, lavender and chamomile, drew him forward. Another inch, three at most, and he could press his mouth to her neck, kiss his way up to her ear. His traitorous mind reminded him she was his wife. He even signed his actual name to the record. *God help me!*

He stood and took three steps back. The faint voice of conscience reminded him he didn't plan to stay. *You can leave a false marriage,* the voice said. *If you bed her, what then?*

"So, wife," he said, forcing a laugh. "I have work to do." His portfolio of notes lay on the secrétaire in the corner of the room. He turned to it.

"Jamie," she said. "Thank you. It's lovely."

"It's nothing, but you are very welcome," he replied.

He pretended to examine his notes; he tried to actually do so. A glance told him Nora had as little luck keeping to her needlework. She repeatedly picked up the cameo from where it lay against her breast and examined it. The sight almost killed him.

Jamie eyed the wine decanter and looked away. *That way leads to disaster*. One more, he knew, would not be enough to cool his blood. An entire bottle would destroy the last of his self-control.

A scratch at the door echoed in the awkward silence. He leapt to his feet, grateful for the interruption, but concerned that any servants were about at that hour. "Enter," he commanded.

Wat Jones entered in his ill-fitting livery holding a small tray with two messages. They never did decide on a role—footman or butler.

"These arrived, Major, one right after the other," the man said. "I thought they might not keep until morning."

Jamie took them and dismissed the servant, who looked at him with a skeptical eye.

"I said you may go, Wat," Jamie told him. "These are probably wedding greetings." The man shuffled out.

"Who are they from?" Nora asked.

"The first appears to be from the Palazzo di Savoia." He broke the seal and scanned the contents. "Wedding greetings, as I surmised," he said, handing it to her. He tore open the other one.

"He must have been informed by Mother Margarita. Congratulations and a summons," she said.

"Yes, we're to be honored with a wedding supper in two days," he said, scanning the second message.

"I suppose we'll have to get used to it," Nora said. "Who is the other one from?"

"Wentworth," he told her, without taking his eyes from it.

"Wentworth? What does he want?" she asked.

"To congratulate us, of course," he said. "News travels as fast in Rome as in London."

"Is that all?"

*My head on a platter and my liver for his lunch*, he thought. He didn't answer her.

The words in the message filled his head.

Bently

Married the chit? Good. Now you can get to work. I expect to hear from you by week's end.

Wentworth

"That's all of it?" Nora asked, reaching for it, frowning deeply.

He stuffed the message in his pocket and yawned deeply. "I fear I need to turn in," he said. "I have work to do tomorrow."

He left her, still frowning, without looking back.

## Chapter 24

"Wentworth can do his own damned work," Jamie growled to an empty room. He slammed his portfolio onto the dainty table in the salon the staff of Palazzo di Savoia had assigned for his lessons and ran an agitated hand through his hair.

*Nora has Isabella. I should leave*, he thought.

Wentworth or his man would see to her formal guardianship. *If I hadn't spent Wentworth's money on a damned cameo, I could be gone by now.*

"Good afternoon." Giovanni interrupted his train of thought, and Jamie forced a smile to greet his eager pupil, glad for the distraction.

"Good afternoon," he said in return.

The young man gave the slightest nod, slipped into his seat, and began to scan the assignment Jamie had given them.

Footsteps in the hall signaled the arrival of the others. He wondered how many of them had bothered with the lesson he had assigned.

Footsteps stopped, and a new voice joined the murmur of conversation—Victor Filiberto.

Jamie glanced at Giovanni and moved toward the door. Three voices met his ears—Eduardo, Luciano, and Victor. *Time to start Wentworth's dirty work.*

"Is a fool." Eduardo's voice. Jamie wondered who he meant but had no way to tell.

"A very powerful fool. You must take care." Victor. *Who is the fool, damn it? The count? Their king?*

"My father thinks saner influence is the way," Luciano said.

Victor mumbled something in a derisive tone. Jamie heard footsteps walking away. He turned and made a show of arranging his papers. Two young men entered. Eduardo looked sullen, but Eduardo habitually looked sullen. *The conversation meant nothing*, Jamie told himself. The thought of reporting it to Wentworth sickened him.

A frustrating hour later in which Luciano looked bored, Giovanni did most of the talking, and Eduardo failed to listen, Jamie had had enough.

"I have no idea," Eduardo said in response to a direct question.

"Why are you wasting my time?" Jamie snapped.

Eduardo yawned lazily. "Why am I wasting mine?" he asked. "Castellimonte wishes it."

"That isn't what I heard," Jamie replied.

"You heard wrong," Eduardo sneered. "Why would I want to listen to some English person force his language on me? What use is it if I get sent back to Turin?"

What Jamie might have responded was forestalled when an apparition burst in the door and threw herself at him, followed by an ineffectual footman.

"She's missing! Oh God, Jamie, she's missing."

Jamie unwrapped Nora's arms from around his neck and took her shoulders in his hands. He glanced at their audience before he spoke. Giovanni had risen from his seat, alarm on his face. Luciano looked worried.

"You misplaced the chit already?" Eduardo asked. "Tsk. That will not do." He remained seated, and his knowing smirk enraged Jamie, but Jamie had no time to deal with him.

"Deep breath, Nora," he said. "Tell me exactly what happened."

"Isabella is gone," she gulped. "She never made it to Santo Spirito."

"Didn't you walk her there?"

Nora avoided his eyes. "Alicia offered to take her. Signora Capello and I had work to plan, and Alicia offered."

She looked up defiantly. "Nursery maids do that! They chaperone children."

"You sent them alone?" Jamie asked through tight lips.

She nodded. "Wat couldn't leave just then. He was cleaning out the massive pots in the courtyard."

"I didn't hire him to garden," Jamie growled. "I hired him to keep an eye on you and Isabella." He gave her a shake and immediately regretted it when her eyes watered up. Awareness of his listeners brought him to his senses.

"Never mind now," he said. "What happened next?"

"I finished and decided to go over early to get her. I thought I could wait in the garden," Nora explained. "When I got there, the sister at the gate told me she never came. They never got to Santo Spirito, and they didn't come home! I ran back, and they weren't there."

"We need to retrace their steps," Jamie said, thinking out loud. He slid his hands down Nora's arms and squeezed both hands.

"I'll go to Castellimonte," Luciano interrupted. "You will need help."

"I will help," Giovanni put in abruptly. "No need to concern Castellimonte."

"Precisely," Eduardo drawled. "So much fuss over one nursery maid and an infant. Leave Castellimonte to his plots and plans."

Jamie spun on Eduardo. "Be quiet while you have any remnants of honor left, you fool." His word may not have quieted the man, but the look on his face certainly did. Eduardo sank back into sullen silence.

"Luciano, I think your friend is correct. Let's keep this to ourselves for now." There seemed little point in alarming the count at Nora's expense until he had more facts. He put a protective arm around her. *If we turn up nothing, it will be time enough to tell the old man,* he thought.

"I have to retrace the usual route from Casa Beaumont to Santo Spirito and question the sisters," he said. "Giovanni, will you take Luciano and follow a different route?"

"Of course," both men said simultaneously.

"Meet me at the convent." Jamie eyed the young man in the back who watched the discussion with hostile eyes. He intended to keep that one close. "Eduardo, you will come with me," he said.

Eyes caught for a moment, Jamie's daring him to say no. He didn't. Eduardo rose with a shrug. "The stupid maid probably had a tryst. We should check the cafés," he said.

Nora's eyes widened. "I didn't think of that," she whispered.

Eduardo's lips twitched, but he held his tongue.

"We'll know soon enough," Jamie said. He turned Nora in his arms. "Listen to me. You stay here."

"No! I'll go with you," she insisted.

"You will not. I have plenty of help. You will only slow us down," he retorted.

"But—"

"No buts," he insisted. "I don't want to have the two of you to worry about."

She walked him to the door. Before he could take the hat and gloves handed him by Castellimonte's footman, the count himself stalked into the room.

*Damn.* Jamie squeezed his eyes shut. "Count," he said with a dip of his head.

"Major Bently, what is this I hear?" Jamie told him briefly, leaving out any part Nora had in the arrangement. The nursery maid took the child to school. They didn't appear.

"We'll call out the guard," the count insisted.

"Not yet," Jamie answered. "I need to verify the facts." He described the plan to trace the route.

"One hour," the count said. "If it is kidnapping, we cannot allow them time." Nora's face turned sickly pale. "If you are not back in one hour," the count said, "I will put the guard on full alert."

Jamie thought a heavy-handed approach might spook any would-be kidnappers, but he withheld his opinion.

"Mrs. Bently will stay here," he said instead.

"Certainly," Castellimonte agreed. "We will see to her."

"I'm not so fragile," Nora insisted. "I can care for myself."

"You are one of the strongest people I know," Jamie told her, "but I need you here in case Alicia brings her here to find us." The flimsy excuse seemed to satisfy. Nora took the count's arm.

"One hour, Bently." Castellimonte's voice followed him out the door.

Eduardo's suggestion to check cafés ate up precious time. Halfway along, they encountered Wat Jones. Nora's frantic questions had alerted the man, and he had similar ideas.

They found Luciano and Giovanni, equally empty-handed, when they arrived at Santo Spirito a half hour later.

"She did not arrive," the sister-gatekeeper insisted.

"Are you certain," Jamie demanded one more time.

"I have been letting Mrs. Nora in every day, and now I let in the little angel. I would know. She did not come."

A rustle of skirts behind the gate alerted him to Mother Margarita's arrival. Hatchet-faced Sister Cecilia towered behind her.

Mother Margarita's voice maintained its usual calm, even as her face showed deep concern. "Until Nora arrived, we assumed Isabella would not join her class today," she said. "The child did not arrive, nor have we seen your maid. Have you any leads?"

Jamie shook his head. "We retraced the route two different ways, with no luck."

Sister Cecilia spoke then. "You have lost her rather quickly, Major," she drawled. Eduardo bit his lip and looked at his feet. The dog appeared to be laughing. *I may have to kill him yet,* Jamie thought.

A look from Mother Margarita silenced Sister Cecilia. "What will you do next?" Mother Margarita asked.

Jamie searched his mind. He would swallow his pride. "Ask help from the Count di Castellimonte," he said. "Broaden the search."

The nun looked regretful. "Good luck, then. My prayers follow you," she said before the gate closed.

Jamie's head fell back, and he breathed deeply. He knew he had no other choice.

"Where is this maid's home?" Eduardo asked.

"In Trastevere," Wat answered. "You think she went home?"

"Perhaps. Or if there is a young man, his place of work may be there."

"Makes sense, Major," Wat said. "I know the place."

That made sense if fault lay with the maid and not more sinister forces. It wouldn't hurt to look.

Jamie sent Luciana directly back to Palazzo di Savoia. "Tell the Count di Castellimonte that I respectfully ask him to wait thirty more minutes, he told the young man. "Tell him we shouldn't be too far behind you."

"We'll go in pairs again. We'll search the cafés," he told the others.

"All respect, Major, but wouldn't it go faster if we divide up?" Wat asked. It would have, but Jamie had no intention of allowing Eduardo out if his sight. If he didn't find Isabella in an hour, he had questions for the young man and his aunt, questions and plans to extract answers.

"Alicia fed me honey cake," Isabella pronounced an hour later, playing to her audience. They found her eating honey cake while Alicia and her young man, as Wat said, "Made moony eyes," just as Eduardo had predicted.

Nora didn't care. She just held the little girl on her lap.

"Alicia said he was handsome and a hero," Isabella went on. "I thought he looked skinny. He had spots!"

"This young woman, where is she?" Castellimonte demanded.

"I would guess her mother's house," Jamie answered. "Unemployed."

The count stood stiffly in the Palazzo nursery. His unbending posture looked out of place among desks and toys. Nora found it endearing.

"'You're fired,'" Isabella mimicked Jamie with relish. "He gave her such a look I thought Alicia would faint," she added to emphasize the point. Nora thought she might have pitied Alicia if she hadn't given them such a fright.

The count smiled at the little one. Nora wondered if he wanted to do more to Alicia. She shuddered.

"That's all it was? A lovesick girl?" Nora asked.

"It appears so," Jamie answered. He didn't look convinced. Neither did Castellimonte. She saw them exchange a look. She supposed there could be more, but she didn't see how.

*What is Jamie keeping from me?* she wondered. She thought again of the note from Wentworth. She felt her heart squeeze as if throttled by an unseen hand. *I should know by now that men with secrets can't be trusted.*

"Your young courtiers deserve credit for the speedy resolution," Jamie told the count. He looked ill at ease. "Eduardo's suggestions led us to Trastevere, actually," he said. "Giovanni and Luciano couldn't have been more help."

The count listened carefully but didn't comment. *What were those two thinking about?*

"Eduardo called me naughty," Isabella piped up. Nora glared over at the young man. Isabella didn't notice. She kept on talking. "He said 'You are Savoy. You command.' He told me I should have ordered Alicia to take me directly to school."

Sitting upright with her proud little chin raised, Nora could see her ordering the nursery maid about. *Heaven help us!*

The count looked amused. He put an awkward hand on Isabella's head. "You are indeed of Savoy, little one. But you must do what your aunt and uncle tell you. You must mind those who care for you—unless they do something you know to be wrong. When you know them to be wrong, then you must speak with authority."

Isabella smiled at the old man who no longer seemed to frighten her. "Luciano said I was pretty," she confided.

The old man laughed out loud. "Why, so you are, little one. So you are."

Castellimonte's unexpected kindness sustained Nora through the interview and a light dinner, hastily eaten in the nursery. They walked home in silence, accompanied by Wat and a Castellimonte guard. Jamie looked grim, and Nora could think of nothing to say.

Nora heard Isabella's prayers and tucked her in while Jamie and Wat checked locks and reviewed security. Her husband hadn't said one word to her directly since they left the palazzo. She paced across the sitting room, dreading the conversation she knew was coming.

Jamie slammed the door when he came in. He stalked across the carpet until he stood in front of her.

"What were you thinking?" he demanded.

"Please Jamie, I know," she begged. "I'll never let her out without Wat again." She wished he would hold her. She needed to feel him close.

He took her shoulders and shook her. "We were lucky today, Nora, that Isabella sustained no harm. Your position hasn't been shaken . . . yet."

"You aren't helping me," she spat back. "You keep things from me and expect me to make good decisions in the dark."

"Damn it, Nora, I gave you clear instructions. I told you to keep Wat close. What didn't you understand?"

He glared at her, breathing heavily. "You could have lost her!" he exclaimed.

Nora's world crashed in. "Lost her!" she cried. "How could I be so careless?" Once tears started, she couldn't hold them back.

Jamie's hands softened, one rose to caress her face. "I'm sorry, I'm sorry," he said. His thumb wiped tears from her cheek, while his other hand slipped around her back.

She looked up through watery eyes to see that profound sadness marred his face.

"You're safe. We're safe," he murmured, pulling her into his arms. When her head lay on his chest and she could feel the steady beat of his heart, she believed him. She snuggled closer.

A deep groan echoed in his chest under her ear. She felt it ripple through her body and send eddies of heat from her cheeks to her knees. One of his hands turned her face up toward his. She thought perhaps his eyes had a question.

She stood on her toes and drew her mouth to his and hoped it was the answer he sought. It seemed to be enough. She fell into his kiss and let fear slip away.

## Chapter 25

A voice in Jamie's head demanded to know what he thought he was doing. His mind churned with questions, but his body knew exactly what it was doing. He bent down, wrapped his long fingers around her little chin, and slanted his mouth across hers to deepen the kiss. She let him. *The little fool.* He tasted deeply.

Nora reached up and put her arms around his neck. She opened for him and attempted to return his kiss, her tongue shyly meeting his. If he didn't know she was a widow, he would think her inexperienced.

*Too damned much thought. I've had enough of it.* He let the taste of her drive all thought from his head. He put an arm beneath her trim bottom and lifted her up for better access. He could feel her breath come fast where she clung to him. She kissed his lips and licked the corner of his mouth.

He stepped forward until he had her pressed against the door, her feet inches above the floor, and her sweet face even with his. Better. Released from the need to hold her with both hands, Jamie began to explore the body that had haunted his nights for weeks. His hopes and fantasies didn't come close. Tiny, but perfect, Nora curved in the right places. When his hand slid up to cup one firm breast, her moan shot fire through him.

He caught her moan with his mouth, and she kissed him fiercely, running one hand through his hair.

"Wait!" Nora broke the kiss. He buried his mouth in the curve of her neck and began to kiss his way to her ear. Nora dropped her head back to give him access.

"Wait," she said more weakly, pushing against him.

"What?" He should think about what they were doing. He didn't want to think; he wanted to continue.

Nora pulled one hand down, groping around behind her. She confused him, but the taste of her skin made coherent thought impossible. He leaned in to run his mouth up her neck and fell forward.

They stumbled into her room when her hand found the door latch. Startled, he let her slide down his body to the floor. The feel of her sliding over the bulge in his trousers almost undid him. He grabbed her to keep her from falling.

When she took a step away, he felt like she had dumped ice water over him. She stepped toward her bed and looked back at him, her eyes black with desire in the flickering candlelight.

*What have I done?*

He had intended only to comfort. He meant to stop her tears, not seduce her. Jamie dropped his hands to his side. *Who am I kidding? I meant to take.* He struggled to gather up the scattered pieces of his self-control and of the respect he owed her.

"Nora," he breathed. "We need to think about this."


Nora didn't want to talk. She didn't want to think. He was her husband. He may leave eventually, but she would never have another. She knew that in her gut. After the horrors of Isabella's disappearance, the interminable hours waiting for news, she needed his comfort. She needed to be his wife fully. She needed his touch. She wanted him now.

"Jamie, please," she begged, "Don't leave me like this. If you want your freedom later, I won't hold you, but we're married now. Let me be your wife, just for now."

He stood still as stone, serious, and unbearably dear. He had no time to clean up, change clothes, or shave since the hunt for Isabella. With his beard stubble, rumpled shirt, and loosened neck cloth, he looked like her shabby major again. Her heart turned over. She loved him.

Exultation overwhelmed her body and soul. She dropped backward onto the bed. She sat upright and never took her eyes from his.

"Jamie," she started again, clasping her hands together.

He stood in the shadows, her bedroom door closed behind him. "There's no going back, Nora," he said, his breathing ragged. "If we do this, there's no going back. I won't sleep alone any longer."

She felt her face stretch into a smile that echoed her joy. "Of course not!" she said.

"I'm not finished. I can't promise I'll stay. You know that. You and Isabella have a life here. I, well, I have my own life to straighten out."

*Straighten out? What does he mean?* She could help. She would make him see that later. She wouldn't let him close her out.

"I promised you freedom. I mean it," she said instead.

She watched his throat work to swallow. "If we're going to carry what we've started to its conclusion, I need take better care. I'm not a ravening wolf," he said. He took a step closer.

Edmund had never looked at her as if he could devour her, the way Jamie looked at her now. She should hate it, but she didn't.

"I quite liked the ravening wolf," she said past the lump in her throat.

Jamie shrugged out of his jacket and tossed it to a chair. A slow smile spread across his face. "I can raven if you like it," he said. His shirt followed the jacket. He unbuttoned the fall of his trousers. Nora felt air against her eyes when she widened them. She couldn't blink.

His hand stilled, and he took a step closer, and then two. Just as she thought he would reach for her, he sat down next to her.

"This might be easier without my boots," he said and reached down to remove them. She watched him, mystified.

A moment later he chuckled deep in his throat. "You know, you stared at my feet just like that the day you came to my rooms to demand my services," he said.

Nora broke her stare and bent to remove her slippers.

"You looked away that day, too," he said, drawing her eyes back.

He slipped to the floor in front of her and brushed her hands aside.

"Let me," he said, holding her eyes with his.

One warm hand slid under her skirt and up her leg. He untied the bow halfway up her calf, unwound the ribbons, and pulled off one of her slippers. He held her silk-clad foot in his hand, caressing the instep with his thumb.

She felt a little humming sound vibrate through her lips. He swiftly did the same to her other foot.

When he tipped her shoulder to turn her, she didn't object. For a man with large hands, his fingers were nimble on the ties of her gown. His lips followed, kissing and licking from the back of her neck, down to the top of her corset cover, to her shoulder. Nora felt heat pool in her lower parts. Her breathing had become erratic. She began to remove the sleeves to her gown. He stopped her.

"I want to do it," he said.

Jamie took her hand in his as if to negotiate an intricate step to a minuet and raised her to her feet. He kissed her fingers then looked her up and down with deep concentration.

"This first," he said, sliding the gown off her shoulders and allowing it to drop. "And then this, I think."

He made short work of the laces to her stays. Corset and cover disappeared under his skilled hands.

"You've done this before," she whispered.

"Only to practice for tonight," he whispered back,

kissing the sensitive spot below her right ear. He ran his rough hands down both sides of her plain cotton shift.

A wish that she had warn prettier underthings flit though her as lightly as a dragonfly and evaporated when he laid her back on the bed and began to remove her stockings. She watched his bent head, the hair thrown forward, golden brown in the candlelight, and his intense concentration.

*I should fear this.* The thought came unbidden. She had learned to fear Edmund and the hurt he caused. Yet, in Jamie's hands, she felt only safety. *Nothing Edmund did came close to the way he looks at me, his fierce kisses.*

Jamie looked up at that moment and smiled at her. She knew with sudden assurance that she had nothing to fear from him. She opened her arms and gave herself over to him.

He stretched out beside her and began to kiss her mouth, moving downward and then back to her mouth over and over, lower each time until his mouth found her nipple under her shift. Waves of unfamiliar sensation blinded her, and she grabbed his shoulders.

"Enough of this," he said. He tugged on her shift, and she moved so he could pull it over her head.

When they lay skin to skin from head to waist, the sensation wrapped Nora in a blanket of heat. She believed she could lie like that forever, until his clever hands found places, so many places, to tease and titillate. Unrest began to boil and swirl until she could lie still no longer.

"Jamie," she moaned, uncertain what to ask.

"Soon," he soothed, sliding one hand down into her drawers to find her most intimate spot. "Soon. You are wet for me already." He stroked her there until she thought she might go mad.

And then she did. Blinded and beyond conscious thought, she gave herself over to the onslaught of pleasure.

By the time awareness returned, he had removed her drawers entirely, knelt next to her, and begun to remove his trousers and smalls. She thought she ought to help, but she couldn't move. He had rendered her helpless. She could hardly move her own body.

"What just happened?" she breathed when he began to spread her thighs.

He paused where he knelt above her, fully erect, fully aroused, his expression arrested by her question. "Don't you know?" he asked.

She shook her head.

A wicked smile spread over his face. The ravening wolf had returned. "We'll have to try it a few times until you learn," he said.

When he pushed against her opening and slid inside, an echo of the earthquake she had just experienced pulsated. When he began to move in her, she wrapped herself around him and gave herself over to sensation. Earthquakes, she found, can happen more than once.

Jamie lay awake with Nora draped on top of him, her rhythmic breathing telling him how deeply she slept. She lived through a difficult day and an earth-shattering night. She needed her sleep. He held her gently and forced himself not to kiss her awake.

With her body warm against his, he prayed she hadn't traded comfort now for greater heartbreak when he finally left or when she found out the truth and forced him to leave. One or the other certainly would occur. Lying there, he thought perhaps he could store up sufficient comfort for the bleak years ahead. Perhaps they both could.

Nora shifted in her sleep, and Jamie's body came to immediate attention. She moaned and lifted her head.

He knew by her gasp when she came to full awareness of where she lay and in what state of undress. She tried to roll off him, but he pulled her back.

"Too late, Love. No point in going shy with me now," he said, kissing the top of her head.

"Did that really happen or did I dream it?" she wondered out loud.

"Do I feel like a dream to you?" he asked.

She shook her head. "But nothing ever felt like you made me feel."

*Nothing. She means no one—the damned husband.*

"Are you telling me your first husband never brought you to orgasm before?"

"Is that the word for it?"

*Worse and worse.* "Yes, Love. It is what people do when they have a care for one another."

"Edmund thought me insufficient."

Jamie's heart stopped. He didn't interrupt her.

"If he came to my bed at all, it was," she paused, choosing her words, "fast, brief. He didn't do the things you do. Sometimes he couldn't manage it at all. He would shout at me then."

"Edmund was an even greater swine than I thought," Jamie said, "and he is dead. I don't want to hear his name in our marriage bed again." He wished for one hot minute that he could wrap his hands around the selfish poet's neck and squeeze. *What kind of weasel blames a woman for his own failures?*

Nora kissed him at that. She rolled to the side and stopped abruptly. She must have felt his arousal hot against her leg.

"Can we do that again so soon?" she asked, shocked.

Jamie bit back a smile. His answer didn't involve words.

## Chapter 26

Jamie enjoyed the company of men. Most of his adult life he enjoyed nothing more than lingering over port and the inevitable conversation about horses, cards, and sparring, the matters dearest to the male sex. Even politics could liven an evening. Not tonight.

Tonight he swirled the count's excellent port around as if trying to decide where red stopped and purple began and thought of Nora. That entire day she had filled his mind even as she filled his senses. *Perhaps tonight we will try my bed.*

"I hear you are teaching English, Major." The portly gentleman to his right addressed him directly. Jamie tried to clear his head. *Did I miss something?* he wondered.

"I'm assisting some of Castellimonte's aides with their studies," he replied.

"I don't understand the need," another, as lean as the other was portly, said. A dueling scar marred the man's gaunt face, Jamie noticed. *Not one to be trifled with.* He groped to remember the name.

Several other voices chimed in on one side of that issue or another. There were six men in all, including Castellimonte and Jamie. Most of the men looked older than Jamie. He had been relieved not to deal with a pack of puppies for one evening.

"They learn English because it is necessary for diplomacy," Castellimonte pronounced, silencing debate. "We send a trade delegation to London in the summer. Even in Vienna—"

"Even in Vienna the English pushed their weight around," Scarface growled.

"How are they progressing?" another asked Jamie directly.

"Well enough. They should manage fine in London." If they didn't get lost in gaming hells or challenge the wrong lordling to a duel over some imagined slight.

"They will be watched. Your country doesn't trust us," Portly said, fidgeting with his napkin. "Since the unfortunate actions of our cousins the Stuarts, we are suspect."

"Nonsense," another said. "Why should the English worry about some craziness seventy-five years ago?"

Jamie wondered if they expected him to have an answer. He didn't. The Wentworths of the world were paid to worry. No one else Jamie knew thought twice about the Stuart claims.

"Why would we meddle in England? We have the throne of Sardinia," Scarface said. His tone made it clear he considered that a much bigger prize.

Portly wagged a finger at Jamie. "If your Bonnie Prince Charlie had sought help from his Savoy cousins instead of the hapless Scots, things might be different."

Jamie certainly didn't care about the twice-damned Bonnie Prince!

"I saw the Piedmontese at Waterloo," he said instead. "I don't doubt it." That seemed to satisfy them. Their presence at the great battle had been unofficial, under the flag of Austria. Savoy always hedged its bets.

"It is the Pope who should worry, not George IV," Scarface said. "Sooner or later a united Italy will show Europe our true strength." Castellimonte scowled at the man.

"It is Victor Emmanuel who should worry," another said. "Malcontents with short memories think the Code Napoleon will save the nation. Do they think that Victor Emmanuel's brother will be better? Carl Felice is a reactionary."

"More power to him," came a voice down the table.

Portly shook his head, "The young always believe different is better."

"The young must be kept busy so they don't have time to make trouble," Castellimonte said. He caught Jamie's eyes.

Jamie looked back at the sharp eyes. *Does Castellimonte know Wentworth has his table watched?* he wondered. *Probably. Spying goes two ways.*

"Busy racing horses?" Portly joked.

"Busy about trade and the business of Sardinia," Castellimonte said, but he steered the conversation to horse racing.

Jamie sank back into silence. At least now he had something for his report to Wentworth. He let his mind drift back to Nora.

---

"What do men talk about?" Nora asked, rounding a stair onto the landing closest to the palazzo nursery. It had seemed safest to bring Isabella with them. The count sent an escort to bring them and return.

"What do they discuss? The weather!" Jamie answered, pulling her into an embrace and nuzzling her neck.

"Jamie!" Nora tried to wiggle free, but he captured her mouth. Heat engulfed her, and she sank into him. The kiss lasted longer than she intended before she finally gave a gentle shove.

"Not here," she whispered.

"Wait until I get you home," he whispered back. He let her go with a great show of reluctance.

They walked in companionable silence toward the nursery, both too absorbed in images of the night before and thoughts of the night to come.

Nora doubted that the fire that raged between them could last. It must sink from conflagration to glowing ember eventually. She thought she might love embers just as much.

Jamie stopped abruptly at the nursery door. Voices echoed from the high-ceilinged room. He put out a hand to hold her back and cocked a head to listen. Nora understood much of it. Her Italian improved daily.

"So little princess, you didn't need rescue?" the one called Luciano asked.

"Of course not. Amelia was just a silly girl. Aunt Nora said so. I am Savoy."

Laughter greeted that. Isabella's giggle rose above the deeper voices. She obviously enjoyed extending her little drama.

"Remember that Isabella. You are Savoy. Servants do as you say." *The unpleasant one. Eduardo*, Nora thought.

"Stop filling her head, Eduardo." A familiar woman's voice broke in. "Her aunt will not thank you." True enough. Nora did not want Isabella to grow up without any sense of respect for her fellow man.

"Why should I care what the English aunt thinks?" Eduardo sneered.

Jamie looked grim. When he pushed the door open, stunned silence greeted them.

Isabella had been lifted to the top of a desk. Luciano leaned on one side. Eduardo stood next to him. In the far corner, another young man sat on a window ledge and looked up from his book. Nora tried to recall the name of the studious one. *Giovanni, that's it.*

The presence of an older woman shocked Nora. Signora Capello clustered with the little group by the desk, her lips pursed tight, her hands clasped in front of her.

The maid who had been pressed into nursery duty by the count's staff fluttered over to Jamie, spewing Italian words too fast for Nora to understand. Her tone sounded defensive. Jamie nodded and dismissed her. The woman scuttled off.

"So, she tells me you came up to practice your English. Did I understand that correctly?" Jamie asked the young men.

Luciana and Eduardo looked at one another. Eduardo shrugged.

"I suggest you do so then. I didn't hear any when I came in."

Jamie turned to Signora Capello. "Is there a reason why you left Casa Beaumont unattended?" he asked acidly. He looked from her to Eduardo.

"Hardly unattended, Major. Your Wat Jones prowls the place like a wild beast," the woman sniffed. "A message arrived for you." She reached into a pocket and handed him a folded vellum packet with a wax seal, like the one that had arrived the night of their wedding.

Jamie looked at it sourly. "It would keep until I got home," he said, examining the seal pointedly. Nora kept her curiosity to herself with effort.

Capello had the grace to look uncomfortable. "I am sorry if it offends you, Major, but I took the opportunity to visit my nephew." She indicated Eduardo with a nod. Jamie looked hard at the young man until he raised his chin and stared back.

"In the future, you might arrange your visits with Mrs. Bently," he said, turning his attention back to Capello. "I don't know your custom, but in our world, servants, even upper servants, arrange such things."

"Yes, Major," the woman said through stiff lips.

"Kindly meet us in the foyer, Capello," Nora said. "You should not be out without escort. You can return with us." As a dismissal, the words were kindly but effective. The woman left.

Jamie picked up Isabella. "Come, princess," he said, "We'll leave your court to the nursery. Perhaps they belong here?" He winked at the little girl, and she giggled.

Eduardo, Nora saw, bristled, but Luciano smiled at the joke. Giovanni had risen and joined them.

"Perhaps we do," Giovanni said, peering at the ornate ceiling and the row of desks. "It is a good enough place to study."

"Gentlemen, my wife and I are for home. I'll see you all at eleven tomorrow, no?" With a nod he offered Nora an arm, and they left.

Nora burned to ask him about the message in his waistcoat, but by the time their escort walked them home, Jamie engaged Isabella in a game of hide and seek involving her favorite dolls, and Nora read the girl a story, thoughts about messages moved to the back of her mind.

Her husband reached for her the moment she entered their sitting room. He pulled her through his dressing room to his bed, and she forgot about the message entirely.

## Chapter 27

Jamie looked over his meager selection of shirts in the dim confines of his dressing room. His wardrobe had grown five times over, but it still looked scant hanging in one corner of the rack. *The whole dressing room feels larger than the hole I lived in until the wedding, until Nora.*

Jamie moved catlike around the room, grabbed a shirt at random, and slipped it on silently. Every cell in his body stood at alert, aware of the woman sleeping in the next room. He had an appointment to keep and couldn't think about her warm body nestled in his bed.

It didn't matter what he wore. "The Boys," as he had come to think of them, would look down on whatever he wore. Wentworth—whose message forced him to rise so early—noticed. He, however, had long ago cataloged Jamie's every detail.

He reached for a jacket and finished dressing in solitude. Madame Capello found his lack of a valet demeaning. He found her snobbery irritating. They were even.

He had dressed himself since his father dismissed the footman assigned to dress him when he was thirteen "to save blunt." Occasionally, one of his friends would assign a servant to him during a house party, but he always declined. He needed no snooty servant to dress him now.

His face in the mirror, soured by thoughts of Wentworth, stared back with a caustic look. He wanted to get to the English spymaster early and get it over with. A sour taste tainted his mouth. *Maybe today I can report enough information to make the persistent muckworm back off,* he thought.

He reached for the door to his bedroom and paused. Gentlemen of his acquaintance would go the other way, through the sitting room, to spare the lady. His mouth twisted in a wry smile. He knew it wasn't gentlemanly, but he couldn't resist one last look at his wife.

The door opened silently on well-oiled hinges. He padded, boots in hand, into his bedroom. Nora lay curled in the center, a tiny presence in the immense four-poster. Her hair feathered across his pillow and hers. She had rolled over to reach for him after he got up. His blood surged at the thought. He moved closer to the bed.

Sleep erased care and stress from his Nora, sleep and good loving, leaving only peace and contentment. His hand went out to touch her, but he pulled it back, remembering his good intentions to let her sleep. He began to step away.

"Jamie?" Nora's voice, thick with sleep, stopped him in his tracks. "I thought you had gone."

"Just leaving. Go back to sleep."

She rose up on her elbows to blink at him. "You're dressed."

"So I am. Go back to sleep," he repeated.

With a deep breath, she sat up, remembering to pull the sheets up to cover her nakedness, to his regret. She peered at him under sleepy eyelids.

"You're carrying your boots," she said.

He looked down as if surprised to find them in his hand. "So I was. I didn't want to wake you."

"Come back to bed."

Every fiber in Jamie's body longed to accept her invitation. Some parts leapt to accept on their own. It took all his waning strength to sit in a chair by the door instead. He began putting on his boots.

"I can't," he said. "I have to go."

"What time is it?" she asked.

"Late," he said.

She looked at the mantel clock Robert Beaumont had installed in the bedroom. His brother-in-law must have been a punctual man. "More like early," she said. "It is only half gone eight o'clock."

He pushed his foot into the second boot and stood. "I have to leave."

She looked adorably puzzled. Jamie needed to leave before temptation kept him there all morning. He leaned two hands on the bed and gave her a swift, husbandly kiss. When she reached up to pull him to her, he stood.

"You don't have to be to Palazzo Savoia until eleven," she pointed out.

"I have business," he said.

"What do you have to do that's so urgent?" She held his eyes.

If he told her he had to see Wentworth, she would want to know why. He could tell her nothing that wouldn't lead to more questions. *By the way, everything you know about me is a lie.* He said nothing.

"You're keeping something from me," she said. *No fool, my Nora.* When he remained silent, she said bitterly, "Secrets don't belong in marriage."

He groaned inwardly. *No secrets? If only she knew.* He didn't answer her.

"It isn't a wife's place to order you," she mumbled. He watched her wilt, dropping her head to study her knees. The tone of her words sounded like echoes of her marriage to Edmund.

"You aren't ordering me. I'm ordering myself," he said.

"You're my husband!" she grumbled, head jerking up. "You should let me share your burdens." *That's more like it, Nora.*

"It isn't my place to tell you what to do about Isabella," he pointed out.

"Your place is to help me!" she insisted.

Her tone of voice made something inside Jamie snap. *My place! What the hell does she mean by "place"?*

"Are you ordering me to know my place in your household, Nora? What is that place? Employee? Lover? Lackey? Our relationship was not supposed to change."

"But it has!"

"Because we share a bed, now I have no right to my own time, my own thoughts? Is that what you want?" They glared across the expanse of the carpet. He could hear himself pant.

"I have an appointment to keep," he said at last. He strode out, slammed the door behind him, and immediately regretted it. He regretted many things. None of them could be fixed now.

An hour later, sitting in Wentworth's office, bile rose in Jamie's throat. He ought to wipe the desk with the muckworm's smug face. The fussy little man in his stuffy little office with dog-eared files in finely carved drawers made Jamie's skin itch. Wentworth would never be satisfied. The bastard dismissed most of Jamie's dinner conversation report.

"General Rambaudi is too much of a nationalist snob to be of any interest," the old windbag said with a snort. "He commanded a battalion for the Austrians at Waterloo. A battalion!" he said derisively. "And he thinks he is Wellington himself."

*General Rambaudi-Scar Face, a soldier's soldier.* Jamie ought to have paid closer attention to names. No wonder he perked up when Jamie praised the Piedmontese.

"You should have recognized the man," Wentworth said slyly. "You did say you were at Waterloo, didn't you?"

*Did I?* Jamie thought furiously. He realized now that he ought to have taken notes after he had met with the man, right after he washed his hands. "Of course I was. I didn't make the connection."

Wentworth dismissed that with a wave of his hand. "The man poses no threat. Tell me more about the young ones."

Wentworth's interest in The Boys made Jamie uneasy. They were young. Some were foolish, others idealistic.

None deserved Wentworth's scrutiny. At least Jamie didn't like to think so.

"Tell me more about this Eduardo Mora."

Jamie recognized the command. Wentworth had dispensed with any pretense of asking.

"Arrogant, sensitive, and chronically unhappy," Jamie said. Eduardo acted like spoiled young men everywhere. Jamie wondered how that made him a threat to England or, God forbid, to Isabella.

"His brother is rising in Victor Emmanuel's court," Wentworth said flipping through a file on his desk. "He may be envious. Is he assigned to the London trade mission?"

"He claims not."

"Find out. What about the others?"

Jamie told him what he knew. Giovanni spoke of the delegation often, as did one of the others who wandered in and out. Luciano never mentioned it.

"What do you know of this Giovanni's background?"

"Nothing." Wentworth must know little also or he wouldn't ask.

"Find out."

"I agreed to pass on what I happened to overhear. I did not agree to probe."

Wentworth gave him a pointed look and went on as if he hadn't spoken. "We need to know who is in the delegation and then we need as much information about them as you can pry out of them."

Jamie let the man think he had won. Jamie would continue as he had been until Nora and Isabella were safe and secure in the guardianship. Then he would leave and to hell with Wentworth and the information he needed.

"When will paperwork for Mrs. Bently's guardianship be filed?"

"I understand you mislaid Mrs. Bently's niece," Wentworth responded.

"Isabella is safe at home and none of your business," Jamie retorted.

"My dear Major, that child is a relative of Castellimonte. That makes her of very great interest to his majesty's government."

Heat rose up Jamie's neck, and he stopped himself from leaning over the desk. He suspected his face looked very much like Eduardo's, the petulant schoolboy. For a few moments all he could think about were the ways he would like to put an end to Wentworth's useless life.

"Come, come, Major. Don't look daggers at me. Of course we are interested in the child. We don't want her used as leverage to move her great-uncle to actions he might not otherwise wish to take."

*Unless, of course, it is you who is wielding the lever.* Wentworth's description of how Isabella might be used matched Castellimonte's so closely Jamie didn't believe it could be a coincidence.

"Touch her and I will kill you," Jamie said through bared teeth.

Wentworth looked genuinely taken aback. "Me? I desire the child's safety as much as you do." Jamie doubted that preposterous statement. "You have peculiar ideas about what I might do."

"I believe you might do almost anything if you thought it promoted what you see as England's good."

"Quite right," Wentworth said. "And that will never include harm to a child. Can you say the same?"

"What do you mean?"

"You find yourself in a comfortable position, sharing a house with Beaumont's sister, dining with the cream of Roman society. Is the child's well-being your primary concern?"

Jamie might be a worthless scoundrel, but he had grown fond of Isabella. Still, he admitted to himself that the child would not be his first concern. He knew with sudden clarity what was: Nora. Isabella made Nora happy, and that made her vital to Jamie's happiness.

"Of course it is," he croaked over the lump in his throat.

"We can help," Wentworth said. "We have sources of intelligence." He waved his hand vaguely. "Friends and so on."

"I'll keep that in mind. However, my family is my responsibility. I'll thank you to remember that. File the papers."

Wentworth's sudden smile pushed Jamie off-balance. "Your family?" he repeated, emphasizing the word with amusement. "Of course it is yours to protect. We wouldn't want it any other way. I believe Archie Campbell plans to file on Mrs. Bently's behalf soon."

Wentworth's knowing smile and sharp eyes followed Jamie out. They lingered in his memory all the way to Palazzo Savoia.

## Chapter 28

Wat returned with Isabella at precisely three that afternoon. Nora spent over an hour practicing language with the girl. They spread picture books on a table set up in the courtyard and sat side-by-side on a stone bench covered with down cushions. Isabella taught Nora the Italian words; Nora taught Isabella the English.

"Pink." Isabella repeated Nora's words. "The flowers are pink."

The bougainvillea, lately pruned, had bloomed, filling their inner courtyard with color and immersing them in its sweet smell. Today it failed to entrance Nora. Neither the flowers nor her niece's dear attempts to teach distracted her from thoughts of her husband.

"Did you hear me, Aunt Nora?" Isabella demanded, putting a hand on Nora's face. "It is your turn. Say '*rosa*.'"

Nora repeated what Isabella wanted without thought. Questions swirled over and over in her mind. *Where did Jamie go so early this morning? What was it that made him look so unhappy?* No answers came to her.

"I think you don't want to do this," Isabella pouted.

"I'm sorry, sweetie," Nora said, her mind elsewhere. He was late, she realized. *What if he doesn't come home at all?*

"Aunt Nora is tired today," Nora said, forcing a smile.

Isabella seemed to accept that. "Can I bring Julianna out here to teach her English?" she asked.

Nora's smile widened to something more genuine. Isabella had been "teaching" the doll since she got her. "May I," Nora corrected, "And yes, you may."

If he didn't come home, she would be alone with Isabella. A month ago that might have been more than enough, as much as Nora had ever allowed herself to hope for. Now the thought left her empty. She feared her insecurity had driven away. She cursed herself for being a fool.

Isabella skipped out carrying her little friend. She propped the doll next to her books and began to chatter in Italian. A smattering of new English words accompanied the lesson.

Nora's eyes strayed continually to the door by the foyer. She had no idea how to go on when he came home. She feared she could not live with silence and secrets. Edmund's secrets usually involved drink, gaming, money, or all three. Edmund's secrets usually resulted in Nora's harm. But Jamie was not Edmund. He had never hurt her. Why, she wondered, couldn't she just trust him?

Her hands would be rubbed raw from fidgeting. She needed to stay busy.

"Aunt Nora needs to fetch her tatting," she said. Isabella merely nodded and went on chatting to Julianna.

Nora had only taken two steps into the foyer when the door opened, and Jamie handed his hat and gloves to the waiting footman. Sunlight on his hair made gold strands shine among the brown; it took her breath away. The door closed, and her husband stood across the foyer, looking wary.

"You're late," she blurted. It sounded like a reprimand, even to her ears.

"So I am. Sorry I didn't send a message. Giovanni wanted me to look at some trade documents and assist in translation." He covered the distance between them.

When he kissed her cheek, she sighed but didn't reach out for more.

"Trade documents? They would share such a thing with an outsider?" she asked.

"Don't you believe me?" Jamie responded, frowning.

"Of course I believe you," she said too quickly. His eyes gave nothing away; she hoped hers did the same.

The pause became awkward. Jamie chewed his lower lip as if sunk in thought.

"Tea was put back," she said to break the silence. Nora had agreed to keep an Italian household, but the cook soon learned that Nora held teatime sacred. "I'll tell the cook you're here."

"Excellent," he said. The ghost of a smile lurked in his sad eyes. "Are there lemon cakes?"

"I ordered them especially for you." If she couldn't speak with him, she could at least keep him well fed.

"Cook's lemon cakes make my day perfect," he sighed, giving her his arm. "Lemon cake and my lovely wife," he added with a wink. "Shall we go indulge?"

His double entendre made her face heat. Her husband had decided to charm her; he succeeded.

She smacked his arm playfully. "Don't be naughty. Here comes Isabella."

The little girl launched herself at Jamie with a gleeful shout. "Uncle Jamie! You are home at last. Did you hear there are lemon cakes for tea?"

Jamie and Isabella walked to the little breakfast room rhapsodizing over lemon cake. Nora followed, her heart only slightly lighter than before he came home.

She would allow him his secrets, but she had no idea how to stifle her fears about the consequences of those secrets. She would have to endure them.

Nora's hands, tiny but graceful across the lacy work in her lap, moved with musical precision. She made needlework a dance. Jamie wondered what she would look like in a ballroom. She—and the count—had drawn the line at balls and dancing while mourning her brother. *Next year then,* he thought, *she will dance.* He wondered if she could waltz and yearned to teach her.

Longing for what he would never have benefitted no one. He dragged his eyes back to the papers on his desk and forced his mind back to the numbers on the document in front of him.

The paper made him ill. The contents, a set of instructions and goals for the English trade delegation, bored him. The manner in which it came to him turned his stomach.

The instructions, written by the English authorities, had fallen into Sardinian hands. It included tariffs to negotiate, wine harvests to catalog, towns in the Piedmont to explore, and much more. Giovanni had possession of an explosive document. Jamie wondered how that had happened.

Nora looked up and smiled at him. He smiled back. He feared he looked as sick as he felt.

"Preparing lessons? Or translating?"

"Both," he murmured vaguely. "What do you call that kind of needlework?"

"Crochet," she said, holding up a tiny silver hook.

He went back to work. The sooner he translated it, the better. Wentworth would want to know they had it. His heart skipped a beat. Perhaps Giovanni or Castellimonte wanted Wentworth to know. Perhaps they fed it to him on purpose. He had no idea why.

A deep shuddering breath put a period to the thought. Between them, Wentworth and Castellimonte had him looking suspiciously under every rock. He would start examining puppies for weapons next. *Translate, Jamie, don't think.*

"Mending is less frivolous," Nora said into the silence.

"What?"

"Mending. Practical and useful. I will have lace shawls a'plenty by the end of the week and be forced to start on dresses for Isabella. We don't need all this fancywork, and it isn't useful."

His English wren had returned.

"What do aristocratic ladies do with the endless piles of needlework they do to keep their hands busy?" she asked while her hands stitched along.

"Seat cushions," he said, looking back at his work. That's what his mother did, in any case, and some of the other grand ladies he had met.

The odd feel of the silence made him look up. Nora's eyes had a question, but she didn't ask it.

"At least that is what I've always heard," he said. She looked away and went back to her work.

"Damn."

Nora's head bobbed up again.

*Did I said that out loud?* "Sorry," he mumbled, "it's the paper." She looked back down, but not before he caught the questions in her eyes. She wouldn't ask him. He hated to see her dampen down her curiosity but was glad for it at once.

He forced his attention back to the page and immediately regretted it. *Damn and seven kinds of damnation*, he thought when one particularly sensitive passage caught his attention.

Victor Emmanuel is amenable to favorable rates. He is easily influenced. We must continue to cultivate him directly.

Favorable to England it meant. If he failed to translate that passage, Giovanni would certainly puzzle it out. Jamie felt his gorge rise. It took all his self-control to write the translation and push through to the last sentence of the report. "We anticipate highly favorable negotiations," he read. Castellimonte, he thought, would see about that. He translated it as written.

He raised his pen, picked up his transcription for Wentworth, and recorded a copy. Even rubbing his hands on his trousers didn't make the dirty feeling go away.

Two words stuck in his mind, "easily influenced." Forces inside the Sardinian kingdom would be unhappy about that, very unhappy.

Jamie stuffed one set of papers into his portfolio with shaking hands and folded the other for dispatch to Wentworth. He attempted to smile at his wife. The smile became genuine at the sight of her.

Nora caught his eyes and returned his smile with one full of promises. His heart skipped a beat when she put her lacy shawl aside and rose to face him. Drawn to her as a moth to light, he closed the distance and pulled her in for a kiss.

"Time for bed?" he asked with a raised brow. He adored her blushes. They turned to her room, with his arm around her shoulder, but he remembered something that made him stop.

"I forgot to warn you. We are invited, or rather expected, at the Palazzo again for dinner in two days."

She groaned. "Again?"

"You don't like state dinners?" he grinned.

"What I like are our quiet evenings at home, just the three of us for dinner, and then the two of us here. Like tonight."

Jamie's smile reached deep into his heart. He preferred that, too, domestic contentment so strong he almost believed it was real.

"And Cook's cakes," he said, making her laugh.

The joy sank away. Contentment would last only until he fled. Better that than to have her show him the door when she found herself married to a renegade aristocrat.

"Perhaps our count enjoys our company," he said, one hand on the door handle to her room.

"Do you think so? He seems to be genuinely fond of Isabella," she replied. "I wouldn't have believed it a month ago."

"Perhaps having us is an excuse to spend time with her. She is expected also. The Palazzo nursery seems to be supplied with new books and toys."

Nora laughed. "Who can resist our little charmer?"

"Who indeed?" he repeated.

He opened the door, swept her up into his arms, and carried her, laughing, to her bed. *A few weeks pleasure will be enough*, he thought, undoing the ties of her dress. He kissed his way down her back. *It has to be.*

## Chapter 29

Jamie didn't particularly mind that protocol consigned both he and Nora to a spot well below the salt at the far end of Castellimonte's table. The dinner proved to be larger and more formal than the last. Protocol kept him far from the pompous elders.

Nora sat surrounded by The Boys, who also rated the bottom of the table. Luciano sat on one side of Nora and Eduardo on the other. Jamie and Giovanni sat across from them, and two of Jamie's occasional students sat at the very end. Jamie noted the shortage of young women at court. Nora had little competition.

Wentworth, at least, should be satisfied with the seating if he saw it. The man had little interest in the old men. He wanted to know about these young ones. Jamie's heart sank. Young they might be, but he didn't think they had any harm in them.

Nora set out to put each at ease initially. Giovanni maintained steady conversation, using the opportunity to discuss fashion and the weather in English, skills he would need in London. Eduardo's attention directed itself up the table in any case. Jamie noted that the boy's ambitions lay with the men in power. His glittering eyes followed every gesture and every word from Victor Filiberto. Jamie finally ignored Eduardo's preening, and Nora gave up on him also.

As the dinner went on, Luciano began to be a nuisance. He flirted with Nora in both English and Italian. Subtle at first, his behavior become more forward with every glass of wine. The Italian began to get much too warm for Jamie's taste. Blessedly, Nora didn't seem to catch the meaning.

"Tell me, Luciano, do you plan to join Giovanni in London?" Jamie asked, as much to take the puppy's eyes away from his wife as to get the answers Wentworth wanted.

"Whada ya want to know?" the boy slurred. He shot a hostile glance at Giovanni. *No, then,* Jamie thought.

"No reason. What will you do when the delegation leaves? Will you stay here?" Jamie asked.

"Shuffle papers f'Caste'monte." Drink made the normally cheerful Luciano an unpleasant table companion.

"What would you prefer to do?" Jamie continued.

Luciana waved his glass at a footman for a refill. Either no one had taught him manners or he lost them in a wine bottle.

"He prefers to be a farmer," Eduardo answered for him. "His papa wanted an educated son. Here he is forced to learn English and"—he glanced at Nora—"become a man of the world."

"Not farmer," Luciano snapped, a bit too loudly. Giovanni looked embarrassed for him. "Wine maker. Hate the city."

"I prefer the countryside also," Nora said.

"English countryside?" Luciano snorted. "Not like my mountains." Nora colored. Jamie wanted to throttle him.

"Do you dislike all cities or just Rome?" Nora asked.

Eduardo laughed. "This is the only city he knows—the only one that matters."

"Rome—dirty, crowded, and full of corrupt cardinals," Giovanni said, catching Jamie off guard. "Only power and opera make up for it. London will be the same."

"No corrupt cardinals there," Jamie pointed out.

"Who needs it?" Luciano asked no one in particular. "C'ruption all the same." He downed another glass and made a face. "They brought out the bad wine."

"You think the city c'rupt?" Luciano asked Nora, leering at her décolletage.

Movement at the head of the table saved Jamie from committing murder. Nora rose with the other ladies, and they all scrambled to their feet, Luciano swaying slightly.

Nora gave Jamie a pleading look.

"I shouldn't be long," he said. He hoped it was true.

Old men's preference for leisurely conversation dashed Jamie's hopes. Most of the young wisely kept quiet. Luciano's loose tongue made one inappropriate comment too many and drew a frown from Castellimonte.

"I will see Luciano to his quarters," Giovanni offered. At the count's nod, he pulled Luciano, who rudely protested, out. A few of the others slipped away with him. Eduardo stayed.

"No manners, the young," Scarface, General Rambaudi, said bitterly. Murmurs of agreement rolled around the table.

"Not all of us, certainly," Eduardo said, offended.

"No," Castellimonte agreed. "Not all young men. He will be dealt with."

*Poor Luciano, the would-be wine maker who can't hold his liquor*, Jamie thought. He looked down at his glass. He had left his dinner wine untouched. Luciano's drunken stupidity gave him distaste for it. He sipped the count's port sparingly and steeled himself to listen to a conversation Wentworth probably didn't care about. At least he could report that Luciano posed no threat.

Nora's face hurt from smiling, and her head hurt from struggling to understand the giggling chatter of the Italian ladies. She almost sagged with relief when Jamie's form filled the doorway and he stepped briskly to her side.

She relished a husband who could see how she felt; he began making their excuses to leave immediately without being asked.

When the receiving room doors closed behind them, Jamie paused long enough to embrace her. He ignored the footman standing guard in his livery, eyes studiously forward.

"Let's fetch Isabella," he said, "and go home."

"Please. Quickly." The word "home" on his lips gave her comfort.

Jamie ordered their wraps and an escort to be brought round and took her by the hand. "Shall we send someone for Isabella? You look too weary to climb four stories."

She nodded. He dispatched a message.

Jamie helped her with her wrap and sat her on a marble bench near the massive entrance to the Palazzo. She anticipated a short wait.

Long minutes passed with no sign of Isabella. The point of discomfort loomed just as footsteps sounded on the stairs. Nora turned at the sound, but her relief proved short-lived. The footman returned alone and alarmed; he rattled on in Italian so fast Nora demanded translation.

"The nursery is empty," Jamie said grimly. He barked orders, demanded to see the nursery maid, and demanded to see the housekeeper. Then he bolted up the stairs at a dead run.

Nora followed as fast as she could while he took the steps two at a time. She heard the nursery door slam open and ran more quickly down the hall. She slid through the door to see Jamie surveying the vast empty room. She saw no Isabella, no nursery maid, no living human being.

Nora began to shake uncontrollably, unable to move while Jamie prowled like a caged lion, shouting for the housekeeper. The dragon herself, dressed entirely in black, her hair piled on her head in a series of tight braids, bustled into the room.

"This cannot be!" the housekeeper exclaimed. "I saw the child here myself after she greeted the count. I assigned a mature, responsible girl to her, not some bird who would flit off to meet her boyfriend."

Nora felt the criticism like a slap.

"Did anyone check the garden?" the woman demanded.

"At night?" Nora asked. "No 'responsible girl' would take the child out at night, even in the walled garden."

"Check it anyway," Jamie told the footman. "Think again," he said to the housekeeper.

"What is this?" demanded the Count di Castellimonte as he swept into the room. A few members of his entourage followed, Eduardo among them.

Jamie explained, fear making his voice harsh. At the sound, Nora's panic threatened to spiral out of control.

"I'll check this hall," Eduardo offered. "Perhaps she ran off, and the maid had to pursue." Jamie looked like he wanted to pull him back, but the young man went off like a shot.

The housekeeper opened nursery bedrooms and the empty room that would have housed a live-in nursery maid. "Nothing here," she said.

"Try the cupboards," Jamie said grimly.

"Foolish," the woman spat, as she yanked open a storage cupboard. "What could possibly be—" Her shriek drew all their eyes to what looked at first glance like a bundle of clothes that had fallen off one of the deep shelves.

The maid lay with her throat cut, covered with blood, and eyes wide open.

Darkness began to envelop Nora, but she fought it off. "Dead," she heard Jamie tell the count. "Dead," echoed in her head. She refused to faint as she had the first time she came to Palazzo Savoia.

She rushed to her husband. "Not Isabella," she said, gulping air. "The maid but not Isabella." She beat on his chest with her fists until he took them gently in his big hands and pulled her into an embrace.

"Find her, Jamie. You have to find her," she cried.

# Chapter 30

"Seal the doors."

Castellimonte gave the order before Jamie could react. He looked at the old man over Nora's head.

"It may be too late," he said.

Nora choked.

"Too late to catch the kidnappers," he clarified, kissing her face. He cradled her in his arms.

Guards, footmen, and courtiers of every level and function began to converge on the upper story.

"We will send a patrol out to the streets," Castellimonte said.

"This happened inside your household," Jamie retorted.

Eduardo skidded back into the room. "Nothing," he panted. "Not on this hall."

"Search every corner from attics to basement," Castellimonte ordered. The men began to divide into groups. Eduardo led one group to retrace his steps, checking cupboards in every empty room.

Giovanni, who had arrived soon after the count, recruited two footmen. "We'll start at the other end, in the cellars," he said.

"Where is Luciano?" Jamie asked.

"Passed out in his room," Giovanni said over his shoulder. He hurried out.

The count conferred with the captain of his guard. Patrols would fan out in three directions.

"What will they look for?" Jamie asked. "Simple-minded thugs dragging a screaming girl?"

The count ignored him. Jamie thought furiously. He had no idea how many of the searchers they could really trust. Whoever took Isabella did it silently and under Castellimonte's nose.

"Come, we will wait," the count ordered.

"No." Jamie would not take orders. "I'm not going to sit and wait," he said. He needed Wat Jones. The two of them could at least scour the gutters of Rome.

"Your time may be best spent comforting your wife," Castellimonte pointed out.

Jamie gripped Nora's shoulders, holding her away to search her face, crumpled with fear. "I'm going to stop at Casa Beaumont for Wat. Can you manage here or would you rather be there?"

Nora looked at Castellimonte and back at Jamie. "Here I think. At least I won't be alone." He kissed her fiercely, breathing in her sweet scent of lilac for strength.

"It may take time," he said.

"Do whatever it takes. I'll be safe here." She glanced up at Castellimonte. The old man needed her as much as she needed company. That thought reassured Jamie. Nora could lean on the count for now, but it might be a different story if they failed to find the little girl.

A vision of Isabella, frightened and alone, filled the space in his heart. He ran like the devil.

Within thirty minutes, Jamie and Wat began to scour the seediest taverns, gaming hells, and brothels, probing for information.

Jamie never believed the abduction could be entirely the work of street thugs, but the possibility that the kidnappers hired local muscle drove him out into the streets. Someone somewhere must know something.

An aging prostitute in filthy dive coyly suggested she had what Jamie needed. He declined, sipping stale ale and eyeing the drunken men around him.

"Did I understand that you need information about a girl?" she asked, rubbing against him.

"Not the sort of girl you mean," Jamie answered, pulling away.

"Pity," the old drab said.

Wat grabbed her hand before she could lift Jamie's purse.

Jamie returned the favor at another prime location, dropping a brutish-looking fellow who took offense at Englishmen in general.

After hours of it, a furtive little man leaned across Jamie's drink to whisper, "I may have the information you need, Signore." The temptation to believe him proved too great to resist.

The weasel rubbed his fingers together. He licked his lips at the coin Jamie offered. "Not here," he whined.

Jamie followed him. By then he felt too exhausted to think of any other option. If the weasel had information, he wanted it.

"You say the girl disappeared from Castellimonte's household?" the man asked.

Jamie nodded.

"You deal with dangerous people, Signore. Dangerous people indeed," he said, and he laughed a toothless laugh.

"You need a keeper," Wat shouted, downing the first of Jamie's attackers. Weasel had many friends. Jamie had a skilled one. It took the two of them twenty busy minutes, several cracked ribs, and the last of Jamie's strength to fight their way out of the alley.

"Do you think he actually knew anything?"

"No," Wat answered. "I know those bully boys. They just wanted drink money."

Jamie groaned.

"Tell me, Major, do you really think any of those dolly-mop Italians at the Palazzo would deal with street vermin? They would never let them in the place."

"Have you been humoring me?" Jamie asked.

"You looked like you needed a fight. I thought I ought to keep an eye out," Wat said.

Jamie sent Wat home. He still needed a fight. He almost got one when he pounded on the door to Hanover's Embassy long after midnight and demanded to speak to Wentworth.

Wentworth sent word to admit him, but the steward kept him in the foyer until the old man wheezed down.

"Major! You look like a refugee from Seven Dials," the old windbag said.

Jamie's jacket reeked filth where it wasn't ragged, blood had dripped down onto his shirt, and his face had an ugly scratch. He didn't care.

"Not London's slums, Rome's," he said and told Wentworth what had happened in a few, short profane sentences.

"Not good," Wentworth said. "Very bad development."

If Jamie believed the man's concern was for Isabella, he might have been impressed. It wasn't.

"We cannot have Castellimonte's support diverted from Victor Emmanuel. We deal with the House of Savoy with difficulty as it is without gaining a king who actually . . ." He let his voice trail off. *Who actually ran the country*, Jamie suspected.

"You think this is aimed at Castellimonte?" he asked.

"Of course! What else would it be? No one really cares about Robert Beaumont's daughter. Family is the man's one weakness."

*Family. How much does Castellimonte know about the actions of his own son?* Jamie had no answer for that. He would dearly like to question the baron.

"Can you help?" he asked Wentworth. "If not, our conversation is over."

Wentworth looked lost in thought.

"We will have to shore up our contacts with the heir, Carl Felice," Wentworth said, lost in his own thoughts.

"What about Isabella?" Jamie demanded.

"Oh, they won't injure the girl, not as long as they need

her to control Castellimonte," Wentworth said absently. He waved a hand vaguely, a habit Jamie had come to loathe.

"But do you have any idea who might want to take her?"

"Any number of people," Wentworth said, acting affronted that Jamie would doubt it. "Victor Filiberto, of course, loathes the king, but it's unclear whether he would act against his father."

Victor again. "I don't doubt it," Jamie said.

Wentworth went on as if Jamie hadn't spoken. "The young ones for certain, but it's difficult to determine which ones."

*The Boys*. Wentworth seemed sure of it. Jamie's blood went cold. He struggled to think who had time to get up to the nursery, snatch Isabella, and kill the maid. Several young men had left dinner together. Eduardo seemed closest to Filiberto, but he stayed behind at dinner as had Victor. They hadn't left early, but Filiberto could easily be paying someone. There had to be more than one person involved.

"You see, Major, why it has been important to gather as much as we could about your students? If you had found out more, we might know, but as it is, one can't be certain," Wentworth pronounced.

"That's it then? I failed and you can't help," Jamie spat.

"Don't get hostile," the old man responded. "I suggest you simply return to Palazzo Savoia and wait. The conspirators will contact Castellimonte soon enough."

Jamie stalked to the door.

"Major?" Wentworth called after him. "You will let me know when they do, won't you?"

## Chapter 31

Castellimonte attempted to distract Nora with chess. Nothing, neither the exquisite inlaid table, nor the hand carved ivory pieces, nor the generous competitor pulled her mind from Isabella. They gave up after two games.

Eventually she sank onto a chaise lounge and pretended to nap. The count never left her.

Guards came and went, saluting with stiff formality. Housemaids came and went, wringing hands and bobbing curtseys. Courtiers came and went, oozing concern and courtesy. Every one gave the same message. No sign of the girl, no note, no demands.

Long after the scurrying stopped, long after the house quieted, long after the last patrol returned, her husband returned, filthy, bloodied, and ragged. His formal obeisance to the count looked ridiculous.

She flew to his arms.

Jamie held her to him in a fierce hug, but he looked directly at Castellimonte and shook his head. He brought no good news.

"What happened to your face? You look like you've been in a fight," Nora said.

"Several," he replied with a wry smile, "and to no avail."

She rang for a servant and asked the sleepy footman who responded for towels and hot water.

"I hope it made you feel better," she said tartly.

"It did, rather. Briefly." His eyes looked bleak.

Nora accepted a basin of water and towels and began to

wipe the blood and grime from his face. He batted her hands away and sat upright.

"Any word?" he asked Castellimonte.

"It may come in the morning," the old man said.

"What may come?" Nora asked.

"The kidnappers' demands," Jamie said, watching the count.

"We have money," Nora said. "Isabella's inheritance may serve."

"They don't want money," Jamie told her. Castellimonte remained silent. "They will want something from our friend here. Isn't that so?" He sounded angry.

"Probably. Yes," Castellimonte agreed.

"You will work with them," Nora said.

"We will see what they want first," Castellimonte replied.

"But you must!" Nora protested. "Isabella is in danger."

Too much time had passed. Too many fears plagued her. Too many secretive looks passed between these men. "You must!" she insisted. She could feel tears threatening to overwhelm her. She willed herself not to wilt.

"We will know soon enough what can be done. Whoever did this wishes to humiliate my house and take power over me. I cannot say what we will do until we know."

Nora faced the count. She opened her mouth to demand his cooperation but immediately sank back. The count had as little power as she did until the kidnappers contacted him. The starch went out of her spine.

Jamie wrapped her in her velvet cloak; he must have ordered it before he even came to her. His arm guided her from the palace, speaking softly to their escort. She allowed him to lead her home in a daze.

Only when they had been admitted by Wat who stood at alert, only when he had led her to his bed and undressed her, only when they lay side by side and his warmth seeped into her, did she speak.

"Is that the great and terrible secret?" she asked.

"What secret?"

"The one you've been hiding. The one that has made you unhappy."

He kissed her hair while he ran his hand up her side. *For comfort,* she thought, *not for passion.* He leaned up and kissed her mouth, looking down with dark sad eyes before pulling her so that her head rested in the hollow space below his shoulder and his arm curled around her. She couldn't see his eyes, and she thought he wouldn't answer.

"Yes," he said at last. "That was it." His hoarse voice rasped over the words.

"Someone wishes to pressure Castellimonte, and they are using Isabella to do it." He didn't contradict her.

"Power," she spat, suddenly angry. "Those who have it, abuse it. Those who don't, abuse others to get it. I hate the nobility. I hate the whole damned upper class."

Jamie went very still. She could hear his heart beating beneath her, fast and hard. After what felt like an age, he kissed her hair.

"That's my wise, Nora," he said. "Once this is over, avoid the bastards, all of them."

Jamie wore a rut in the carpet of the Castellimonte's private office for two hours before word came, goaded by the knowledge that he had failed the women in his life again. He had slept fitfully and left a swollen-eyed Nora, too exhausted to rise, behind in spite of her protests to the contrary.

He arrived at Palazzo Savoia before the sun rose high, clean, shaven, and as angry as he had been the night before. Castellimonte had affection for Isabella, but he refused to make commitments. His position demanded priorities beyond the well-being of one little girl.

Jamie and Castellimonte waited for a message in a state of truce. They almost overlooked it when it came.

The old wolf, who sat at his desk and pretended to attend to administration, nodded regally when asked if he wished luncheon brought on a tray. The meal arrived with three footmen, several covered platters, and a maximum of ceremony. A portable table had to be set up. Chairs were arranged, covers lifted.

"We will eat," Castellimonte announced, dismissing the servants.

Jamie never refused food. He had nibbled biscuits, mounted and ready, just before the first charge at Waterloo. That morning food tasted like ashes. He began to nudge the exotic morsels with his fork, moving them around.

"Wine?" the count asked. Jamie shook his head and reached for the water pitcher.

"What is that?" he asked pointing ivory vellum under the edge of a platter. "Does your staff send you messages from the kitchen?"

Both men reached for it at once. Jamie grabbed it first, upending the platter and spilling gravy down the side of the table linen. The vellum, folded over and sealed, read, "To his Lordship, the Count Di Castellimonte."

The count reached out an imperious hand.

Jamie fought the urge to tear it open and handed it over.

While Castellimonte read, Jamie called back the three footmen. "Who filled this tray?"

The three men looked at one another. None answered.

Jamie shouted, "Who touched it? Damn it, who had put the dishes on the tray?"

"Fruitless, Major," Castellimonte said without looking up. "A dozen hands touched that tray, and more passed it on the way up from the kitchens. These three won't know."

He waved the folded paper with a deep frown. "Childish," he snapped. He handed it back to Jamie.

"'Come alone,'" Jamie read, his eyes noting the location in a public park. "It sounds like a bad novel."

"Quite. As expected, our conspirators are amateurs," the old man said.

"You can't go alone," Jamie told him.

"Of course not," he replied.

"How shall we proceed?" Jamie asked.

"We?" Castellimonte repeated, glaring down his aristocratic nose.

The threats might belong to the count, but Isabella belonged to Jamie. "You'll need a guard," he said.

"Nothing so indiscreet. A subtle assistant or two."

"They'll know The Ferret."

Castellimonte's lips twitched. He didn't need to ask which assistant Jamie meant. "True enough," he said. "But they would know you also, Major. You are not a subtle man. There are others."

The meeting request implied immediately. The count rose and excused himself. "You will hear from me soon," he said. "Once we know their demands, we can plan our next steps."

The door shut with a whisper. He left Jamie cooling his heels like a poor petitioner. A roar burst from him in an explosion of frustration. Wine spilled across the table linen, and the decanter hit the wall; a red stain dripped down the velvet wallpaper. Shards of etched crystal sprayed across the floor.

"Isabella matters first and last, you old fool," he roared. *Nora's Isabella, mine to protect.*

He sank onto a sofa and ran a clenched hand through his hair. Meeting with kidnappers just meant more delay. Isabella wouldn't be there. Castellimonte and his enemies played games with her life while a tiny girl sat alone and afraid, or worse.

Jamie's thoughts raced. *Did Isabella actually leave the Palazzo? Wat seems to think not, but how can we tell?* There had been no sign of forced entry. Guards on every door would have seen something. Yet, the inside search turned up no trace.

Jamie strode to the window. He tried but failed to shake the feeling that the searchers could not be trusted. The kidnapping had to be the act of insiders.

Jamie would rather search than wait like a kept dog for the count's orders. If he could retrace the search of the Palazzo on his own, he might turn up a clue.

He couldn't remember where Eduardo had looked. Giovanni, with his typical good sense, had suggested they start in the cellars, the farthest point from the nursery. Jamie would begin with the cellars.

## Chapter 32

Nora arrived at the Palazzo soon after the count left with one discreet bodyguard. She dismissed Wat Jones with whispered instructions to follow them discreetly.

Ten minutes later she thought she would scream if one more patronizing servant attempted to mollify her. Mrs. Bently's husband had been there, but his whereabouts were unknown to any of the upper servants.

Her footsteps echoed on the marble hallways of the formal court wing of the palace. Her rising voice bounced off walls.

"My niece is missing. This is no idle visit. I demand to know where my husband went!"

The housekeeper had been called in to soothe the wild woman who spoke their language so poorly. "I do not know, madam. I have been told he is not with the count. That is all I can tell you. The facts will not change if I tell you again." The dragon's voice rose also. With a flick of her skirt, she left Nora gaping.

"Signora?" a soft voice called from a partially opened door. A tiny girl, clearly one of the lowest in the servant hierarchy, peered out. "You seek the Major Bently?" she whispered.

"Do you know where my husband went?" Nora demanded.

"I came to clean. He—" the girl glanced over her shoulder, embarrassed "—had an accident with the lunch."

Nora saw an overturned lunch table and broken glass in the room behind the girl. "Was there an argument?"

"I cannot say. His Lordship left, and the Major . . ." She shrugged eloquently.

"But where is he?"

"I do not know, but I heard him ask the way to the cellars." The girl looked furtively down the hall and began to withdraw.

"Wait! Did he go there?"

The girl shrugged. "That is all I heard." She began to shut the door in Nora's face.

"Wait!" Nora exclaimed. "What is your name?"

The answer came as a faint whisper, the sound mingled with the hush of the closing door. "Clara."

Nora stomped back toward the entrance. The footman stationed there looked at her with lazy indifference.

"Can you tell me how to find the cellars?" she asked.

He looked affronted. Guests did not wander the count's cellars.

"I believe Major Bently has gone there," she said. "I wish to find him."

"How do you plan to do that?"

"I need to find the cellars, you oaf!"

Suddenly, the footman transformed his insolent slouch into an attentive stance. "What about the cellars?" a familiar voice broke in. Nora's tension eased. She looked around, with relief, to find Giovanni approaching.

"Giovanni, thank goodness! Have you seen Major Bently?"

"He sent word there would be no tutorial today, understandably. Isn't he with Castellimonte?"

"There must have been word from the kidnappers, but the count went out alone. Someone overheard my husband asking for the cellars," she told him.

"Who said such a thing?" he asked.

"It doesn't matter. I need to look for him. I can't imagine where else he would be."

"Surely not. Perhaps he has returned to Casa Beaumont," Giovanni suggested.

"I just came from there. I didn't pass him on the way."

She took hold of the young man's sleeve. "Please, I'm worried. Can you show me the cellars?"

"To the dirt and damp? It is no place for a lady," he insisted.

"I'm not so weak! Show me the way," she demanded.

"There may be rats." If he was trying to frighten her, he didn't know his target. "I cannot allow—" he began.

"It isn't for you to allow!" she snapped. "I ask only the direction."

Giovanni's perpetual mask of calm slipped a bit. A flash of something ugly flew across his face and confused Nora momentarily.

"Very well," he said with his normal good manners. "But I insist on accompanying you. It isn't safe for a lady to go down there alone."

She took his arm with relief.

Deep in the cellars, Jamie's lungs ached from the damp air. His muscles ached from one fight too many the previous night. Nothing impeded his hearing. The sound of a weeping child, faint but unmistakable, tore his heart out.

"Silence! You make my head hurt," a voice growled in Italian.

The weeping continued. Jamie felt along the damp walls, searching for an opening he missed, a hallway he failed to find. He pressed his ear to one side of the wall. Nothing. He took a step back and listened again. The sound came from the other side, low down, and over to Jamie's right. It came from a spot where wooden kegs had been stacked.

The muffled voice spoke again, "I told you my head hurts. If you don't stop that whining, I will leave you alone here."

A wail drove Jamie wild. He began tossing kegs left and right until they rolled in every direction. He tore at them until he found it. A door of rough nailed planks covered an opening that came to Jamie's waist. He knelt and pressed his ear to it.

The crying had faded to sniffles. "You hit me," Isabella complained.

He knew he should move with caution so as not to alert Isabella's jailor, but the sound of rolling kegs made it much too late for that. He broke open the door with a roar and charged in, ducking under the doorway into a hidden storeroom.

Isabella crouched beneath a thin blanket on a large barrel shoved against the far wall. Two rusty lanterns hooked high on the walls cast flickering shadows.

"Uncle Jamie!" she cried, throwing off her cover and scooting toward the edge. Even in the dim light, Jamie could see that she clutched two little dolls.

Next to her, Luciano slumped on a campstool, holding his head in his hands. He looked up at Jamie with red-rimmed eyes but made no effort to get up. The entire conspiracy, with one hung-over jailor and no weapons that Jamie could see, bordered on farce.

"You," Luciano moaned so calmly Jamie wondered if surprise, disappointment, or relief lay behind the word.

Isabella flew into Jamie's arms and wrapped her hands around his neck.

"Did you doubt that I would find her?" Jamie growled at Luciano.

"We knew Castellimonte would not. He makes great show, but he trusts everyone."

"I knew you would find me," Isabella said. Jamie kissed her head.

"You trusted me." The thought warmed him.

"Yes, I did," she said. Isabella looked uninjured and as spunky as ever. "I called and called you until he told Luciano he had to stay to keep me quiet."

"He?" Jamie looked at Luciano.

Voices in the hall interrupted whatever answer Jamie would have gotten. Nora was calling him.

Jamie ducked back out of the little room, holding Isabella with her dolls clutched tightly in his arms.

"Over here, Nora," he called.

Nora turned the corner ten feet away; Giovanni followed behind her. Her face lit up with joy.

"Thank God," she said, taking a step forward.

"I told you hiding her down here would not work," Luciano whined.

"*Stupido!*" Giovanni exclaimed.

The pieces fell into place for Jamie even before Isabella pointed. "Him," she said. "That's who told Luciano to keep me quiet 'no matter what.'"

## Chapter 33

Nora felt Giovanni's left arm snake out and grab her from behind. His right fist came around her chest. It held a thin but lethal blade pointed upward toward her chin.

"What are you doing?" she demanded.

"Stubborn woman. You insisted on the cellars." He shoved her forward a step.

Jamie pushed Isabella's face into his shoulder. A growl came from deep in his throat. Nora could see his eyes calculating the distance to Giovanni, but he stood fast. He could not move, not with Isabella.

The sight of Isabella on his shoulder focused Nora's attention and narrowed her world to a few sharp sensations: the constriction of Giovanni's arm cinching her waist, the feel of cold metal against the open bodice of her gown, and the sight of growing panic in Jamie's eyes. *Dear God, he must not move!*

"You English, always so smart," Giovanni sneered, the polished student gone. "Take the girl, Luciano. I will deal with these two."

"Give it up, Gianni," Luciano said. "We failed."

"Take the girl. We need her. We have to have Castellimonte's support. We don't need these two." Nora felt the rise and fall of his chest, his breathing, coming faster as his agitation increased.

"Get her yourself," Luciano whined. "You promised this would be simple. You promised I would go home."

"Stupid boy," Giovanni replied. "Do you think they will let you go after this?"

"Luciano is right," Jamie said, clutching Isabella tightly.

He would not let her go without a fight. "You can't expect to murder us and get away with it. Castellimonte knows I'm here. They will hunt you down."

"As they hunted for the girl?" Giovanni sneered.

Jamie would die for Isabella. A vision of him doing exactly that and bleeding on the stone floor as a result, horrified Nora.

"Think, boy," Jamie went on.

"I am no boy," Giovanni spat, enraged. Nora felt the hand with the knife move fractionally upward.

Jamie's body jerked forward and fell back. He couldn't move, not with Isabella. Nora knew she had to act.

She slumped at the waist, made loud gagging noises, and pushed her rear into Giovanni's legs. She forced her upper body as far forward as she dared and gagged as if she might vomit. Giovanni groaned in disgust.

Nora felt a pinprick below her neck when Giovanni jerked his head away. His stiletto slid sideways up her chest until the side of his hand pushed against her chin and the blade pointed off to the left of her ear. She dropped her chin and bit down hard. She bit until she tasted blood and the blade clanged on the floor.

Jamie closed the space between them in seconds, covered the stiletto with his boot, and thrust Isabella into Nora's arms. He pulled Giovanni away and began to pummel him.

Nora took savage satisfaction in the beating until a sound from Isabella brought her to her senses. By that time, Jamie had him down on the floor and had slammed his head against the stone.

"Jamie, stop! You'll kill him," she shouted. "Jamie! Isabella!"

She tried to cover the girl's eyes, but Isabella twisted around to look.

"Stop, Uncle Jamie, you are scaring me," the girl cried.

Behind them Luciano retched uncontrollably.

Jamie stood and staggered to Nora, pulling both of them into an embrace. Giovanni lay bloodied on the stones; he did not move.

## Chapter 34

"Stop staring at me as if you expect me to keel over," Nora whispered.

Jamie stared, transfixed on the tiny red spot on Nora's neck. *That animal could have killed you,* he thought, *would have done it without remorse*. He didn't dare say the words out loud.

"You won't," Jamie said instead. No woman who took on an attacker with a knife at her throat would keel over—unless an overheated salon full of excitable Italians did her in.

"Then stop looking as if you want to eat me," she hissed.

Jamie pretended to look affronted. "Not in front of people," he whispered. Her blush rewarded him. The wound looked as minor as she claimed once it had been cleaned.

His wife pretended to listen to Castellimonte's description of Sardinian law regarding treason, but he doubted if she understood it. Her real attention lay with the child in her lap.

Isabella cuddled her two dolls, Marietta and one whose name escaped him. He heard her murmur, "The bad men won't take you again. Uncle Jamie won't let them."

It felt like a knife to his heart. The conspirators had used her toys as bait to entice her to follow them quietly. Now she clutched them as if they would be taken away again. Isabella didn't look as calm as she claimed.

"They must hang immediately!" Victor Filiberto's voice carried across the room. The count responded with studied calm about the need for a trial.

Jamie watched the pallor on Nora's face. Isabella didn't

need to hear such things. He needed to get his family away from wagging tongues.

"What trial?" Filiberto continued. "They have admitted their crimes!"

Jamie had enough. *Giovanni hasn't even regained consciousness enough to confess to anything.* He rose to his feet. He didn't want Nora reliving what they heard in the cellars.

"I demand it!" Filiberto shouted. Abrupt silence greeted that.

"You demand?" his father asked. He stared his son down.

A burst of talk erupted again. The entire court seemed to speak at once. Some believed the criminals should be shipped to the court in Turin in chains. Some sided with Victor, advocating for immediate execution.

One voice with a heavy English accent carried to Jamie. "You must do as you see fit, Count," Wentworth soothed oozing oil. "I'm sure you will make certain you have all the facts before you act and know exactly how deeply this conspiracy goes."

Wentworth had arrived in the confusion of revelations and arrests. His paid informers worked efficiently. The whole web of them made Jamie sick.

"We need to take Isabella home," Jamie told Nora.

"Is it safe?"

"Safer than it was last night," he said. "Safer than any time since we met her." He believed it. Jamie refused to believe Giovanni and Luciano acted alone. He glared over at Filiberto, so anxious to silence the two young men. He shook his head to cool his rage. Whoever the conspirators were, they wouldn't try the same ploy twice.

He shepherded Nora and Isabella toward the door. A familiar voice cut him off.

"Courageous work today, Major," General Rambaudi said. "Courageous and ingenious."

"Not I, General. My wife is the hero."

"I doubt that, Major," the general said. "Your Mr. Wentworth tells me you fought at Waterloo." Jamie saw the windbag sidle up to Rambaudi.

"Indeed," Wentworth said. "14th Foot, wasn't it?" The man knew full well what Jamie claimed. His knowing eyes watched like a spider in its web.

"That's correct," Jamie said, taking Isabella from Nora's arms. "Let me carry her, you must be exhausted," he told her.

"I want to go home," Isabella whined. *Good girl*, he thought.

"14th Foot?" Rambaudi mused. "I do not know it, but there were many of us, no? Were you with Colville?"

Nora leaned against his arm, eyes bright. Isabella whimpered.

"Er, no," Jamie said. He shifted Isabella to his opposite shoulder. He felt pathetic using a child as a shield. "I was with Grant," he said to close off the topic. He immediately regretted it; Grant commanded cavalry. He cursed silently.

Rambaudi looked puzzled.

"My wife and her niece need their rest, General. They have had a troubled day." He nodded his head in a vague attempt at a bow and guided Nora toward the door with his free arm.

A tweed-covered arm reached around him to open the door. Nora walked ahead. "I think, Major," Wentworth said before Jamie could follow her, "you didn't fight with the any regiments of foot, did you?" Jamie didn't stick around to give an answer.

Nora didn't hear Wentworth's words. She busied herself requesting their wraps and, he noted, an escort.

"I didn't know you were at Waterloo," Nora said. "I should have."

"You must have been very brave," Isabella put in with a yawn.

"I don't talk about it," he said, in a massive understatement. Nora and Isabella, he knew, would feel safe once they realized the conspiracy was over. He wished he felt the same.

In the end, Nora heard they had executed the conspirators. Giovanni regained consciousness only long enough for them to tie him to a post and shoot him.

"No trial, no hearings. I am horrified—or I ought to be," Nora said for what must have been the tenth time in as many days. She still hadn't come to terms with her own blood lust in the cellar.

"Sad," her husband replied. "Not just the ending but what it took to get them there. Poor Luciano listened to the wrong person." Luciano, they heard, never stopped protesting his innocence and blamed the crimes entirely on Giovanni.

"And Giovanni?" she asked.

"I don't know," he said. "I would feel better if I knew who he reported to. Perhaps Castellimonte's people got it out of him before they shot him."

Nora shuddered at how that might have occurred. She continued to mend Jamie's shirt.

"We have servants for that, you know," he said.

"I want to mend my own husband's shirt," she replied tartly. "Allow me something useful to do before I bury Casa Beaumont in lace."

Jamie smiled at that, drawing an echoing smile from Nora. He smiled less now than before. She had hoped that the great secret, the one he and Castellimonte shared about their fears for Isabella, had been the cause of his chronic sadness. That hope died within days of the execution.

Secrets, regret, and sorrow. She knew him well enough now to see them all milling around beneath the charm and disarming playfulness. Something ate at her husband.

"Wentworth says he's invited to dine at Palazzo Savoia," she said.

"Wentworth?" Jamie asked sharply. "When did you talk with that old windbag?"

"Odd really," she said. "I found him talking with Mother Margarita when Wat and I went for Isabella this afternoon. I don't think she likes him much."

"She has good sense," Jamie said. He looked like he had bitten into a rancid plum.

"I told him we would not be there," she said.

"Good. We won't."

Jamie had warned the count in terms that brooked no contradiction that they needed time alone. Nora appreciated that, but still, she wondered at the fierceness of it. She knew the Palazzo held bad memories for both of them, yet he continued to go daily. His band of folk needing English lessons had grown.

"It has been three weeks," she said. "Perhaps a dinner out wouldn't go amiss."

"No," he said.

"I thought you liked the Palazzo's exorbitant table."

"Our own cook makes magic in the kitchen. I have no need to look elsewhere," he said, rising from his seat. "Besides, my own wife is all the entertainment I need."

Jamie stalked toward her, miming predatory gestures until he scooped her up. She let out a shriek and grabbed on for dear life, still holding his shirt. It trailed over his shoulder where her right hand held fast.

"Foolish man, put me down."

"Not on your life," he said, nuzzling her neck. "My room tonight?" He didn't wait for an answer.

"Let me put my mending away," she protested as they swept through his dressing room.

"It will keep until morning," he said, sliding her down to stand on her toes.

So it would. She dropped the shirt when Jamie's talented

fingers on her gown suddenly became more urgent than the mending. She opened for his kiss.

He had changed the subject rather thoroughly, and she let him. She had promised herself she would never question him. When he laid her, naked and open, on the bed and began to remove his clothes, she forgot about it entirely.

## Chapter 35

Beating a traitor near to death seemed an odd qualification for a teacher. Jamie found it amusing that his English tutorial grew with his reputation for violence. Several courtiers and a guard who planned to accompany the trade delegation joined his class.

Even more amusing to Jamie, a servant girl with ambition to be a lady's maid begged to participate. The count gave permission when Nora told him the girl, Clara, had been helpful to her the day they found Isabella.

Eduardo emerged as his star pupil. His radical change of heart amused Jamie most of all. He had become the lead student. Two days after Nora's encounter with Wentworth, Eduardo even lingered to help clean up after class. The boy puffed out his chest while he handed Jamie a file folder.

"So you see, I'm to go to London," the young man bragged. That would account for the sudden turn about in his attitude. "I was overlooked before. Now I will make my country proud."

Jamie bit back a smile.

"You'll be ready, I think, if you buckle down and study."

"I have done," Eduardo declared, outraged.

"So far. You must continue," Jamie told him.

"Of course. I will lead a delegation someday. Now even Victor Filiberto pays attention to me. Before, he favored Giovanni, always Giovanni. You see? Even Castellimonte's own son made mistakes about him."

Jamie paused in his packing. *Giovanni and Victor. Would the count's own son conspire against the old man? Perhaps*

*I should discuss it with Nora.* He knew that keeping things from her had been a mistake.

"See, there is Victor now," Eduardo said, strutting toward his new sponsor.

"Ah, Baron, how may I help you? Do you need something?" Jamie asked. He searched the baron's face, looking for deceit but finding none. *I should tell Nora my fears this time.*

"Nothing at all, Major," Filiberto replied. "Eduardo and I have an appointment." Eduardo preened, but Jamie thought Filiberto secretly laughed at the coxcomb.

"You missed dinner last night with the English 'visitors' from Hanover's embassy," Filiberto said.

"As I explained to your father, we have no need for such exalted company. My family needs quiet time together."

"Pity. Your Wentworth is not the most urbane conversationalist. You might have livened up the table. General Rambaudi was eager to refight Waterloo as always," Filiberto sneered.

"Since I have no desire to relive that particular experience, I would be no help whatsoever," Jamie said, snapping his portfolio shut.

Victor Filiberto's cold smile froze Jamie momentarily. "Oh, I think you are most interesting, Major. Don't underestimate yourself." He left with Eduardo dogging his steps.

When the baron departed, Jamie relaxed. The force he used to keep his jaw clamped shot pain from chin to ear. He slammed the valise down on the desk.

*"I think you are most interesting, Major." What the hell did the little worm mean by that?*

"You do not wish to dine with the count, Major?" a soft voice asked, interrupting his thoughts. The maid Clara sat in the far corner of the room, so quiet he had forgotten her. "The food is good," she went on.

Jamie forced a smile. "The food is excellent."

"You do not like the talk, cunning—sly like, um, foxes, I think?" she went on.

Jamie gasped back a laugh and looked more sharply at her. "You don't miss much, do you?" he laughed.

Clara shrugged. "I serve. I see things."

"No, I don't like the 'cunning,' but it is wolves that I dislike, not foxes." Jamie could feel the truth closing in on him, coming closer every day. He could feel Wentworth and Filiberto circling him, like wolves, a hungry pack looking for weakness to feed their own hunger for power.

"Yes," the girl said knowingly. "Beware of the teeth, Major." She blushed at her own boldness and scurried down the hall.

The odd conversation haunted Jamie on the long walk home. He strode down the gently sloping road past the Villa Borghese. He walked without seeing the massive carved gates, without hearing the songs of birds that nested in its massive park.

If a serving maid could see through him, he thought, Wentworth had no trouble. Every day he didn't confess to Nora, he dug his grave more deeply. He no longer doubted that she loved him, but his secrets could destroy that. Delay wouldn't make the inevitable any easier. *Better she hear it from me than Wentworth. Worse,* he thought, *what if she heard it from Filiberto?*

He paused in the Piazza Barberini where the afternoon sun glinted off the water-drenched shells of the Triton fountain, casting apricot highlights on the baroque façades around the square. *Rome*, Jamie thought, turning his face to the sun, *has become home, and my secrets threaten to snatch away the first home I've known in decades.* He wanted to howl like an abandoned dog.

He had finally come to believe he should tell her everything. Perhaps what they had built was enough to hold their marriage together. The closer he got to home, the more he hoped he could put it off a few days longer.

Wat met him at the door with little formality and a worried expression.

"You have visitors. We put them in yon drawing room," he said, nodding in that direction. "Come from Wentworth looking for some baron."

*Some baron.* Jamie felt the jaws of death closing in. He walked with the stiff gait of a man going to the scaffold, but he struggled not to give up hope prematurely. *Perhaps my visitors are seeking some other English expatriate.*

One look at Nora's distressed face put that thought to flight. One look at the man next to her finished it. *Too late to tell her now.* Hope died.

"Jamie! Thank goodness you're here," Nora exclaimed. She clutched a cream-colored calling card so hard she bent it. "The Duke of Sudbury," it said. Nora had no idea what to say to a duke. She could only hope Jamie did.

Jamie ignored her greeting. He glared at the man sitting beside her who had introduced himself as Mr. Andrew Mallet. He had the look of a bespectacled scholar and a kindly manner that almost put her at her ease. His badly scarred face spoke of a past beyond scholarship, however.

"Hello, Jamie," Mallet said.

Jamie stood frozen in place.

"You know this person?" Nora gasped. "Do you know the baron they are seeking?" She looked in confusion between Jamie and the man to her side.

"You've led us a merry dance, my friend. You led us here," Mallet said.

*Friend?* Nora searched Jamie's eyes. He looked directly at the man, but a veil of bleak regret clouded his expression.

"Yes, Heyworth, you have indeed led us a merry dance and I, for one, am ready for this charade to be over," the other man, the one she understood to be a duke, said.

Nora's breath caught in her throat. The duke called Jamie "Heyworth," the name of the man they sought.

Jamie jerked to look at the duke who stood at ease behind his left shoulder lit by sun from the courtyard.

Nothing in Nora's experience prepared her for such a creature's presence in her drawing room. His gold brocade waistcoat and priceless lace gave him aristocratic elegance that surpassed what she thought she had gotten used to at the count's dinner table. His white blond hair and ice blue eyes gave him an otherworldly air that unnerved her. Jamie, she could see, had no such difficulty with the man.

"Hello, Richard," Jamie rasped. "Shall I make you known to my wife?"

"We've made our introductions," the tall man said. "I wonder if we ought to introduce you to your own wife instead."

"Who are these people?" Nora demanded. She waved the calling cards she held. "I mean, I see names, but I don't understand."

"This personage, Nora, is Richard Hayden, the Marquess Glenaire," Jamie said, never taking his eyes from the man.

"But it says Duke of Sudbury here," Nora corrected, indicating the card.

"You've been gone three years, Heyworth," his erstwhile friend said. "I've come into my title."

"Do I wish you happy or offer condolences?" Jamie asked with a sad smile.

An aristocratic eyebrow rose. "Whichever pleases you. You've missed many things your friends might have wanted to share."

Jamie looked sick. He turned to the other man. "This man, Nora, is the duke's brother-in-law, Andrew Mallet. Plain Mister. I don't think he's come into a title since I saw him last."

Mallet chuckled. "No, but you did miss my second son's birth. Bad of you, Jamie."

"And this," the duke said, "Is Lord James Heyworth, 7th Baron Ross."

The words did not make sense. *My Jamie? The man they seek?* Nora's heart stopped momentarily then jerked to life erratically. *How,* she wondered, *can Jamie call the duke by his first name?* Her husband's familiar face belonged to a stranger. She didn't know him at all.

"Did you think we would give up?" Mallet asked without malice.

"You? Yes. Richard? Never," Jamie said.

"Quite right. We have much to discuss," the duke said. He looked at Nora with raised brow.

Nora believed no aristocrat, no matter how exalted his title, had the right order one about without even speaking. Resentment rose in her throat. She would not be ordered from her own drawing room by the raise of a ducal eyebrow.

"Is there an office or study we might use?" the duke asked as if he had read her mind.

"Yes. The way you came. On the right," she felt a fool for babbling. *Damn the man. Damn them all.*

"Thank you," he said with a slight bow. He pinned Jamie with a look and went the way she described.

Mallet's mouth quirked up. "Don't mind Richard," he told her. "Rudeness was bred in his bones. He fears you'll see the good heart under all that ice." He winked and limped to the door.

Jamie rose to follow.

"Jamie," she called after him. When he turned, she hesitated. "Your name is Jamie, isn't it?"

He squeezed his eyes shut.

"Yes."

"Why are they here?"

"They worry. Richard makes it a profession."

"What . . ." she began. Questions rushed into Nora, one crowding out the others. *Who are you?*

"We'll talk later," he said with the air of a dying man, and left her.

## Chapter 36

"Take help from your friends," Andrew repeated for what felt like the twentieth time.

The interview had gone on far too long. Desperate to get to Nora, Jamie tried to cut it short.

"There is nothing to discuss," he said.

"Rome has twisted your sense of honor if you think calling on your friends in time of trouble is dishonorable," Richard said. "In that case, half the aristocracy of England has no honor." His cold voice had pounded Jamie relentlessly for over an hour.

"My father used his friends and anyone else he could suck dry," Jamie spat.

"Your father was a worthless reprobate, and we all know it," Andrew put in.

Richard stood against the window in Nora's tiny office, graceful but haughtily erect, and looked down his well-bred nose to where Jamie sat. Andrew eyed him sympathetically from across Nora's desk.

"Why would I deny it?" Jamie asked.

"You are not your father!" Richard burst out with uncharacteristic force. "Damn it, Jamie, is that what you're afraid of, call on your friends in time of trouble and you become him?"

The guttural voice of that crude old man echoed in Jamie's head.

*Ask Glenaire for the blunt, boy. He's well to pass. Sent you to Harrow so's you could make them friends of yours, didn't I? Use 'em boy. Use 'em.*

Too often, he had done exactly that.

"Honor permits a major to live off his friends, but not a baron?" Richard demanded when Jamie didn't answer.

"I developed backbone eventually," Jamie mumbled. They had been through the entire discussion twice before. He wanted it over. Nora's face, confused and alarmed, haunted him. He needed to explain; he had to make it right.

"You can't order everyone's life, Richard," he insisted. "There are some things even you can't make right. A man can't damn well ask his friends to rescue an estate gone barren, coffers gone bankrupt, and—"

"And your sister?" Richard suggested.

Jamie leapt to his feet and glared, but remorse filled him. He hadn't been able to protect the women entrusted to him. He dropped back to his seat and leaned his elbows on the desk. It always came back to that. He had abandoned his mother and his sister. And soon, he would fail Nora.

"You're right," he said at last, his words muffled by his sleeve.

"What? Do I sense agreement?" Richard raised an eyebrow.

"You're right, blast it, Richard." Jamie lifted his head. "For that I should have asked for help. Your mother would have sponsored Arianne if you had asked her, and you would have if you knew we needed help."

"My sister," Richard corrected.

"I beg your pardon?" Jamie said.

"My sister sponsored her."

Jamie looked at Andrew. Richard's sister was Andrew's wife.

"You gave my sister a season?" The thought stunned Jamie. Richard would have borne an enormous expense.

"It is a trivial matter to me but of some great importance to your sister. You will understand if we had no time to ask your permission."

Jamie didn't doubt that. "She is well?"

"Very well. She's married," Andrew told him.

Jamie stared at his hands.

Richard continued without pity. "She wanted to wait until we found you. When our first efforts were not successful, your mother persuaded her to go on. Your mother, you will appreciate, felt anxious that the marriage proceed."

"Who is he?"

"Baronet. Small but prosperous estate in Kent. Well-off enough to manage a wife. I saw to the marriage settlement. We had no time to wait." Jamie felt Richard's blue eyes bore into him.

"No time to find me. Yes, I believe you've made that point. I presume I am even deeper in your debt," Jamie said.

Richard waved a dismissive hand. Andrew wouldn't meet his eyes.

"Your mother has gone to live with your sister," Andrew said. "She is relieved to be free of her nip-cheese sister-in-law, I believe."

Jamie couldn't digest the thought of Arianne married. "What is his name? Is he good to her?"

"Sir Walter Canfield. I haven't seen her since the wedding, but she seemed happy enough then," Andrew said. "If you are concerned with their welfare, you should visit them."

Jamie's head snapped up. "I can't," Jamie shouted. "You know I can't go back."

He went on more softly, "Arianne is settled. You said that yourself. I am worthless to them. My name is bankrupt, long since published in the *London Gazette*. Only the bailiffs wait for me. The vultures will have taken everything by now, and they're entitled to it," he paused for a moment, "not that the house contained anything worth a farthing."

"Mumford is entailed. No one can take it."

"They'll have taken the rents. Worthless in any case. Tenants driven off by my father's neglect. Farms barren. House falling down. The crown can have it when I'm gone." Jamie didn't pretend to care. The old place made up the stuff of his nightmares. He had spent a lifetime escaping it. "I don't want it. Never did."

"But isn't it your mother's home?" Andrew asked.

"Miserable place. She's better off with Arianne and this Canfield person." He didn't know that though. He saw with sudden clarity that even with Richard's news he couldn't be sure the women entrusted to his care were well provided for. He couldn't know it unless he went back.

"It is your son's birthright, and your grandchildren's heritage," Richard pressed.

"It may have escaped your attention, Richard, but I have neither." *Nor am I ever likely to.* He had to talk to Nora. He would make an apology at least. He owed her that much. He would apologize and give her freedom. He would not tell her about the Avante; he couldn't bear it. Grief threatened to overwhelm him.

"Exactly what do you want?" Jamie asked. "Let's be done with it."

"Come back with us." Richard's eyes bore into Jamie's.

"Face it, fix it, and be done with it," Andrew said.

"I can't. I'm wanted for debts I can't pay." A sudden thought made him hesitate. Something in their faces made him sure. He fell back in his chair. "You paid those, too, didn't you?"

Neither man denied it.

"Will helped," Andrew said. Will Landrum, the Earl of Chadbourn, made up the fourth of their group. They had called themselves "The Cohort" as foolish schoolboys, but the name stuck long after they had grown. Jamie ought to have known he was involved.

"I'll owe you for the rest of my life!" he shouted.

Neither man responded. They looked back with calm determination. *They don't know about the Avante. If they did, they would have said. If they did, they wouldn't insist on helping.*

"Besides," he went on, "I—" he meant to tell them

everything, but it stuck in his throat "—am married," he finished at last.

"Your family will, of course, travel with us," Andrew said.

"Isabella cannot. She is to stay in Italy. Nora won't leave her," Jamie told them.

"The will and the house in Rome." Richard looked down at neatly manicured hands. There seemed to be little he didn't know, even the conditions of Beaumont's will.

"The little girl must remain behind." Richard continued, "Your wife, of course, will stay with her. There is no help for it. You'll have to come alone. She will wait for you." In the man's mind, Nora's compliance was never in doubt.

Jamie knew better. Nora wouldn't allow some duke to arrange her life. *I'd like to see him try it,* he thought with bitter amusement.

He wondered if she would wait. He wouldn't bet on it. She would bar the door if she had any sense.

The fight went out of Jamie. "Give me a day," he said, "and I will do what you want."

"I can't. I'm needed in London, and a ship sails with the tide before morning."

*Tonight?* That gave Jamie no time to repair things with Nora. His heart sank. *I've most likely damaged things beyond repair anyway.* He agreed.

Richard's look implied that he had taken too much time from affairs of state to deal with the petty problems of his friend already. Arrangements took but a moment.

Jamie left Wat to show them out and hurried down the now-darkened corridor to Nora's sitting room. He found it empty and the door to her bedroom firmly closed.

Jamie hesitated. More than a door lay between them.


"Nora, open for me, please," Jamie pleaded behind the door.

Nora sat up in bed, hands splayed over the unread book in

her lap, and tried to ignore the muffled voice of her husband.

"I know you must be angry," he began.

*Angry? Hurt. Confused. Enraged. But angry?* Her heart began to pound again as it had when he left her alone in the drawing room.

"I should have told you in the beginning, but I didn't think it mattered."

She married a shabby major. Now she had a duke parading around her drawing room. *How could it not matter? She didn't even know her own husband.* She grabbed a book and threw it at the door.

"Go away!" she told him.

"Good. Be angry. You have every right," he said. "At least I know you aren't prostrate."

"You know me better than that!" she yelled back. "I at least have always been authentic with you. I do not collapse when, when faced with a—"

"A rat-faced lying husband?"

She had no answer for that.

"Open, just for a few moments and then I'll leave you alone," he pleaded with her.

She had nothing else nearby to throw.

"Nora, please!" he shouted.

She turned the key and opened the door a crack. "It's late. What is it you want to say to me?" Jamie pulled the door part way open and looked at her in the dim candlelight.

She met his gaze wearing her old muslin night rail, her much patched wrapper, and a wary expression.

"It's very late," she repeated.

"Richard kept me," he said.

She glared back. *Richard. His close friend. The duke. How could I have missed the signs? Of course he had highborn friends. The damned man made a fool of me.*

"Nora, I'm sorry it took so long. I—"

"Oh, pardon me. Obviously the demands of a duke outweigh simple honesty to a mere wife," she spat. Another thought struck her. "Am I even your wife?" she asked. "Who are you?"

"Damn it, Nora, don't say that. Things have to be sorted out."

"When?" she demanded.

He stood mute.

"You're leaving," she guessed. His eyes confirmed it. Her lying husband planned to leave her. *He probably planned it all along.*

"Tonight," he said.

*Oh God! Jamie is leaving.* No words made it to her mouth.

"I have to return to London," he said. "I left some things, that is, my life—"

She held up a hand to stop him. "You don't owe me an explanation."

"Of course I do," he sputtered.

"No! You don't." She pulled the wrapper more tightly around herself and hugged her waist with her arms. "I always said you were free to leave. You obviously have responsibilities. Someone in London must want an accounting, and . . ." her voice trailed off, "you must be needed."

"Nothing so noble. You knew what I was when you met me," he began.

"Did I?" she asked.

"The drunken major without two coins together was real and beneath your notice," he asserted. "The rest of it, what I left in England, lies in shambles. I left people dependent on me. I left debts."

"Were you married?" she demanded to know.

His shocked expression gratified her. "Only to you," he said.

Her throat convulsed, pride stuck like glue. His title, his name, and the extent of his debts—those were the hidden things she had feared. Something else, more secrets, lurked under his hesitation; she knew it in her bones. "Is there more?" she finally managed to grind out.

A shadow crossed his eyes. He looked away. "We have to leave immediately," he said. It was not, she knew, an answer to her question.

"Richard is needed in London," he went on. *The wretched duke again.* "I'll write to you at Casa Beaumont. The quarterly allowance Robert arranged should—"

"Yes, Robert provided well for Isabella. We'll do fine." She didn't try to keep the bitterness out of her voice.

"I'll write to you," he repeated. "You could reach me via"—he hesitated, groping—"via Richard at the Foreign Office, if you need anything. Wentworth's office can help with that."

Nora nodded glumly. "If I need anything," she repeated dully.

"Nora, I have to leave before dawn. We should talk more. There are things I ought to explain."

"There is nothing to say." *Nothing I can bear to hear.* "Isabella will be hurt when you don't say goodbye."

"Please, Nora, don't dismiss me like this." His eyes pleaded.

"I think it would be better," she rasped without dropping her eyes. She couldn't bear to have him in her bed, not after all his lies. "Go to your friends." She began to pull the door shut.

"Where is Isabella?"

"With me." Nora put Isabella to sleep in her room. She needed her close, needed one more thing to put distance between herself and Jamie.

He walked into Nora's bedroom before she could stop him and lifted the flickering candle from her bedside. Books lay scattered across rumpled covers still warm from Nora's body. He gave her a look of longing and regret that tore her heart to shreds before moving to the foot of the bed.

Isabella lay there on a little cot. He knelt and tucked the covers up snuggly around the dainty face.

"Sleep well, Princess," he whispered. "Uncle Jamie has

to leave for a while, but he won't forget you." He kissed the top of her head without waking her.

He took a scrap of paper and a piece of the child's charcoal from Nora's table and wrote:

Goodbye, my princess. I have to leave you for a while. Care for Aunt Nora for me. I know you can, for you are strong and brave.
Uncle Jamie

Nora hugged the ends of her wrapper tightly, watching his every move. *Be done with it Jamie,* she thought, *before I shame myself by begging you to stay.*

He put the note on Isabella's cot.

"That's it then," she said. "You're leaving her—leaving us."

"Nora—" he began, but no words came. He stared at her for a long moment. "I will come back. We'll fix this." He took her mouth in a fierce kiss before she could deny him.

She turned her face away when he released her. He left her with no words to say, no hope to cling to. She gave herself over to grief and wept.

## Chapter 37

"Where the devil is Archie Campbell?" Nora demanded of an empty room. She paced the foyer of Casa Beaumont, as empty as it was cold. She slapped one hand that held a piece of folded vellum against the other one in a rhythm that matched the tap of the heels of her fashionable half boots.

*What,* she wondered, *could be keeping Wentworth's blasted clerk?* They were two days short of the final hearing that would make Isabella hers and give Nora legal authority, and now she had been sent a notice of a challenge from the court.

She had no idea why there could be a challenge so late in the process. The notice burned in her hand. She needed advice. She needed to talk to Archie Campbell.

She needed Jamie more. He may have lied and deceived her, but he would have known what to do. *Blast the man.* He had been gone six weeks and had not bothered to so much as answer her letters. He knew their case depended on married respectability.

"Lady Ross! I came as soon as I could. What has upset you so?" Campbell bounded through the door and practically tossed his hat at a frowning Wat Jones. He bowed over her free hand and pressed his look of concern on her. "What is it?"

"Castellimonte. He has challenged the guardianship." She handed him the papers.

Campbell let the air empty from his lungs. "You had better tell me everything."

Moments later she watched anxiously while he reread the court summons seated in her courtyard.

"There isn't much to go on," he said. "It is simply a notice that the Count di Castellimonte challenges the petition for guardianship. Has the count contacted you?"

"I haven't seen him since he left Rome for Turin a month ago. I thought we had satisfied him. I thought he came to trust me. I thought he agreed to the arrangement."

"Obviously not." Campbell ran a hand through his hair and twisted his neck as if to free it from the high collar above his intricately tied neck cloth. He gave Nora a guarded look. "Have you heard from Baron Ross?"

"No." If Jamie were here it might be different. The count made it clear from the beginning that he didn't approve of a single woman as guardian for Isabella. "No, and I believe that is the heart of the problem." *Damn you, Jamie*, she thought.

"I fear you may be right, but we can't tell from the notice. All I can do is look into it. If we understood the challenge, we could be prepared to counter it."

"If he challenges my marriage, what then?" Nora wasn't sure how to finish.

"He can't. We covered that. Your marriage is perfectly legal, at least in Italy." Archie had explained that even in England the withholding of full title might not have invalidated the marriage.

"But Jamie is gone," she said.

"Do you mean Castellimonte might pose you as an abandoned wife?" he asked.

Nora felt the blood drain from her face and the hope from her heart. Campbell voiced the thought that haunted her nights.

"Nora!" Campbell sprang in alarm, "Lady Ross," he amended, "are you well?"

Nora sat up straighter. "I'm well," she said, "but Isabella deserves better than being used this way." *Isabella*, she reminded herself. *Isabella matters, not my pathetic love life.*

She saw Archie Campbell to the door with some hope and more relief. The man's obvious attraction to her, one he made less and less effort to hide, had become a problem. Whether he would prove capable enough to ensure that she obtained sole guardianship of Isabella constituted a different problem.

When the case concluded, she would find a kind way to send him away. For now, she needed him, her only English ally in Rome.

An hour later she sat with her one true friend. Mother Margarita, her black eyes warm with concern, watched Isabella dance around the convent garden chasing butterflies.

"No word from the major?" Mother Margarita asked. Nora never heard the woman call him "Baron Ross."

"No." Every week it was the same answer. Jamie had not written. Nora conversed comfortably in Italian these days.

The older woman's face lost none of its serenity. "You will hear from him."

"What if I don't?"

"Then you will manage. You are strong and good, Nora. You can manage."

"I may have to. Castellimonte has challenged my guardianship."

Mother Margarita gaped at her. "Why on earth? The old fool!"

"Perhaps he sees me as an abandoned wife. He liked Jamie. I'm not sure he ever warmed up to me."

"Nonsense. That patriarchal old reprobate may not be particularly warm, but he admired you as soon as you stood up to him. He likes that."

"Yes, but he still insisted on the marriage."

Mother Margarita had no response for that. She appeared to ponder for a moment before asking, "Are you certain the state of your marriage is the reason for the challenge?"

Nora let out a long sigh. "No," she said, "I don't know what to think."

"I will see what I can find out. Perhaps my cousin Barnabas can look into it, although he is somewhat preoccupied lately."

Mother Margarita worried her lower lip. "I may not be able to reach him. You know you have my prayers."

Nora smiled at the idea of that old dear attempting to help. "Thank you, Mother. I appreciate your support."

The older woman patted Nora's hand sympathetically. "We may not find out in time. What will you do?"

*If Jamie were here, he would know what to do. If Jamie were here, there might not even be a problem.* He was not. She would have to manage the thing herself.

"What will I do? I will fight, of course. Isabella needs me, and the court must be made to see that. I will take on the count, the court, and the Pope himself if I have to. Robert left Isabella in my care, and care for her I will."

A wide smile spread across Mother Margarita's face. She sat back and beamed.

"You think I'm a fool?" Nora asked warily.

"I think you are a warrior. You would march into hell for Isabella."

At the sound of her name, Isabella's head bobbed up from the flowerbed. She grinned at Nora, and Nora smiled back. They had become family, and no court could change that.

## Chapter 38

"What else could there be?"

Will Landrum, Earl of Chadbourn, and the third of Jamie's dearest friends, sat in his dark paneled library, redolent of beeswax and brandy, with an air of absolute contentment.

The Cohort, the old friends who were now his creditors, had been busy since they dragged him back to London. Richard, Andrew, and Will owned all of Jamie's debts and had settled the matter to their own satisfaction.

"What else?" Will repeated. His uncharacteristic inebriation might have amused Jamie if the question hadn't crushed him. They still knew nothing about his most shameful secrets.

"Sister married," Will enumerated on his fingers, "mother as content as those creatures can be. Mortgages consolidated. Tattersall's paid. Tailor satisfied." Will smiled foolishly into his brandy. "Done," he said.

Jamie put his name to the last of the legal papers that transferred all the income from his crumbling estate to these, his closest friends, (all, that is, but a small quarterly allowance for his mother) until all debts were satisfied. He refused to take any income for himself. The papers designated Chadbourn, the most honest man Jamie knew, as executor. Will had reason to be pleased.

"Don't forget Waylon's gambling den brought low," Andrew, the steadiest one in the group by the fire, pointed out. "Waylon's utterly destroyed," Andrew repeated with a flourish of satisfaction. "No one lamented the demise of that nest of low-living cheats." Bob Waylon's dishonest tables drained much of Jamie's father's pockets.

"No," Jamie replied. A moment later he added, "But those who need to gamble have plenty of other places to go." His father would have.

"Hph." Will gave a drunken belch and continued their inventory on his fingers. "Waylon's. Tenant houses well on the way to repair, north fields—"

"Spare us the agricultural detail, Will, before you begin to enumerate the turnips, the drainage ditches, and the wool production." Andrew had no interest in farming. "Let's all agree the estate escaped the brink."

"Decent little estate. Crime the way old Ross ran it down." Will lamented. "Recovering though." He should know; his steward managed the miracle.

"Old Ross depleted everything and everyone to feed the tables. Old Ross was a pig, and his son hasn't done much better," Jamie answered bitterly.

"Lord, Jamie, give it a rest!" Andrew broke in.

Will spoke at the same time. "Ridiculous, man! Mumford's in fine shape. It should start producing again this year. Better next."

Jamie poured a glass of brandy in the sputtering light of a half dozen candles, thought better, and poured it out. He hadn't depended on drink in Rome; he wouldn't depend on it now.

"Perhaps the estate will earn what I owe you in ten more years," he growled.

"You're a damned fool, Jamie. You're paying your debts," Mallet said in a voice laced with impatience. "It wouldn't take much longer to earn out if you had taken an income like we proposed."

"Don't start again, Andrew."

"You have a wife, Jamie," Andrew began.

"Leave my wife to me," Jamie sputtered. He would not have them interfering with Nora. They could spare him that much.

Andrew ignored Jamie's outburst. "So when are you going back to her? Have you heard from her?"

"No." Jamie spoke so softly Andrew leaned closer to listen. "Not once."

"Then go, man. What else is there to put right?" Will asked.

"Nothing that can be fixed," Jamie said.

"No such thing," Will told him. "Can fix anything if we all put our minds to it."

*They have a right to know,* he thought.

"Can you bring one hundred and thirty-two Africans back from the dead? Even Richard can't do that." Jamie blurted it before he could cower from it again.

Will and Andrew stared at him, eyes wide, for a long moment before all three men turned their faces to the far corner of the room where Richard silently sipped his wine.

"Quite right, Jamie. Even I can't raise the dead." He raised one brow and a glass in salute.

"Africans?" Andrew asked. "Jamie? What is this about?"

He had been right; they didn't know. Richard must. Jamie assumed he had told them. They deserved to know. They deserved the whole truth about the kind of man they rescued.

"Jamie," Will prodded, "what Africans?"

"Slaves," Jamie murmured. "They went down on the Avante, a slaver out of Jamaica. Dead, every one of them."

"The African trade has been illegal since '07. In America, too." Will looked puzzled. "Jamaica's one of ours." He always believed in the good in people.

Andrew spared Jamie from responding. "Since when did making highly profitable activities illegal put a stop to them? We banned the trade but not slavery itself," he said hotly. "As long as the plantations rely on slave labor, men will run the patrols to get at the profits, the blood money!" Andrew choked off his words. He looked at Jamie and then at Richard.

"Quite," the duke affirmed, looking steadily at Jamie. "Bloodsuckers who profit have blood on their hands as much as the plantation owners."

Jamie felt sick.

"Jamie," Will whispered, "what does the Avante have to do with you?"

Their expectant silence lashed him like a whip, but he still couldn't answer. *How do you tell men who love you, who moved the earth to find you, to rehabilitate you, that they helped a murderer?*

"What else is there to do, Jamie?" Richard asked, at last. It wasn't really a question.

"Nothing," Jamie said. "There is nothing left to do. Nothing I can do. My inheritance, meager as it was, financed the Avante. Mine! I'm responsible for the dead at the bottom of the Atlantic, and there is nothing you can do, singly or together, to fix that."

Andrew and Will stilled, drinks in hand, waiting for Jamie to continue.

"I didn't know," he said. "You must believe I didn't know. The bastards lied to me."

"What did they tell you?" Andrew asked.

"They told me she was leaving with a cargo of manufactured goods and returning with sugar," Jamie told him. "They didn't mention the part in between, the middle voyage, the trip between Africa and Charleston."

"You believed them."

"I wanted to. I was desperate to repair the mess he left me. I didn't ask questions. I didn't think that the profits they promised were more than sugar profits, much more. I sat in London and waited for the money to roll in so I could pay my father's debts, waited until word came that the Avante went down."

"You didn't know," Will repeated.

"I didn't try to know. I didn't ask." Jamie's voice rose to a shrill pitch.

The confession, wrenched from his gut, left him weak, but he didn't see revulsion in his friends' eyes. He saw only sympathy. *Would Nora understand if I dragged up the courage to tell her?*

"Perhaps you can't make the Avante right," Richard drawled. He paused for effect, waiting until he had their attention. "But you might wish to make reparation."

"What? How?" The duke's air of mystery annoyed Jamie more than ever.

"The Slavery Bill?" Andrew guessed.

"What bill?" Jamie asked.

"Wilberforce and others have introduced bill after bill since 1816 to put teeth into enforcement of the Slave Trade Act and even to get slavery totally banned from the colonies," Will said.

"The move now is for full emancipation," Andrew explained.

"'Bout damn time!" Will exclaimed. "Parliament outlawed the trade thirteen years ago. I speak on it when I can in Lords—Richard supports it in the corridors." That was Richard's way, always in the background.

"I almost let these two convince me to take a seat in Commons over this issue," Andrew added. They could certainly have ensured one for him. "I have no stomach for politics. The fight has dragged its fetid being through parliament for years with no sign of success."

"How does this bill fix what happened to the Avante?" Jamie asked.

Andrew shrugged. "It doesn't, not directly, but your story might influence votes. Stop the blighted institution, stop the illegal trade, stop the ships—is that it, Richard?"

The duke nodded, his eyes on Jamie.

"I can't. I'm no politician. I don't want a seat in Commons."

"Lords, Jamie—you're entitled," Will corrected.

"No! Wilberforce gave his life to the slavery issue. I can't do it."

"I rather think not. Politics, as Andrew shows, is not for everyone. You wouldn't last a month," Richard said, "but your story may have influence if whispered in the right ears."

"Or shouted from the rafters," Will said.

"I'll look a fool. I can hear what people will say: 'That simpleton Baron Ross didn't know a slaver when he saw one. Let the scum pull wool over his eyes.'"

"Probably—at best." Richard agreed. "Do you care?"

Jamie realized he didn't care about the opinions of the ton, or any opinions but those of the three men in front of him.

"No," he said out loud, the word a rumble deep in his throat. These men and Nora were the only people whose opinions mattered.

"You may have to tell your story several times. Dinners can be arranged, parties planned," Richard said.

"Will I have to make speeches?" Jamie asked.

"In parliament? No," Richard said. "Give your story to Chadbourn here and to others. Let them use it."

"We can publish it," Andrew said. He had the connections for that.

Chadbourn had asked what more he had to fix. *Only this*, he thought. His story would be a tiny restitution for a great wrong, but it gave him something to take back to Nora, one small shred of pride to show for his time in London. He had nothing else.

"Let's do it," he said.

A smile started in the left corner of Richard's mouth and spread across his face. *Damn his devious hide!* He had known about the Avante and planned Jamie's anti-slavery efforts all along.

## Chapter 39

"What do you mean there's been another delay?"

Nora looked at the three men—Campbell, Wentworth and Salvia—arranged awkwardly in her drawing room and hoped the outrage she felt made its way through their thick heads.

"Why is Robert's will being heard in the Rota Romana?" she demanded for good measure. "I thought that was an ecclesiastical court."

"In the Papal States, it is all the same. The Rota is the only court of law for all matters," Wentworth explained with pursed lips, wary eyes, and exaggerated patience.

"Can't we object?" she demanded.

"Goodness, Lady Ross, one can't object to being heard in the only court of law," Campbell blurted out.

"Not to the venue," Nora corrected impatiently, "to the delays. Can't we object?"

"One does not 'object' to the proceedings of the Rota Romana," Salvia advised her. "These delays are not unusual. Roman legal procedures move slowly. The auditors want more time to study Robert's will and the challenge." He had explained that auditors presided over the court, not judges.

"Why can't I just appear and state my case? Surely these men can see that the child is better off with her own aunt!"

"That would be ill-advised," Wentworth told her. "A woman can't just appear before the Rota. We will present your case in due time."

Nora sputtered in outrage.

"Considering the challenge is from Castellimonte, the delay is a good thing," Wentworth continued. "It is damned surprising really."

"Good?" Nora sputtered.

"Castellimonte's objections might have been accepted without question," Wentworth told her. "Given his position, that would not have surprised us. The delay means the auditors are considering both sides. They are reviewing the will."

"If I can't speak, how can that be so?" she demanded.

Salvia gave Wentworth a pleading look. Wentworth pursed his lips as if choosing his words carefully. "My dear Lady Ross, it is most unusual for a woman to have guardianship. My colleague Mr. Salvia would of course stand as executor during the child's minority, but, still, it is unheard of for a single woman to have custody."

"I am not single!"

Campbell cleared his throat. "That much is true, Wentworth. Castellimonte has accepted the legality of the marriage, has he not?"

Again, the two older men appeared to be in nonverbal communication. Salvia answered for both of them.

"Castellimonte's representatives withdrew the challenge, yes, but they raised other claims. They claim instead that you have separated from your husband—a far worse charge than if your marriage was invalid, I believe."

"Have they questioned my fitness to be a mother?" Nora asked. She looked from one face to the other. She saw surprising sympathy on Salvia's face. Wentworth looked merely exasperated.

"We requested letters of support," Wentworth said.

"I offered," Campbell asserted.

"Yes, well," Wentworth said, "Such a letter from a single young man may be more hindrance."

"Mother Margarita has written on your behalf," Salvia said sympathetically. "The Reverend Mother is very well connected."

Wentworth nodded. "One suspects her influence is the only reason we haven't gotten a summary judgment already."

Nora shot a prayer of gratitude, not the first one, for her stalwart friend at Santo Spirito. The thought of "summary judgment" made her blood run cold.

"If we might be blunt, Lady Ross, my colleague Mr. Salvia and I are quite agreed. Unless Lord Ross can provide evidence of his support for you and/or the child, your case is weak indeed. Have you written to him?"

Nora tried not to think about how many times she had written or how frantic her letters had become. Now was not the time to sound like a desperate lovesick female.

"Lord Ross," she said in her firmest voice, forcing the image of Jamie from her memory, "has not yet responded. His business in London prevents his return. We should hear from him soon."

"Until then, madam, I suggest that the delays, painful as they may be, are in your best interest. Castellimonte has contacts in the Curia. His influence is strong." Salvia emphasized each word. "Strong," he repeated, pinning her with his eyes.

Nora dropped her gaze; she couldn't hold against the man's grim determination. She clasped her hands together to still their agitation.

"Then, Signor Salvia, Mr. Wentworth, I will try to accept the delays quietly," she said.

Nora watched the older men go with relief. Campbell hung back in the foyer.

"I should go." His voice lacked conviction. Hopeful eyes looked down at her under tousled hair. "I hate leaving you alone here."

Nora took a hard look at him. "I'm not alone, Mr. Campbell. I have Isabella," she said.

"Yes, yes of course. I know. It's just that—damn it, I wish I could do more."

"There is one thing you can do." She stepped to a marble side table and picked up a sealed packet.

"Another letter, Nora?"

The skin on the back of Nora's neck crawled. *Who gave him leave to call me Nora?*

"I have to keep trying, Mr. Campbell," she said.

Angry color rose up the man's cheeks. "There is little point to it!" he growled. "He's gone. When will you get used to it?"

"You have no right to anger on my behalf. I'll thank you to remember that," she snapped. *If I didn't need him, I would throw this impertinent man out.*

He looked as if he wanted to argue. She rushed on. "I have to try. I need him. Isabella needs him." Nora hated the catch in her voice. "We are fortunate that you have access to diplomatic couriers and grateful for your help, *Mister* Campbell." She held the letter pointedly in front of her.

Campbell stared at it for a moment, before he finally took it from her. "Very well. One more. But he won't respond," the clerk sniffed.

"What my husband does or does not do is not your concern. Will you or will you not send my message?" Nora snapped.

He took the letter and took his leave.

*Come back to me, Jamie,* she prayed.

## Chapter 40

Rain, cruel and unrelenting, pounded on the windows and on Jamie Heyworth's heart. It fell in torrents against soot-darkened glass and trapped him in a third-rate inn an hour from the ship that would take him to Rome.

"They approached you at a dinner party?" Mr. Emmet, the honorable MP from a district near Whitby exclaimed. His cheeks shook with outrage.

"Yes." Jamie responded as Andrew had instructed. He focused his tale on the duplicity of the slavers and not his own guilt. "They became aware of my financial difficulties, and they sought me out. They knew precisely how to gain my interest." Jamie had become the poor helpless victim of his own story. It didn't seem fair.

"My dear sir, that is outrageous!" Emmet reacted exactly as they hoped.

Andrew, Jamie's partner in storytelling, moved in for the kill. "You see, sir, how insidious it is? The very nature of slavery, even in the colonies, brings out the worst sort of greed and abuse."

Greed paled next to the horror of the slave ships. Jamie wanted to howl about the far greater evil, but they needed Emmet's vote. Outrage, however justified, wouldn't influence the votes they needed.

"They withheld the purpose of their voyage? What sort of man deceives a gentleman?"

"They did not conceal their purpose." Jamie corrected grimly. "They admitted their purpose was to make money—lots of money. They didn't say how."

"Yes, yes," Emmet replied. "Of course, flattery and the promise of profits, but they never revealed the risk, man, did they?"

"No," Jamie admitted, the word catching in his throat. *They didn't tell. I didn't ask.*

Emmet launched into a tirade about the respect due a gentleman and honor among peers. Jamie let Mallet nod politely. He moved to the window where the rain continued its relentless assault.

Rain held Jamie prisoner halfway between London and freedom, forced to endure one more telling of his shameful story.

He had recounted the story of his sad victimization by slavers through six dinner parties, one interminable reception, and an awkward interview with the Colonial Office Secretary. He had done it all, and yet England held him in a strangle hold. He wanted to go home to Nora.

"You can't make it stop by glowering at it." Andrew's voice broke through Jamie's grim despair. "You did manage to drive Emmet away with that face, however."

Andrew limped to a wingback chair close to the fire and pulled out a sheaf of papers. "Come, look at the changes we discussed."

"Give it up, Andrew. You heard the story enough times. Write what you wish." Jamie stared out the window.

"It's your story," his friend said.

"No." Jamie looked back over his shoulder and choked on a laugh. "I gave it to you. Write whatever will do the most good." They had fussed over Jamie like mother hens until he could tell it over and over, the way they wanted it said. It was no longer Jamie's story. "Write what you wish."

"Then sit with me, and tell me about your Nora." Andrew removed his spectacles and rubbed his nose.

Nora. *Why hasn't she written? Why hasn't she responded to my letters?* Grief clawed at him. "I prefer to repeat my tale of woe," he said. "Where is Emmet?"

"He found pressing business in the taproom," his friend said.

"Was I that bad?" Jamie asked.

"You were not a great deal of help, but you planted a seed. He got the point. 'Disreputable types prey on honest gentlemen.' We can't have it!'"

"Why not simply rail against slavery? You have the passion for it," Jamie told him.

"For the same reason I won't run for office. They don't care," Andrew explained. "The ones who will vote for the bill because slavery is evil don't need persuading. We have to find ways to win the other votes."

Jamie dropped into a chair next to his friend, leaned his head back, and closed his eyes.

"Will it never end?" he moaned.

"The rain will stop eventually if that is what you mean," Andrew replied reasonably. When Jamie didn't answer he went on. "Nora—you love her."

"Yes." He didn't open his eyes.

"Does she know about the Avante?" Andrew asked.

"No."

"Ah. Do you plan to tell her?" his friend went on.

"I have no choice. If I don't tell her everything, there is no hope for us at all," Jamie said.

"And if you do?"

"There still may be no chance for us, but I'll have tried." Jamie understood that now. Truth, open and total truth, held his only hope.

The door to the inn exploded open, and an odd little man wrapped in coats and dripping buckets stood just inside. Jamie sat straight up and turned with Andrew to gape.

"Mr. Harvey?" he asked. He had never seen the Duke of Sudbury's secretary quite so travel-worn or quite so wet.

"The very one, sir, and glad I am to see you. Glad indeed." The little man bustled over to the fire and began to rub his hands. "Searched for you at every inn from the waterfront at Portsmouth up the length of road until the rain stopped me at a snug little inn a short distance from this one. Better than this one, I must say!"

Harvey looked around himself, disapproval on every line of his round little face. "I began to worry you hadn't left London. His Lordship was anxious, very anxious that you meet the Honorable Mr. Emmet on your way."

"He needn't have," Jamie said bitterly. "Emmet is the reason we stopped at this foul establishment."

"Ah. I did wonder, sir. Not His Grace's usual, not at all."

"Nor mine," drawled Andrew, "but you may tell your employer we did as he bid."

"Very good, sirs, but that isn't why I was sent to fetch you, no indeed."

Jamie waited; he dreaded what he might hear.

"What then?" Andrew asked.

"Why, Lord Ross's ship, sir!"

Dear God. It sailed without him. It might take a week to book another. Jamie leaned forward. "Is it gone?" he asked.

"No, but it sails with the tide tomorrow, sir. I was worried, what with the weather. Carriages can't manage the roads. I brought horses."

Jamie leapt to his feet, crossed the room in four strides, and threw open the door. The rain lessened somewhat. He could go. He could go to Nora and get it over with once and for all.

Long wet hours later, Jamie shivered on the Portsmouth docks with Andrew and Richard, who met them looking dry and elegant as always. The ever-efficient Harvey hovered nearby.

Jamie hated long good-byes. His mother had clung to him when they parted, but he thought relief and gratitude had as much to do with it as sorrow.

"I may not be back to England."

"Then we shall come to Rome," Andrew said. "The air is conducive to one's health I hear."

"And conducive to diplomacy as well?" Jamie asked.

"That too," Richard said, and he gave Jamie one of his rare smiles.

"Good luck, Jamie. You have the letters?" Andrew asked.

Jamie patted the letters of recommendation in his pocket. They meant well, but he wouldn't use his friend's influence to find work unless he had to. He'd had enough of that.

"Letters! Bless me sir, I forgot!"

Jamie turned to see Harvey rooting about in his ever-present valise. The little man pulled out a large bundle of letters. Jamie thought it was odd.

"Didn't Harvey tell you?" Richard asked.

"Tell me what?" Jamie responded.

"Quite strange," Harvey blustered. "Most peculiar. A pouch arrived at Whitehall from Rome two days ago. These letters were tucked inside for you, the whole pile of them. They appear to be from Lady Ross. I meant to give them when I met you."

Jamie snatched the bundle of folded papers. Nora's handwriting covered the top one. He turned them over and over in his hand. "I don't understand," he said.

"People give letters to our officers abroad frequently. They trust our couriers will bring them safely to England," Richard said.

"Just as I gave mine for Nora to send via courier."

"Exactly," Richard replied. "Occasionally one may wait until there is room in the courier's pouch, but we can't account for these many at once."

"She wrote," Jamie breathed. "She wrote to me."

"It appears someone in Rome delayed them," Harvey frowned. "Someone performed poorly indeed."

"I'm sorry, Jamie," Richard said quietly. "We will look into it."

Jamie didn't care who did it. He stared at the letters. *She wrote!* She hadn't given up on him.

"Sorry to interrupt, sirs," the flat American voice of the captain broke in, "but we can't miss the tide."

Jamie slipped the bundle into his jacket, cradling them against his chest. With a nod, he turned to board the ship for Rome and Nora.

"I suppose I will have to bring her my response," he called back to his friends.

## Chapter 41

Nora sat on a wooden bench in an empty corridor of the Lateran Palace, sick with fear, while men judged her fitness as a woman, her fitness to raise Isabella.

Fury made her determined to overrule them. Fear held her in place. She might have tried to demand entrance, but for one thing: the man who followed Wentworth and Salvia into the courtroom.

The Count di Castellimonte sauntered down the hallway and into the court in full silken splendor accompanied by pike-carrying bodyguards and two black cassock-clad counselors. Only it wasn't the old count. Victor Filiberto avoided her eyes until the last moment. Just as he passed through the door, he shot her a look of triumph. Then he was gone.

If Filiberto was the count, the gruff old man who loved Isabella was dead. Victor would take Isabella just to prove his power. Grief and new fears added to Nora's burden of emotion.

Her heart skipped a beat when the door opened and a man came out. It sank when she recognized him. Only Archie Campbell.

"What," she croaked, "what news?"

Campbell scowled at her obvious disappointment.

"Nothing yet. I thought you might worry about the time." He reached for her hand on the bench. Nora moved it to her lap before he could touch her.

Campbell's scowl deepened.

"What are they talking about in there?" she asked.

"You, of course, and Isabella," he said smugly.

"Don't be a fool, Mr. Campbell. Tell me what goes on!" she insisted.

"Legal maneuvering." The man crossed his legs and pursed his lips. "The solicitors lay endless procedural points on the table. The count's representatives—*juris consultus* they call them, 'legal consultants,' and clergy both, I must say—shake it aside and point out over and over that a woman separated from her husband is not fit."

Campbell's cold eyes made her shiver when he spit out the words "separated from her husband" made her shiver. He did not take her rejection well.

"Did you tell them Isabella needs me?" she asked desperately.

"You know I support you, darling Nora," he soothed unctuously, "but I wasn't given a voice. You must see your situation for what it is."

"I will not let that animal get his hands on her no matter what this court thinks," she said.

"We cannot antagonize the House of Savoy!" he exclaimed, every inch the petty bureaucrat.

Nora thought he would throw Isabella in front of a carriage if he thought it would advance his career. She took breath to tell him what she thought of him, but the sight of movement at the end of the gleaming marble corridor stopped her.

A small veiled figure moved smoothly toward Nora, Mother Margarita. Two of her sisters floated discreetly at a distance behind. A soberly dressed man walked at her side, adjusting his stride to hers. The familiar grace of movement rocked her. She forgot to breathe.

Jamie had come.

Campbell rose abruptly to bow to the nun. She ignored him, gave Nora a brief smile without stopping, and walked purposefully to the door.

"Reverend Mother! You can't go in there," Campbell shouted, moving to stop her.

Mother Margarita shot him a scornful look, her hand on the door.

"This man," she said, "is central to the case."

Campbell paled. He gasped. "Lord Ross."

Nora's eyes devoured her husband.

"Jamie … when?" she stammered, flooded with questions.

Tender brown eyes met Nora's. "There is no time to talk now, little bird. I have to deal with this court."

Nora nodded. She didn't trust herself to speak.

Mother Margarita pushed the door firmly, causing a soft whoosh. A guard in renaissance livery put out an arm to stop her. Mother pinned him with a glance that brought color to the young man's cheeks.

Nora saw several gentlemen grouped around tables at the end of the room rise and frown in unison at the intrusion.

Mother Margarita stood in the doorway and announced in her commanding voice, "Forgive the interruption gentlemen, but Baron Ross is newly arrived from London. I was certain you would want his testimony today."

Victor Filiberto, who hadn't risen, turned toward his representatives who merely wrung their hands. Salvia smiled, and Wentworth leaned to speak to him. The chief officer of the court gestured Jamie forward.

Mother Margarita smiled up at Jamie and stepped back into the corridor.

Jamie entered the chamber, and the door swung silently shut behind him.

Nora stared after him. "What," she whispered, "do I do now?"

"Now, my dear, you wait." Nora felt a comforting hand on her shoulder.

Jamie breathed in to clear blood red rage that blinded him at the sight of Filiberto, now the count, sitting at his ease in court.

Jamie knew with absolute certainty that he had engineered Isabella's kidnapping. *This animal should be caged.*

He forced a polite smile for the three auditors who sat at a raised table watching him curiously. He forced his eyes to focus on those men with the power to take Isabella from Nora.

He hoped he looked more confident than he felt. Walking past Nora had already sapped his self-control. He had walked right into the hornet's nest, and his defenses were weak.

"I apologize for the interruption, Your Honor." *Honor? What does one call an auditor of a papal court?* They looked like bishops, except two of them wore red. *Your Reverence?* "It has come to my attention that you wished to speak to me."

"You are Baron Ross?" the oldest looking of the three auditors asked.

"James Heyworth, Baron Ross, Your Reverence." The old man nodded, one hand raised with a pen as if he had been about to write something when Jamie interrupted.

"Husband of Lady Ross," Jamie went on.

"Of course, of course," the old man said.

The auditor scribbled notes. Jamie heard movement to his left. He recognized Wentworth and Salvia, who rose to his feet.

"I believe, Your Eminence—" Salvia began.

*Eminence!* Jamie thought. *That was it.*

"—it should be obvious to all of us that Baron Ross's arrival invalidates any claims the House of Castellimonte might wish to make."

*Damn right,* Jamie thought.

"Perhaps so, Signor Salvia, but you will understand the court's desire to be certain?" another auditor, a younger one with a cynical air about him, asked.

Salvia opened his mouth to object but appeared to think better of it. He nodded. The elderly cleric went on, "If the baron would please sit. There are questions . . ." His voice trailed off as he flicked a glance toward Castellimonte. Jamie refused to follow the man's eyes. He would not look at Filiberto.

"We have seen your marriage lines, Baron, and the House of Castellimonte conceded their earlier claims that the marriage was a sham," the senior auditor said.

Jamie made a silent prayer of gratitude that he had signed his true name.

"That leaves the questions that arose about the current state of your marriage," the younger man went on.

"My marriage, Your Eminence?" Jamie asked innocently.

"You have been gone from Rome, Baron, gone from your wife," the man said.

"Business took me to London, Your Eminence. I returned as soon as messages reached me."

"Messages reached you?"

"From Lady Ross. Apparently they had gone astray. I departed the day they reached me."

"Is the court to understand that you only came home because of those messages?" the auditor asked.

"No. That is, yes." Jamie wished he knew what the court wanted to hear.

"Which is it?" the auditor demanded.

"My business kept me but was drawing to a close. The letters sounded urgent." *Urgent? She sounded frantic.* "I, of course, hurried my affairs to conclusion and came immediately." He thought that close enough to be true.

"Let me be blunt, Baron. Do you and your wife live apart?" the younger cleric asked.

"Apart?" Jamie acted affronted.

"Do you share a house—when you are not on a business trip of course?" the man pushed.

"We're married," Jamie answered. "Married people share a house."

"Yes, Baron, but there is some question about whether or not you and Lady Ross do so," said a voice, sharp and high-pitched, from Jamie's right. It came from one of the clerics representing Filiberto. The hair on Jamie's neck rose; he didn't turn his head.

"There is no evidence!" Wentworth bellowed.

"There is the evidence of Baron Ross's behavior. By his own admission, he only returned here because of today's hearing," Filiberto's representative said.

"The child does not belong in a broken home," his partner added. "If Lady Ross's marriage is not as it ought to be, then we object to guardianship."

"Lady Ross's marriage is her husband's concern, not yours," Jamie hissed, turning toward the plaintiff's table. He felt his beating heart raise heat in every limb of his body at the sight of the new count, his long silk-clad legs crossed at the ankle, looking on with smug amusement.

"Gentlemen, gentlemen," the elderly auditor shouted, "we will have order!"

Jamie subsided, eyes forward.

"Baron Ross, can you unequivocally vouch for the state of your marriage?" the old man asked.

"Of course," Jamie bit out. "My marriage is in order."

"Lady Ross has given assurance she will remain in Rome while the child is a minor. Do you agree to that?" the senior auditor asked.

"Of course. It is the stipulation of Robert Beaumont's will. The child is to be raised in Rome," Jamie agreed.

"But your business in England, Baron Ross—" Filiberto's representative began.

"Has been concluded," Jamie said.

"In spite of your precipitous return? You have no further business in England?" one of the auditors asked.

"That is correct. I have none." *If only you knew*.

The three auditors whispered among themselves.

"You will then, ah, cohabit with Lady Ross and the minor child in the house of Robert Beaumont?" the eldest asked.

"Of course." *If she doesn't throw me out on my ear.* Jamie's jaw hurt from clenching.

"May we have a word, Your Eminence?" one of the new count's representatives asked.

Jamie wondered what they were up to. To his left, Wentworth and Salvia had an agitated, whispered exchange. The Italian rose and faced the auditors; they waved him forward.

Jamie heard little of the conversation and didn't like what he heard. Nora's Italian representative came back looking grim. The man shook his head. He leaned over, two hands on the table in front of Jamie and Wentworth.

"Just answer their questions, Baron Ross. Answer honestly but carefully." Salvia sat down and ignored Wentworth's look of inquiry.

"Baron Ross, the House of Castellimonte has raised an issue on behalf of the minor child, the count's cousin," the younger auditor said.

*I know who Isabella is, and I know Victor doesn't give a damn,* Jamie thought. "What is the concern?" he asked.

"Robert Beaumont's will provided well for the care of his child. As guardian, Lady Ross will, of course, live in Beaumont's villa, which belongs in trust for the little one," the auditor intoned in a nasal voice.

"Yes, I know these things," Jamie agreed.

"The will, my dear Baron, does not extend to the guardian's husband. The count's representative points out that the will provides no stipend for you," the man continued.

*They accuse me of being a fortune hunter? Why not.* "What is your point, Eminence?" he asked.

The little priest wriggled uncomfortably. "There is some question, that is, the count has just revealed the results of some investigation."

"What investigation?" *What had the weasel found out?* Jamie almost stopped breathing.

"It appears your estate is bankrupt," the auditor said.

Breath left his body in a long slow thread, his heart regained its beat, and his shoulders relaxed in relief when they didn't bring up the Avante.

"That's true, gentlemen," he said. "My business in England allowed me to arrange for the settlement of my debts."

"How do you plan to support yourself in that case, sir?"

"Unlike most gentlemen of my class," he said, "I do not disdain work for hire. I plan to seek employment."

Hushed voices and rustling paper erupted on his right. He could make out Filiberto's voice, strident and demanding, but not his words.

"Does Castellimonte object to honest labor?" Jamie asked. "The count's father put me to work as a teacher. I found I quite liked it."

"Surely the court does not consider employment as a common teacher fit for the guardian of a child of Savoy," one of Filiberto's lackeys attempted to say.

"That matter is irrelevant to the case at hand, Eminence," Wentworth was on his feet objecting like a true solicitor.

Once again the auditors demanded silence. Jamie spoke into the quiet.

"Eminence, I believe we can settle this in a friendly manner. If I could have but a few moments alone with the Count di Castellimonte, I am certain I can provide the assurances he seeks, and we can resolve it." *That or I'll kill him*, he thought.

Jamie pinned his false smile on those at the judging table and waited.

"May it please Your Eminences," one of the lackeys oozed, "Baron Ross obviously fails to appreciate the seriousness with which this court takes its responsibility."

"Actually, Monsignor, the court values Baron Ross's offer. If this matter can be resolved within the family, so to speak, the court would be grateful," the senior auditor said. Relief gave the wizened old cleric the look of a benign leprechaun.

Within moments guards ushered the count into a small salon off the courtroom. Jamie, as protocol demanded, followed him. He turned to the guards when they moved to close the door. "Don't go far," he said, "we won't be long." *And you may be needed*, he thought.

"What game are you planning—Ross is it?" Victor spat as soon as the door closed. "Do you think you can challenge Castellimonte?"

## Chapter 42

The vision of her husband's retreating back filled Nora's mind, burned there long after the merciless doors closed. She remained cut off again from the proceedings that would decide her future one final time. Now she also sat cut off from the exasperating man who came to speak for her.

"He came," she murmured.

She sank down on the bench and put her shaking hands in her lap and repeated herself. "He came."

"Of course, my dear, did you doubt it?" Mother Margarita smiled from the seat next to her.

"I wrote and wrote, but he never answered," Nora said through a throat thick with a knot of confused feelings.

"He didn't receive your letters."

Nora's head jerked up to face the kind black eyes of Mother Margarita. Her eyes darted to Archie Campbell.

"Didn't receive them, how can that be? I gave them to Archie Campbell." She gestured toward the man who stood at the courtroom door as if he couldn't decide whether to stay or go. "He said they could go in the diplomatic pouch. He sent twenty-three letters for me. One of them must have gotten through."

"The major did get them eventually. It seems they had been held up." Mother Margarita shot Campbell a shrewd look. Nora followed her gaze and glared at the man. "One might expect the British courier system to be more efficient," the nun continued.

"I may be needed inside," Campbell said abruptly.

"Good day, Mother Margarita," he said through stiff lips, bowing, "Nora." He slipped into the room.

Nora waved a hand as if to brush the subject aside. "He got them," she sighed. "He came. It isn't too late, is it?" She sounded more hopeful than she felt.

"We'll pray that it is not. Baron Ross is a good man. He'll show them reason."

"How did he know to come here?"

"He came to me when he found you gone from Casa Beaumont," the nun said.

"How will I ever thank you?" Nora wondered.

"Don't be foolish," the older woman said tartly. "You love Isabella, and so do I. We do what we can." She rose in a graceful movement and took both of Nora's hands in hers.

"Now, be strong. Sometimes waiting takes the most courage."

"Must you leave?"

A wry smile twisted the little nun's face. "If I haven't broken the order's rules, I've certainly bent them today. It is better if I go about my duties. You will be strong, and someone here loves you." She gave Nora's hand a little squeeze and left. Her two companion sisters fell into step behind her as silently as they had come.

*Someone here loves you.* She wondered if it were possible that her husband actually loved her, or if perhaps Mother meant Campbell. *Surely not.* That thought made her nauseous.

Nora rose and began to pace, but the polished marble floors and her unsteady knees made it difficult. She leaned on the deep sill of a tall window to see Piazza San Giovanni's sun-dappled stones surrounding their ancient obelisk. She wondered if San Giovanni could move the minds of the men deciding her fate. A sudden vision of her father's reaction to her praying to a Catholic saint made her laugh.

Down the corridor, the door, the cruel door, stayed firmly shut.
*Jamie, what are you doing in there?*

The old men would ask about her marriage. She could only hope Jamie could reassure them. *Did he want to? He must. He came.*

She had walked halfway back when the door swung open. She hurried forward, expecting Campbell, hoping for Jamie.

Filiberto stormed past the guards, the Furies in his eyes. He barged past Nora, threw her a hateful look, and charged down the corridor. His bodyguard trotted behind, and the two monsignors who argued his case struggled to keep up.

Standing outside the open doors, Nora watched Signor Salvia and Jamie at a table with the auditors signing papers. While she hovered in the doorway, Wentworth and Campbell approached her.

"The will," Wentworth intoned, "has been settled, not without complications."

"Complications?" Nora's heart reached her throat.

"The count questioned the baron's ability to support you." Campbell sneered.

"Why does that matter?" Nora asked. "Isabella is well provided for."

"Quite," Wentworth said, "But Castellimonte demanded that the estate not provide support for the baron."

"He is penniless, Nora, did you know that? His estate is bankrupt." Campbell's polite mask slipped. His face twisted with spite.

"I was not aware he had an estate," she responded.

Campbell made an ill-bred snort. "He lied to you."

"He didn't tell the entire truth, no," she replied, focusing her eyes on Wentworth, "but that is irrelevant now. I don't care about any estate."

Wentworth returned her look shrewdly. "Listen carefully. Your husband has agreed to accept no funds from Isabella's trust. None. Not for the clothes on his back or paper to write on."

"But how?" she began.

Wentworth waved her words away impatiently. "Signor Salvia, as guardian of the trust, made written surety that you and the baron may live in Isabella's house and receive benefit of food and shelter. You, as her guardian, will of course receive a stipend for your lifetime. Your husband receives nothing."

That sounded reasonable. Nora felt her face relax. "That's it then?"

"He'll live off his wife's stipend," Campbell sneered.

"You must cohabit," Wentworth began at the same time, cutting off the younger man. "The court insists on it. The case depended entirely on Baron Ross's testimony that you have a whole, normal, valid marriage and that all accusations that you have been, in fact, separated are false. I must say his firmness impressed the court."

Nora breathed a prayer of thanks for Jamie. Whatever might pass between them now, she would always be grateful.

Wentworth looked as if he had more to say, something that made him uncomfortable. "I think it is fair to say, Lady Ross, that you would do well to be careful."

"Careful, Mr. Wentworth?" she asked.

"Questions have been raised about the state of your marriage, questions that raise doubts about your fitness as a guardian," he explained.

"People will be watching Baron Ross, and quite rightly!" Campbell gloated.

Nora wondered if Campbell had even attempted to send her letters to Jamie. She had been a fool to trust him. Wentworth turned slowly and glowered at his clerk, obviously annoyed by the man's behavior. Nora wondered if Archie Campbell's career had come to an abrupt end. She devoutly hoped so.

Before she could open her mouth to take exception to Campbell's remarks, Wentworth rushed on, "I did not mean to say they were correct, only that those implications were made. You must be doubly careful about any sign of impropriety."

"What he means, my dear wife, is that you and I must show the world our wedded bliss and not hide our light under bushel baskets." Jamie's familiar baritone came from behind Wentworth.

England's agent in Rome moved sideways at the sound, and Nora breathed in the familiar scent of sandalwood soap. She fought tears that threatened when faced with her husband.

*How dare he stand there looking calm, confident—and too ridiculously handsome—while I am about to shatter apart?*

"Gentlemen," Jamie said smoothly, "Lady Ross has had a trying day. I suggest you let me take her home. Signor Salvia, you understand, I hope, that long separations are difficult for husband and wife. Could we perhaps conclude our business tomorrow?"

Salvia smiled his most paternal smile. "But of course, Lord Ross." He beamed at Nora, expecting, no doubt, her acquiescence.

Jamie took Nora's right hand and placed it over his left arm. "Gentlemen, if you will excuse me?"

Nora felt herself led away. She felt Jamie's breath warm near her ear. She felt, or perhaps heard, the beating of his heart. His voice, a whisper against her cheek, caressed her ear.

"Smile, lady wife. Look the part, at least until we are alone."

## Chapter 43

Her silence during the ride to Casa Beaumont almost killed him. Drowning in the immensity of it, he sat immobile across from her. If she would not speak, he could not.

Of all the words he might have said, the ones that needed saying remained unspeakable. *Here it is—the final truth. Your husband is a slaver. No. Your husband is a greedy bastard who didn't know he was a slave merchant until he sent one hundred and thirty-two souls to their death.*

That thought lay between Jamie and the person he loved above all like an impossible gulf.

Nora sat still as marble; only the tremor of her fingers showed how agitated she was. He wished desperately that she would speak, that she would bridge that gulf.

Her face turned to the window, looked pale as alabaster, so pale he wondered if she was ill. She had filled out in their weeks apart. That delicious shade of blue that always flattered her eyes now also flattered the lush curves of her body.

The carriage lurched uphill past Santa Maria Maggiore where it turned toward the Quirinale neighborhood. His time ran out with every turn of the wheel. If she would not have him, he might not have another chance to speak.

"Nora, can you bear to look at me?"

Her head jerked toward him, tears glistening in her eyes. "Of course," she rasped, "I, I can't seem to decide how to thank you, how to begin to tell you how grateful I am."

His heart lurched. The little wren's silence stemmed from an excess of gratitude, not anger. He took a deep breath to steady its beating.

"Thank me? For what? For failing in a husband's most primary duty to protect you? For arriving like Galahad at the last moment to that ludicrous trial to say the words you could have said, that the fools should have let you say?" Jamie burst out. "If there was any justice in Rome, you wouldn't have needed my help."

"They shut me out," she sobbed, swallowing convulsively.

Jamie reached forward to comfort her instinctively. She pulled back with the shake of her head.

"The suit wasn't the Rota's fault, but they shut me out!" She went on as if a dam had broken. "They let Victor in. They let him speak!"

Bitterness tightened her mouth, until a sudden memory made her light up. She wrinkled her brow. "Victor! They said he withdrew his suit. What did you do to him?" She sounded concerned.

"I didn't hurt him," Jamie said, "if that's what you're afraid of."

"It would serve him well if you did. He might learn from it," she said.

Jamie felt a smile stretch across his face at his wife's ferocity.

"What did you say to him?" she persisted.

"I told him we knew about his treachery, of his attempts to supplant the king. London knows also. There are letters outlining what he did."

"Really?"

"The letters are real. I may have let him believe we found proof," Jamie shrugged. "He believed me."

"Good!" she said fiercely.

"London believes me, in any case," he went on. "If you or Isabella experience discomfort at the hands of Castellimonte, those letters will make their way to Turin and to their allies in Vienna."

She relaxed into the seat. "It really is over then?"

"Dispute over Robert's will? Yes. The Rota's findings will stand. You are the guardian. He can't hurt you, Nora." Emotions that Jamie wasn't fool enough to try to interpret played across her face. She seemed to study his face. He let her look in silence.

"My stipend will be enough," she said at last. "We will live in Robert's house."

*We will live in Robert's house*. His hopes rose, but caution kept them in check.

"I think not."

She blinked rapidly. "Not enough?"

"Not mine. The only thing I've ever agreed with Filiberto about is that," he said. "I can't take money from you, Nora. When we married, your brother's money paid for everything, even the clothes on my back. No more."

"But how—" she began.

He stopped her with a raised hand and leaned forward, elbows on knees. "Aren't you getting ahead of yourself? You said 'we,' 'we will live.' There's much unsaid between us."

Her nod was wobbly, but her voice was firm. "Mr. Wentworth said we must. He said you agreed."

"Wentworth exaggerates. With no one to challenge, no one is going to sniff around our domestic arrangements. You always have a choice."

The blue eyes widened and then narrowed when her brows drew together. He watched her adorable lips slip between her teeth and then out again with a pang of longing. His little bird looked confused, exhausted, and undecided.

He needed to give her room to think, but he reached for her hands, giving in to the impulse that had plagued him since the Lateran.

"You have to decide, Nora. You have to know what you want," he said.

"What do you mean, 'want'?" Her pink tongue moistened her upper lip. He beat back the vortex of desire she caused.

"You've won what you wanted most—Isabella. You can care for her comfortably thanks to her father's will. You don't need me."

She didn't deny it.

"Is there room in that life for me? What do you want from our marriage?"

She didn't speak, but she didn't pull away. He rushed on. "I have to warn you, I don't want what we had before, based on lies and misconception. I won't be a piece of furniture in the home you've envisioned for Isabella, a hanger-on in your brother's house. It is far, far too late for that."

Nora pulled her hands from his and looked away. "You left," she said, "and you never wrote. I don't know what to think—I don't know who you are."

"I wrote. The letters didn't reach you, but I'm here now."

"Baron Ross." She didn't try to disguise the bitterness.

"Yes—the bankrupt son of a wastrel father, but yes, Baron Ross."

"Were you a major?"

"Yes. I always told you the truth. I just didn't tell you all of it. I was a better major than I will ever be a baron."

The carriage stopped with a jolt, and hands flung open the doors. Casa Beaumont. Servants in livery looked on in anticipation, ready to help Nora climb down. He moved to the door first. As one foot struck the pavement, a glimpse of bouncing black curls in the window caught his eye. Isabella.

Jamie couldn't let himself be caught in the web of family yet. Unless Nora wanted him, all of him, with the entire truth out in the open, he couldn't stay. He had to leave before his little princess caught him.

Nora took his hand and stepped out of the carriage. He leaned over and kissed her hand, savoring the lavender scent of her.

"Signor Salvia comes tomorrow at one to finish up the guardianship business. I will join you then, if you wish it. We will settle things." He prayed she would say yes.

"Of course, yes. But what things?" she asked.

The carriage pulled away before she could demand an answer. Jamie watched her until they pulled around the corner out of sight and turned toward the river, back to his dreary little room in Trastevere.

He wondered if he had lost her and thought it likely. No matter the outcome, she had given him life. He wouldn't throw that gift away. He would live on with half his soul, but he wouldn't throw it away.

Tomorrow he would lay the entire truth at her feet, and he would know.

*Where the devil is he? He said he would come.* Nora detested waiting. She wondered what the infuriating man meant by "things" while she paced the foyer. She encircled the courtyard. She fidgeted in the drawing room.

A knock at the massive front door came at five past one. She slid into the foyer to see Wat Jones admit Signor Salvia. Her eyes flew past him to Jamie who followed right behind and handed his hat to Wat with a wink. If Salvia thought Jamie's arrival odd, he didn't say.

Jamie took her arm with exaggerated formality, and she let herself be led to her little office. Salvia droned on. Papers appeared, and she signed them. Words were exchanged. She heard none of it. Her mind swirled over and over with one question: what did Jamie need to "settle?" She knew it didn't involve Salvia.

Jamie took her hand and kissed it with exaggerated care, one eye on Signor Salvia, before suggesting she wait for him in the courtyard. The wretch took his time seeing the man out. Nora reached a boiling point just before he stepped out into the sun.

Sun gave Jamie's hair a golden glow. She noticed for the first time how his fashionable new cut flattered the lean lines of his face. The air of health and peace looked new also, new and yet fitting. Only his eyes showed concern, an old wariness creeping in.

"What are these 'things' we need to settle?" she demanded.

"You asked yesterday who I am," he said, moving her to a bench beneath the bougainvillea. "Most of it you know."

"You're a major."

"Was. A wild hell-for-nothing cavalry major who by rights should have died in the Peninsula, if not at least at Waterloo."

"After that a baron?"

"After that a care for nothing. I especially cared nothing for the barony. My father—" he paused, and she let him choose his words "—cared nothing at all for his estate, his responsibility, his family. He died drunk in a gambling hell."

"You aren't like him," she state emphatically.

He laughed bitterly. "I wanted to think so. When he died, I had been drifting, living on the charity of friends."

"The Duke of Sudbury?" she guessed.

"Yes, and Andrew and others. Left with a mother and sister to care for, an estate to rescue, I had an opportunity to redeem myself," he told her.

"Mother and sister?" she prompted.

He nodded. "I'll tell you about them later. Let me finish."

She composed her hands in her lap and bit back her questions. He rushed on.

"The debts buried me," he said. "I felt desperate to redeem myself. When two men who appeared respectable enough approached me at a dinner party and offered me an opportunity to invest, they found me easy prey."

"Predators?" she asked.

"So I came to understand. That night, though, I thought them saviors. I would invest money in shipping and gain tenfold on my small inheritance. I would rescue the estate and care for my family. Stupid, stupid, stupid." He threw his head back.

"How so?" Nora prodded him to go on.

"The gains they promised sounded good—too good. I ought to have been warned that something smelled foul. I asked no questions."

"The venture failed," Nora guessed, her anxiety growing by the moment.

"Spectacularly. The ship sank," he said flatly.

"Unfortunate, but not uncommon," she mused. "Shipping is high risk." *What can possibly be so terrible?*

"Yes. I felt a fool, but then came the worst." Jamie looked ill. He wouldn't meet her eyes.

Nora's heart ached for him. She reached over to touch his arm, but he pulled away. He stood and took two steps away before turning back to her, his face pained and his body stiff with grief.

"The Avante was not the merchant vessel I took her for, Nora. She carried human cargo."

"Human cargo?" For a moment she didn't understand, but the full horror dawned quickly. "Slaves?" She gasped and covered her mouth with her hands. "Oh my God!"

His face crumpled. "One hundred and thirty-two went down with the Avante. Dead. Every one. And I financed it." He ground out the words with a hoarse voice, thick and wet. He sank to his knees and grasped her hands so hard they hurt.

"I didn't know, Nora," he said hoarsely. "You have to believe me. I will regret it for the rest of my life. I didn't know, but I should have." The words wrung out of him as if torn from his soul.

Nora froze, unable to respond, visions of chained, drowning men filling her with revulsion. Jamie moved after a long silence.

"I'll leave you now," he said. "You deserved the whole truth about your husband, and now you have it." He lurched to his feet and left her.

## Chapter 44

Jamie almost made it through the open French doors to the foyer before responsibility stopped him. He should stay to make arrangements for their separation, for meeting the terms of Nora's guardianship, but he couldn't. One more moment and he would shatter into a thousand pieces.

"Jamie! Wait," Nora called.

Hope flared. He looked at her, and it died. *How can she forgive the unforgivable?*

"We'll manage something," he said, breathing hard. "You don't have to tie yourself to me."

Nora looked up at him, her eyes reservoirs of sorrow.

"You carried this alone for a long time," she said. "Do your friends know?"

He nodded and hung his head. "They do now." His friends knew and understood his need to redeem himself. He could live with himself if he had to.

"Now I do," she said.

The blue eyes that shone up at him held compassion and something else. She held out her arms to him.

He dragged her close and clung as if he himself were drowning. Tears began to fall; he couldn't stop them. His wrenching sobs might have toppled them both if she hadn't pulled him down to a bench and held him until the storm abated.

"I didn't know," he repeated over and over.

"Of course you didn't," she said at last.

He told her about England, about his efforts to create anti-slavery propaganda. "It isn't enough," he said in the end. "It will never be enough."

"In many ways, no, but you are a different person now, a better one," Nora said.

Seeing it in her eyes, he believed it. He leaned to her, never breaking eye contact. She met him halfway in the kiss he longed for, a kiss full of forgiveness and promise. His arms tightened around her; she slid her hands up his back to tangle her fingers in his hair.

How long they might have lingered in healing embrace, he would never know. A lyrical voice interrupted them.

"Uncle Jamie! You're back!" Isabella bounced into the middle, hugging them both.

"Princess, back from Santo Spirito so early?" he laughed.

"I knew you would come. I told Mother you would, and she let me go." Isabella sat up straight, shook her head until her black curls trembled and pointed her finger at him. "You left yesterday without coming in. You are very naughty."

"I'm sorry, Princess," he said, as joy welled up inside him. "It won't happen again." He looked at Nora. "I'm never going to leave again."

## Chapter 45

"She's off to school," Jamie announced, popping the last bite of a lemon biscuit into his mouth. He climbed back into bed. "I promised gelato this afternoon, or she might never have gone."

Nora smiled up at her husband, content to look at his brown eyes and see them free of shadows and sorrow, filled with love for her.

Jamie snuggled close. "How shall we spend the day?" he teased, kissing his way from her chin to her breast.

"I don't know," Nora teased back, her voice thick with pleasure. "Don't you have to look for work?"

He flopped to his back. "I did promise the court, didn't I?"

She nodded, running her hand up his flat belly to his chest, reveling in the textures.

"Mm," he moaned. "Keep that up, and I will forget to tell you."

"Tell me what?" she demanded.

"I don't need to look," he said. "I have work."

She sat upright so fast the sheets fell away.

"The most beautiful sight in Rome," her husband sighed, leering at her.

"Tell me," she demanded.

"You are very distracting," he said, slipping a hand between her thighs.

She slapped his hand away. "Tell me first," she demanded.

"First?" he asked, cupping her breast with one large hand.

"Jamie! Stop teasing."

"I'm not teasing. I am very serious." For several moments he concentrated on what he started.

When he pulled away abruptly, she fell down on her back with a moan of frustration.

"Very well," he said, giving her a quick kiss on the lips. "We are free to linger in bed a few more mornings."

She raised a questioning eyebrow.

"I start work on Monday," he said.

"So soon? Doing what? Where? And how did this come about?" she asked.

"Yes, teaching English, the Vatican, and I found out the day of the hearing after I left you," he answered, reaching for her.

She pushed him away several long kisses later. "How did you get hired at the Vatican?" she asked.

"Mother Margarita's cousin," he said, taking her mouth again.

She slid sideways. "Padre Barnabas?" she asked, puzzled.

He rose up on one elbow.

"Yes," he said, "the very one. Did you know the man wears red shoes in his spare time?" His lips twitched suspiciously.

"I don't understand," she said.

"Mother Margarita's cousin's other name is Pius VII," he said, holding back a laugh. "When he isn't looking in on his cousins, he rules the Papal States. Padre Barnabas is the pope."

She gasped, trying to take it in. "When did you find that out?"

"After the hearing when I kept an appointment set up for me by Mother Margarita and discovered who had summoned me." A laugh escaped him; he pressed his lips together.

"No wonder our marriage could be easily arranged," she mused.

"That's the least of it. He most certainly made sure that you got a fair hearing. We always had a powerful protector, little wife. We just didn't know it."

He began to laugh in earnest. He laughed until the bed shook, and she couldn't help but join in.

They hugged each other until laughter subsided and passion took over.

Laughter and passion, she thought much later, would see them through whatever life gave them. She smiled at her husband, curled around her in his sleep, and knew it was so.

# Author's Note

Only a few actual historical figures put in an appearance in Jamie and Nora's story. The historical milieu, however, is quite real.

Italy as we know it did not exist. When Napoleon was defeated and the French withdrew, the Papal States, Sardinia, the Kingdom of the Two Sicilies, and the Kingdom of Venice, along with a number of lesser duchies, struggled to reestablish territorial rule. Significant political unrest and reactionary suppression took place all over Europe. Castellimonte's political fears had a firm foundation.

The Count di Castellimonte and his wicked son are my creations. The House of Savoy did, however, rule the border between France and Italy as I described it. Victor Emmanuel II of Savoy, born during the year in which *Dangerous Secrets* takes place, became the first king of a united Italy in 1861.

The one great liberty I took in this novel has to do with the Piedmontese troops at Waterloo. A Piedmontese regiment fought there, but it fought on behalf of the French. That Savoy might try to play both sides struck me as a reasonable stretch. They certainly landed on their feet after the Congress of Vienna. However, the suggestions that Piedmontese fought with Austrian troops or any other than France has no historical truth that I could uncover.

The French Revolutionary Army invaded Italy, including the Papal States, in 1797 and annexed them to France in 1809. In the midst of this, my Padre Barnabas, Barnaba Chiaramonte, Pius VII, was elected pope as a compromise candidate in 1800. Some perceived him as soft and suspect due to his support for democracy and attempts to work with Napoleon. He agreed to the Concordat of 1801 that restored some church rights in France and upheld the principles of religious freedom and separation of church and state. Nevertheless, after the annexation in 1809 he was carried to Paris as a prisoner. The most famous image of him can be found in David's "Coronation of Napoleon I," looking on sadly while Napoleon, who has snatched the crown from the pope and crowned himself, crowns the empress. A Benedictine monk, he was by most reports a good and humble man. He has been proposed for canonization, but his cause moves slowly. Mother Margarita is fictional.

England's relations with the Papal States continued to be complicated by old religious conflicts. They did, indeed, use the services of Franz von Reden, the minister of the Kingdom of Hanover, in communications with the Papal court. Wentworth is fictional.

English travelers, however, poured into Italy during this period. Nora might have had her pick of Englishmen to serve as interpreter in 1820, including "that poet Keats." He went to Rome for his health, probably a few months later than the novel reports him living there. He died in Rome in February 1821 and is buried in the Protestant cemetery there.

Britain passed The Abolition of the Slave Trade Act in 1807, with William Wilberforce's help. The Abolition of Slavery, however, did not pass until 1833. Wilberforce and others put forth a series of bills to try to add teeth to the ban on the slave trade and, eventually, bills requiring full emancipation beginning around 1816. Thomas Fowell Buxton, an MP from Nora's Dorset, was one of them. The Society for the Abolition of Slavery came into existence in 1823, after Jamie's visit to London. I know of no specific bill under consideration in 1820.

One final note: in the words of the traditional Scottish ballad, "lonely cairns lay o'er the men who fought and died for Charlie." If that is so, where is the Bonnie Prince himself buried? The answer may surprise. He is buried next to his father, his brother Henry Stuart the Cardinal of York, and a long line of popes in Saint Peter's Basilica in Rome. When Henry died, the Stuart claims passed to the descendants of Charles I's youngest daughter Henrietta whose own daughter married the King of Sardinia. The claims passed to the House of Savoy, even if no member of that family ever made such claims. By a twisted line of descent, the succession fell to Duke Franz of Bavaria in 1996.

CPSIA information can be obtained
at www.ICGtesting.com
Printed in the USA
BVHW092327010223
657620BV00007B/690